11/02

Spanish Jack

Also by Robert J. Conley

THE "REAL PEOPLE" NOVELS

Spanish Jack

ROBERT J. CONLEY

ST. MARTIN'S PRESS ≈ NEW YORK

www.stmartins.com

Library of Congress Cataloging-in-Publication Data

Conley, Robert J.
   Spanish Jack : a novel of the Real People / Robert J. Conley.—
  1st ed.
     p. cm.
  ISBN: 0-312-26231-0
1. Spaniard, Jack, d. 1889—Fiction.   2. Cherokee Indians—Fiction.
3. Outlaws—Fiction.   I. Title.

PS3553.O494 S63 2001
813'.54—dc21

                                2001019265

First Edition: August 2001

10 9 8 7 6 5 4 3 2 1

Spanish Jack

I

1841

Jack rode the narrow trail slowly. He was deep into Osage country, and he was looking for a fight. The long and bitter war between the Western Cherokees and the Osages was supposed to have ended, but for Jack it could never end. He hated the Osages, as he knew they hated him, and he was determined that he would fight them for as long as he lived. At thirty years or so, he had known nothing else most of his life. He had been born in Missouri of a mother who had left the old Cherokee country with a band of disgruntled Chickamaugas, the Cherokee faction that had sided with Great Britain during the American Revolution. They had done so because they knew that the rebel colonists who were then calling themselves Americans wanted to move onto Cherokee land. Jack's father had fought with the great Dragging Canoe, but in the end, they had lost.

They had lost, and a new country had grown out of the conflict: the United States of America. The Chickamaugas were stubborn though. Some had continued to fight the new country, Jack's father among them. Then when things had gotten too hot in the old country, with the United States and the majority of Cherokees, who had made their peace with the Americans, all against them, some had moved west. They had moved into Missouri and made new homes there. That had been in 1794. Jack's parents had made that move.

But in 1811, a major catastrophe had occurred. The largest and most destructive earthquake in anyone's memory had caused rivers to run backwards and change their course, had leveled mountains, had caused the earth to shake for distances of many miles in all directions. The Cherokees in Missouri decided that that was not a good place to live. They decided to move again, and this time they moved southwest, settling along the Arkansas and White Rivers in land the Americans were calling Arkansas Territory. And they organized themselves into a new nation which they called the Cherokee Nation West. They selected their own chiefs and made their own laws. The U.S. government, already planning to move all Cherokees west, was glad to have the Cherokee Nation West located in Arkansas Territory. It would give them some more leverage in dealing with the rest of the Cherokees. Happily, the U.S. dealt with this new Cherokee Nation West under that new name.

But the Osages did not like the presence of this new nation in territory which they claimed for themselves, had claimed for as long as any of them could remember, and the Cherokees had not been long in their new homes before they found themselves embroiled in a bitter and bloody war. The Cherokee war chief, Degadoga, advocated complete extermination of the Osages, whom he called "a nation of liars." And the Osages felt about the same toward the Cherokees. The Osages, trying to get the U.S. Army to take their side, pretended to be pitiful.

"We are naked and have only bows and arrows," they said. "The Cherokees have guns to kill us with."

The blue-coated soldiers at Fort Gibson tried constantly to get the Osages and the Cherokees to sign a treaty and agree to stop fighting, but the war continued. Now and then, an uneasy truce would be established, but always something would happen to cause the fighting to flare up again. Then in 1838, the United States forced almost all of the Cherokees from the old homelands back East to move West. They moved them to a new homeland just west of where the Western Cherokee Nation was already located, and then they made the Western Cherokees move across the line with them. Jack had been forced to move his own home. He resented the move.

Jack hated the Osages. He hated the United States. And now

he was coming close to hating the Cherokee Nation, for it had reabsorbed the Western Cherokee Nation into its own ranks. The nation Jack had known and been a part of for his whole life no longer existed. And the war with the Osages was over. The Cherokee Nation said that it was over. The United States said that it was over. Even the Osages said that it was over. And the Western Cherokee Nation was gone, so it could have nothing to say in the matter.

But Jack had plenty to say about it. For Jack the war would never be over—not until he was dead. He rode north into Osage country in proud defiance of the Osage Nation, the Cherokee Nation and the United States of America. He meant to find some Osages and either kill them or be killed by them. This had become a private war for Jack, for he had become an outlaw, wanted by all three nations. He had become a man without a country.

He had already been a man without a family, for years earlier, when he had been a young man, during a lull in the war, he had met and married an Osage woman. He had lived with the Osages for a time, for it was a long-standing tradition among the Cherokees that a man live with his wife's people. He had learned the ways of the Plains Indians from the Osages, and he had learned to speak their language. He had learned to steal horses from other Indian tribes. He had learned the Plains method of hunting buffalo. He adapted easily and well to the ways of his wife's people, and he could have forgotten the old animosities and lived away his life as an Osage.

Then came the day that still burned in Jack's memory. He had been away on a trip to New Orleans to sell some horses he had stolen from Comanches. While he was away from home, some Cherokees had encountered some Osages in the disputed hunting ground, and there had been a fight with men killed on both sides. When Jack had returned from his trip, he found the war raging again with a fury, and his young wife murdered by her own people, presumably for having married a Cherokee man. He would never forget that day, and he would never abandon his mission. He lived alone. He lived for revenge. He lived to kill Osages. And he did so in defiance of three governments.

He rode along the narrow trail in a hilly, rocky and tree-covered terrain. Off to his right, at the edge of the trail, was a steep drop down to the river and its rocky shoreline far below. As he rounded a curve in the tree- and brush-lined trail, he saw ahead three mounted Osage men. They were armed with bows and arrows, lances and war axes. Jack carried his long rifle, a brace of pistols, a hunting knife and a war ax. He stopped his horse in the middle of the trail to study the three men ahead. They had also stopped and were looking at him. Finally, one Osage rode forward of the other two and stopped again.

"You're a-that-thing-on-their-heads person," he said to Jack. His reference was to the turban that Cherokee men wore wrapped around their heads. "What are you doing in our country?"

"I go where I want to go," Jack responded in the Osage language.

"Ah, you speak our language," the man said.

"Along with several others," Jack said. "But I'm glad that I speak your language. I have many things I want to tell you."

"Are you hunting here in our country?" the Osage asked. "Are you killing our animals?"

"I killed one just yesterday," Jack said, "a big buck, and I ate all its best parts and left the rest on the ground for you."

The Osage stiffened in his saddle and scowled. He was about to respond, but Jack spoke again before the Osage could form his words.

"But my main reason for being here is to kill you," he said.

"The war is over," the Osage said.

"Not for me," said Jack. "I am your worst enemy. I am called Spanish Jack."

"Spanish Jack," the Osage said. "I thought as much. No other that-thing-on-their-heads person would ride into our country this way. But there are three of us here, Spanish Jack. Do you think you can kill all three of us?"

"I wish there were six of you," Jack said. "I'd kill you all."

The Osage looked back at his friends. "He's going to kill all of us," he said. They all laughed. "If we kill you, Spanish Jack," the Osage continued, "we will be rich with white man's money, for your own people will pay us a bounty, and so will the blue coats."

"See if you can," Jack said. He raised his rifle and thumbed back the hammer. He aimed at the chest of the bold Osage. All three Osages shrieked and kicked their horses to ride full tilt at

Jack. Jack pulled the trigger, and the hammer struck spark from the flint. An instant later, with a great boom, the powder in the chamber exploded, sending the large, lead ball hurtling through space. It tore into the bare chest of the lead Osage, flipping him backwards off his horse. The confused animal ran loose in circles.

The other two Osages came closer. They were almost upon him, as he dropped his rifle to the ground and pulled out his two pistols, one in each hand. Jack fired one pistol, and a second Osage dropped from his horse. As the third Osage rode past Jack, he swung his war ax, but Jack ducked under it as it whooshed over his head. He turned in the saddle and fired his second pistol, but it missed fire.

"Damn," he shouted, resorting to English. He tossed both pistols to the ground and jerked his war ax loose from his belt. He turned his horse to face the Osage man who had ridden past him. Ahead, the Osage had turned his own war pony. The two men raced toward one another, brandishing their war axes. Side by side, both men swung their axes. The clubs clacked together and locked. The horses kept running, and both riders tumbled off their backs, landing hard on the trail. Still locked together, they rolled over and over in the dirt and rocks. At last, Jack got a foot into the stomach of the Osage and gave a kick, tossing the man head over heels. The man lit on his back and rolled to his feet, as Jack scrambled up from the ground. The two men faced one another, on foot, both now armed only with war axes.

"Now we are evenly matched," the Osage said. "You killed my two friends with white man's guns. See how well you do now."

"I could kill you with a rock," Jack said, "or my bare hands."

They ran together, swinging their axes, and again the axes locked together. With his free hand, each man grabbed for the other man's wrist. They struggled upright for a long moment. Then suddenly Jack swept both legs out from under the Osage with his own right leg. The man hit hard on his right shoulder, but he rolled quickly away from Jack. When he came to his feet again, he still clutched his war ax. They stood facing one another again, readying themselves for another rush.

Just then four more mounted Osages came riding down the road. They stopped their horses when they saw what was happening. Jack backed away from his opponent when he saw them, his eyes darting back and forth from the one on foot to the four mounted ones. The one facing Jack glanced over his shoulder when his tribesmen rode up. One of the mounted Osages nocked an arrow.

"No," said Jack's opponent. "I'm going to kill this one by my-self. You just watch, all of you."

The mounted Osage lowered his weapons and looked at his companions. They shrugged and sat still on their horses. When Jack saw that he would not have to fight five of them, at least not all at once, he returned his full attention to the one on foot there in front of him.

"Come on then," he said. "Try again. Try to kill me."

"If I should fail," the Osage said, "my friends will kill you. Either way, you'll die here today."

"But you won't be here to watch it," Jack said. "Come on. I'll take you with me. When we get to the other side, we'll fight some more there."

With a loud and long yelp, the Osage ran at Jack swinging his ax, but Jack ducked under the swing and drove his own ax into the Osage's stomach, knocking the wind out of him. The Osage doubled over. Jack took hold of his topknot and raised his club high for a death blow, but the Osage hooked his club behind Jack's right foot and jerked, throwing Jack off-balance. Jack staggered back and nearly fell, but he managed to stay upright. While he was off-balance, though, the Osage ran at him again. This time, he ran into Jack so hard that both men fell over. Jack landed on his back, the weight of the Osage bearing down on him, but he grabbed the man's shoulders and rolled.

They kept rolling, one man on top for an instant, then the other. In one of his moments on top, Jack pulled his right arm loose and swung his ax, but it pounded earth just beside the Osage's head. The swing had thrown Jack off-balance just a bit, and the Osage took advantage of the situation to throw his weight and cause them to roll over in the opposite direction from the one in which they had been moving. They rolled right to the edge of the precipice, and with a mighty effort, the Osage threw Jack over the rim.

Jack clutched the man's hair though. *If I go, he's going with me,* he thought. For an instant, Jack swung in midair, and the

Osage grimaced in pain, pushing both hands hard against the lip of gorge. Knowing that Jack would pull him over too, he reached for the knife at his belt, thinking to cut Jack's hand or his own hair or something, but with only one hand holding him against Jack's weight, everything broke loose at once. The Osage went flying through the air. Jack let go his grip on the man's hair and dropped straight down. Astonished, the four mounted Osages rode over close to the edge. They leaned forward.

"I don't see them," one said.

A second one dismounted and walked even closer to the edge. He leaned forward to look, but he still could not see anything. He dropped down to all fours and crawled to the edge, leaning out as far as he dared. Straightening himself up, he shook his head.

"I can't see either one of them," he said. "They're gone."

"Should we go looking for them?" the third one said.

"It's too dangerous," said the first one. "It's straight down, and it's rocky. It's a long drop. If we try to go down there, we might fall."

"Let's go home, then, and tell the others what we saw here," said the fourth.

"We'll tell him that our friend is gone," said the third one. Believing their friend to be dead, he had refrained from mentioning the man's name. "But we'll tell them also that he took one with him, one of the that-thing-on-their-heads people."

"Not just any that-thing-on-their-heads person," said the first one. "Do you know who that was?"

"No," said the second. "Who was it? Do you know?"

"I've seen him before," said the first one. "That was Spanish Jack."

The eyes of the other three opened wide in astonishment.

"Spanish Jack?" said the second.

"Then there will truly be peace at last," said the third. "With Spanish Jack gone, the war will really be over."

"We'll mourn for our three lost friends," said the first one, "but when the period of mourning is over, we'll rejoice in the death of Spanish Jack."

They turned their horses, kicked them in the sides and rode hard toward their home village. One of them slowed down long enough to pick up Jack's guns.

On a jagged ledge, perhaps a third of the way down toward the rocky riverbank, Spanish Jack lay bruised, broken and bloody. In a semiconscious state, he thought that he was dying. He rejoiced in the knowledge that he had taken the Osage along with him.

2

J ack lay on the ledge, not so much in pain, more numb than anything else. He could tell, though, that both arms were hurt badly, maybe broken. He would know better if he tried to use them, but for the time being, he lacked either the strength or the willpower even to try. He was breathing heavily, panting for his breath. It came to him that he might just lie there and slowly die of thirst or starvation. It would have been a less cruel death had he plunged all the way to the bottom and been dashed on the rocks below. He decided that he wouldn't fight it. He was damn near helpless anyway. He might just as well lie there quietly and take it as it came to him.

Then slowly feeling came creeping back into his battered body. The first thing he noticed was that his back hurt. Then he felt the pain in his ribs. His legs began to ache, and so did his head. The last misery to come into his consciousness was the sharp, stabbing pain in his arms. It was the worst, and it had waited until last to mainifest itself. It was almost more than he could bear, he thought, and he considered the possibility of rolling himself off the narrow ledge in order to finish the deathly plunge. Why prolong the agony when it was all over with anyway?

In spite of the logic of his reasoning, he did not throw himself off the ledge. There was something in him that against all logic insisted on hanging on to life as long as possible, something that said to him, "all may not be lost, no matter how bad things may seem." He told himself that it was a foolish thought, this thought that held out hope in the face of hopeless odds. Yet he clung to that thought, and to keep himself from thinking the worst, he forced his mind back to memories of more pleasant days.

He recalled his childhood in Arkansas before the Trail of Tears, before the United States had forced him and his people across the line to rejoin the much larger and more recently arrived Cherokee Nation. He remembered roaming the woods under the watchful eye of his mother's brother, the man who taught him everything he knew about tracking, hunting, surviving in the woods. He remembered being at home with his mother, recalled her voice and her touch. But this tactic did not work for long. These thoughts led to other thoughts.

He remembered then the time when the Ridges and Starrs and others, families headed by men who had signed the fraudulent removal treaty, had come into their settlements. It was clear that, having signed the hated treaty illegally and against the wishes of the majority of the Cherokee people, these men had fled west for their very lives. They had come into the midst of the Western Cherokees and declared their intention to live under the laws of the Western Cherokee Nation, and they had been accepted.

Then when the Cherokee Nation had pulled the Western Cherokee Nation back into its fold, many had accepted the situation. But others, like Tom Starr, had not. Starr was leading his own private war against the Cherokee Nation. He and his brothers and a few friends harassed voters at the polls. They attacked the homes of other Cherokees who were loyal to the government of the Cherokee Nation, and they had been declared outlaws by the Cherokee Nation.

Jack understood them, but he had not joined them. He had his own private war, and it was not against the Cherokee Nation. It was against the Osage Nation. Perhaps if he had not built up such an intense hatred for the Osages, he would have joined the ranks of Tom Starr. Perhaps. But that was not the way things had worked out for Spanish Jack.

Those were his thoughts when he heard a moan, and it had not come out of his own mouth. He was sure of it. He listened, all his senses suddenly alert. He heard it again, and this time he was sure. There was a man moaning, somewhere below him and somewhere, well, in the direction his feet were pointing. It had to be the Osage. So his fall too had been broken in some way, and he too was still alive and somewhere on the side of this cliff. Jack tried to quiet his own breathing. What if the Osage was not as badly hurt as was he? If the man discovered that Jack was still alive, he would try to climb up to him and finish him off.

In fact, that is just what Jack suddenly wanted to do. Find a way to get to the Osage and kill him. It was difficult to believe that anyone could have taken the kind of fall Jack had just survived and not be at least as banged up as he was. And the man was moaning out loud. Jack thought, if I can just find him and reach him, I can throw him the rest of the way off this cliff. But he hated the thought that the man might survive and reach safety, and he himself die from his injuries. He had to get up. He had to locate the man and try to finish the job. He tried to sit up, but when he tried to use his arms at his sides to push with, stabbing pains shot through his body. He almost cried out, but because of the nearness of the Osage, he swallowed the noise.

The pain caused by the effort had turned the world black and started his head spinning, and he had to lie still with his eyes closed for a period of time. When at last the spinning stopped, when he could see again, he tried to sit up without the use of his hands and arms. It was difficult, but he managed it. This time, the worst pain was in his ribs. He had decided by then that both arms were indeed broken. He wondered if some ribs were not broken as well. Sitting upright, he breathed deeply for a long moment. Then he started moving his legs, trying to get one knee bent in order to get a foot underneath himself.

The scraping and dragging of the leg were bound to have been heard by the Osage, but Jack did at last manage to get both feet under him. He was on his knees. He inched forward, his useless arms dangling at his sides. He thought that it would have been crazy, what he was trying to do, were it not for the fact that the worst thing that could happen would be if he fell from the ledge. That would only bring it all to an end a little sooner, so it did not really matter. He kept scooting along, scratching his knees as he went.

Looking off the edge, he could see the rocks below, and he could see the river rushing past. The thought of the fall was dizzying, but the water looked cool and inviting. He moved a little farther. Then the ledge suddenly narrowed and disappeared. He had come to the end of his little world. The little world on which his life would likely end. But wait. Below him a scrubby and tenacious tree grew right out of the wall of rock. He thought that if he could somehow lower himself into that tree, he would be able to see from a whole new vantage point. He had nothing to lose. He decided to try it. But how would he climb down with no hands?

Turning to face out into space, he shuffled his feet out from under him and sat on the edge of the ledge as on a chair. His feet dangled just above the tree. It was only a short distance down to the tree, but without hands to use for grasping, it seemed an impossible distance. Even so, he had made up his mind. He would try it. He scooted out as far on the edge as he could without falling and reached with his feet toward the largest branch of the tree beneath him. If he stretched his foot, his toes would not quite touch it. He would have to drop. It was the only way. It was a fool thing to try.

Using the muscles of his legs and buttocks, he inched himself forward until he fell. He felt a sensation as if his stomach had left his body, and then he felt himself hit the tree, straddling the largest branch. He fell forward, his face in smaller branches and twigs and leaves, and he felt himself sliding sideways. Desperate, he bit a small branch and held himself in place with his teeth. Slowly, straining, he straightened himself up. He looked to his right. The face of the cliff was no longer sheer. He had fallen to a place where it began a gradual slope down to the rocky riverbank. And there lay the Osage. Jack could tell immediately that the man had one badly broken leg, for the leg was bent and twisted at an unnatural angle. He could also see that the man was looking at him.

"Ah, Spanish Jack," the Osage said through teeth clenched from pain, "so you too survived the fall."

"Our fight is not over until one of us is dead," Jack said. Gripping a small branch in his teeth, Jack swung his left leg over the branch he straddled and dropped to the sloping ground. When he hit, he slid for a ways. When he finally came to a stop, he was farther down the slope than was the Osage. He looked over his shoulder.

"We're both dead, Spanish Jack," the Osage said. "Your arms are broken. I can tell by the way you move."

"I can kick you off this mountain," Jack said.

"Come on over here if you can, no arms," the Osage said.

Jack struggled, but the more he kicked with his feet, the farther down he slid. The Osage laughed out loud.

"You have no arms," he said. "and I have no legs. We are both useless. We can do nothing but watch each other die."

So both his legs are broken, Jack thought.

"I can outlast you," he said. "At least I'll see you dead before I go."

"We'll see which one dies first," the Osage said.

Jack looked up over his shoulder again. He could tell that the Osage was suffering mightily, and that gave him some pleasure. He had a sudden urge to curse the man.

"Do you speak English?" he asked in Osage.

"No," the man said.

"Damn," said Jack to himself. "I can't even curse him."

He tried again to shuffle his feet to push himself farther up the slope, but again, all he could find to push against was loose rock, and all he did was cause himself to slide farther down the hillside. He quit moving his feet and pressed his back against the unstable ground. In a moment he came to a stop again. He looked over his shoulder. He was farther away from the Osage than he had been. He could not get to him. He laid his head back and tried to relax. He went to sleep.

It was early morning when Jack came out of his deep sleep. He hurt all over, and he had developed gnawing hunger pangs. His mouth was dry, and he was craving a drink of water. He had not thought before that a man could have so many different things tormenting him all at the same moment. His situation slowly came back into his mind, and he looked quickly back up and over his shoulder. The Osage had not moved. He wondered if the man had died yet. Then he saw the Osage slowly lift his head and look in his direction.

"So you're still alive, Spanish Jack," the Osage said.

"I'll outlast you," said Jack. He wanted to add, you son of a bitch, but the Osage would not have understood the English words, and a translation into Osage would not carry the same impact.

"So what do you want to do?" the Osage asked him. "Lie there like a wounded deer and wait?"

"I'd do more if I could," said Jack.

"We can do more," the Osage said.

"What?" said Jack. "What do you mean?"

"You have legs, and I have arms," the Osage said. "If we work together, we can survive this. Then, when we're both healed, if you still want to fight, we can fight."

"I wouldn't help save you," Jack said. "Not even to save my own life. I think you're crazy."

They were silent for a time, each staring into space, each longing for food and water and relief from the pain and the general situation. Jack thought about what the Osage had said. It did make a kind of sense, but he would never trust an Osage. Degadoga had called them "a nation of liars." Then the Osage spoke into the space again.

"Maybe you're afraid that if we live and if we heal and then we fight," he said, "that I will be the winner."

It was the opening Jack needed. "How could I fear such an impossible thing?" he said. "What do you propose we do?"

"I saw you sliding on the hillside in the loose rocks," the Osage said. "Do you think you could slide like that all the way to the bottom?"

Jack lifted his head to look downward.

"I think I could," he said.

"Then I should be able to do the same thing," the Osage said. "Once we're both down there, we can figure something out. On the side of this hill, there's nothing we can do."

"Then here I go," Jack said, and he began to shuffle his feet again in the loose rocks. At first he did not move, and he thought of the irony. When he had wanted to move up, he slid down. Now that he meant to slide down, he could not move. He started trying to shove himself upward again, and then again he began to slide. He did not fight it, and he slid faster. His useless arms got caught on the rocks and pulled this way and that, and he ground his teeth to keep from screaming out with the pain. Then suddenly he stopped. He was down on the riverbank. He turned and looked up.

The Osage suddenly flopped himself off the small ledge where he had been resting, and he began rolling down the sloping hillside, his broken legs flopping wildly. He cried out in agonizing pain, and Jack winced at the sight in spite of himself. At last the man stopped some feet away from where Jack waited. Jack stood up and walked over to his side. He looked down at the Osage who was still in much pain. The bent and twisted legs were ghastly in appearance. The helpless man looked up at Jack.

"Now you can kill me," he said. "You can kick me or stomp me to death."

"I wouldn't last much longer," Jack said, "with these useless arms. What do you suggest we do now?"

"Look around for some sticks," said the Osage. "Long and straight ones. If you can kick them over here, we can splint our broken bones."

Jack began to walk up and down the stretch of riverbank searching for fallen branches. Each time he came across one that looked as if it might serve the purpose, he kicked and pushed at it with his feet until he got it back over to the Osage. Then the Osage said, "These are enough. Let's see what we can do."

"Your legs look worse than my arms," Jack said. "Let's take care of them first."

"No," the Osage said. "I've seen men pass out from the pain of straightening a broken limb. If we fix my legs and I pass out, then who will fix your arms?"

"Even so," said Jack, "the legs are worse. Let's fix them first."

"All right," the Osage said.

"Tell me what to do," Jack said.

The Osage selected one of the longest and straightest of the branches. He pulled a knife from his belt and hacked the twigs and smaller branches away. Then he laid it beside his leg.

"This one should do," he said, "but I need something to tie it with."

The Osage was nearly naked, but Jack was dressed in his leather hunting clothes. He knelt beside the Osage.

"Cut away my jacket," he said. He watched as the Osage knife came close to his skin and slid underneath the leather jacket. He felt the coldness of the steel against his flesh as the man cut the jacket off him. Then the Osage cut strips from the jacket and laid them beside the stick.

"Sit on my foot," he said, "to hold it still."

Jack straddled the Osage's leg between the knee and the ankle and lowered his weight on it. The Osage put his hands on the ground and pushed, straightening his broken and twisted leg until it was back where it should be. Jack watched the man's face contort as he went through the painful process. He was afraid the man would faint, but he did not. The leg more or less straight again, the Osage laid the stick alongside it and tied it in place with the leather thongs he had cut from Jack's hunting coat. He sat panting, recovering from the ordeal.

Ready at last to go again, the man selected another stick and cut some more leather strips. He laid out the stick and the thongs as before. Then he looked at Jack. "Now this one," he said. Jack put his weight on the second leg, and the Osage repeated the grueling process. This time, he shouted out loud at the pain, and when the broken bone snapped back in place, he fell back.

"Are you all right?" Jack asked him, but he got no answer. "Osage," he said. "Answer me." But the man did not. Jack studied the man closely, and he saw that he was still breathing.

Jack looked around in desperation. The clear, cool, running water was not that far away, but it could have been miles for a man with no arms and no container to carry water in if he had good arms. At last, he had a thought. He walked to the water's edge and got down onto his knees. Leaning forward slowly and carefully, he dipped his face into the water. It felt good. He took a long drink, and then he held as much water in his mouth as he could.

He struggled back to his feet and walked back over to the unconscious Osage. Lowering himself to his knees again, he leaned over the man's face and dribbled water from his mouth onto the forehead and then the lips of the Osage. The Osage blinked. He opened his eyes. He wiped his face, and then he sat up. He realized what Jack had done. He took a deep breath, and then he took up his knife again. He prepared two shorter splints and cut more thongs. Soon he had Jacks arms straightened and bound. Exhausted, both men lay back on the hard rocks and slept.

When Jack woke up again finally, he found the Osage sitting up and looking around.

"We need to get down close to the water," the Osage said.

Jack got up. He turned his back to the other man, moved in close and got down on his knees.

"Put your arms around my neck," he said, "and hold on tight."

The Osage reached around Jack and held tight while Jack stood up and walked over to the water. Then, as carefully as he could, he knelt again and lowered the Osage back down to the ground. Both men sat panting for breath and recovering from the pain of the latest ordeal. At last, the Osage managed to get his face into the water for a long, cool drink.

He got himself back up to a sitting position and began moving rocks around, digging out a space for each of them to be able to lie down in comfortably. Jack watched him for a moment, then stood up.

"While you're doing that," he said, "I'll go see what I can find."

Jack walked along the riverbank, along the water's edge and over at the foot of the steep hill at the base of the cliff. When he came across anything that looked as if it might be useful, he kicked it all the way back to the Osage. Mostly what he found were sticks. But he did find one dried gourd and one broken and dried cane pole. The most difficult thing for him to kick along, however, was a piece of old, rotted tree stump. By the time he had done all this, he sat down exhausted.

The Osage took the tree stump, some sticks and a couple of carefully selected rocks, and he soon had a fire going. They now had themselves a small and primitive camp. Over the next few days, together, they figured out how to catch fish and crawdads. More time passed, and the Osage fashioned himself a pair of crutches. He could stand and move a little bit, awkwardly and slowly, but it was progress. Days passed, and weeks.

Slowly the bones mended. Jack began to use his hands and then his arms. The Osage took off the splints, and Jack flexed his arms. They were sore and weak, but he could use them. The splints came off the Osage's legs too, and he stood, still with the aid of the crutches, but he could move over the rocks much more easily, taking care where he put down the crutch tips. They moved out a little farther from their camp each day, always searching for anything that would be of use, and they found the wood they needed to make a bow and some arrows, and the Osage found the right rocks and made some arrowheads. They shot a rabbit and some squirrels.

One day after finishing a meal, they sat across the fire from one another, and it was as if they both had the same thought, and they both knew it. They sat in silence a bit longer though. At last the Osage spoke.

"Our wounds are healed," he said.

"Yes," Jack agreed. "I can even pull the bowstring now."

"Yes," the Osage said. "And the bow I made has a hard pull."

"You made a good strong one," Jack said.

"I may walk with a limp, but I can walk," the Osage said. "I think I could even run if I had to."

"No one would believe what we two have lived through," Jack said. "I myself would not have believed it once."

"Especially with an Osage?"

"Yes," Jack said. "Especially with an Osage."

"Well, now," the Osage said, "there is no longer any reason to delay this thing. Do you still want to fight me?"

He stood up. Across the fire, Jack stood. They faced one another for a long moment.

"No," Jack said finally. "I don't. I think the war is over."

He reached out a hand and the Osage took it.

"I'll always know you as my friend," the Osage said, "but I can't speak for any of my people. They hate you, and they'll try to kill you if they ever see you again."

"I'll get out of your country," Jack said. "I won't come back, but if I ever see you again, in some other place, some place where we two can sit together in peace and share a meal, I'll be glad of it."

"I will too," the Osage said.

They found their way back up the hill to the trail where the whole episode had begun, and there they parted company, each man headed toward his own home. But for Jack there was no home. He was an outlaw in the Cherokee Nation. Still, he moved in that direction. He had no other place to go. Walking along, he thought that he must have a horse. Surely somewhere along the way, he would come across a place where he could steal one. Then, once he was mounted again, he would decide where he would go and what he would do. His whole purpose in life had been to kill Osages. Now that was gone. He did not know what he would do.

3

Walking the trail, alone in Osage country, armed only with his hunting knife and war club, Jack knew that he was in grave danger. He would have to stay alert to any movement anywhere around himself. He was not afraid to fight any Osage, but he had just declared an end to his long-standing private war, and he meant to live up to that declaration. But he had to get out of this Osage country as soon as possible. He had made his formal peace with only one Osage. Others were not likely to recognize that peace. Jack had probably made more Osage enemies than any other man alive, and in his vulnerable situation, he was keenly aware of that fact.

It was in the middle of his second day of walking the trail. He was hungry, and he was tired. He saw off the trail to his right smoke from a chimney. At first he thought that it might be someone he could get a meal from. He had never traveled this country before on foot. He had always in the past been on horseback. Because of that, it took him a moment to orient himself, but at last he did. He knew exactly where he was, and he knew whose smoke he was watching. It was the smoke of a missionary who had set himself up in that location in order to be able to preach to the Osages.

Jack had no use for missionaries. It was one of the things he had learned from old Degadoga. He saw the work of the missionaries as being a direct assault on all of the old Cherokee beliefs, an attempt to change their entire way of life. Degadoga had once said they were trying to "learn the Cherokees to wear breeches," and that simple statement had meant a whole world of change to Jack. It made no difference that this particular missionary was in the Osage country rather than the Cherokee country. In Jack's mind, the missionaries were all alike, all worthless. But the missionary should have a horse.

Jack cut off the trail and made for the mission. In a short while, he was laid up on a hill overlooking the log building where the white man put forth his messages of attack. There was a small corral just behind the building, and in the corral were two horses. They looked from the distance to be good horses, but he wanted to take a much closer look. He could see from his vantage point that a saddle was thrown on the top rail of the corral. That was good too. He had no way of knowing who or how many men were inside the building though.

While he watched, a half dozen Osage men came riding up to the small house. They all dismounted and went inside. This was not good, to Jack's thinking. He turned things over and over in his mind. Now there were eight horses down there. He thought about getting as close to the place as he could without being seen, and then running for the Osage horses, jumping on one and spooking the rest. He could get well away before the Osages could round up the other five horses. He told himself that stealing one horse was not really conducting war, so it would be all right. He changed his mind about the arrival of the Osages.

His only other alternative seemed to be to wait for dark, sneak down, saddle and steal one of the horses in the corral. The Osage horses, on the other hand, were all ready to go. He could jump on one immediately and be on his way. He longed to be out of this Osage country. He longed to find a place where he could get himself a good meal. He also needed guns. He decided to go for one of the Osage horses. It was time to be moving. He looked around, studying the surrounding terrain.

He could creep down the back side of the small hill he was on, move a distance to his own right into a patch of woods, and work his way down pretty close to the cabin. He would come up on its back side though, and he would have to get to the cabin and around to the front all out in the open. If anyone chanced to come out of the cabin during that time, he would be spotted. Of course, the missionary would do his best to keep the Osages from killing Jack, but the Osages might not choose to listen, and even if they did, he would still be trapped in this Osage country. At last, he decided that it was worth taking a chance.

He worked his way down the hill and through the woods. Standing at the edge of the woods, the distance across the clearing seemed greater. He considered the wisdom of abandoning this plan, but shrugged off the idea. He took a deep breath and ran. He made it to the back of the cabin and stopped. Leaning against the logs, he waited to catch his breath. Then he eased himself around the corner. He saw no one. He had apparently made it thus far without alerting those inside the house. He began edging his way along the side of the cabin, moving toward the front. There was a window halfway down the wall, and he got down on his hands and knees to crawl under it.

At the front corner of the house, he stood again. He looked at the horses just a few feet away from him. He looked carefully around the corner. No one had come out the front door. He looked the horses over carefully, assessing their qualities, and he selected a small paint pony. It was not the nearest to him, but that was all right. He walked calmly toward the horses, glancing back and forth between them and the front door of the cabin. At the hitching rail, he jerked loose the reins of all six animals, then vaulted onto the back of the paint. Turning the paint, he slapped the long reins at the other five, then yelled out and rode hard.

He heard loud protesting voices behind him, and looking over his shoulder as he sped away, he saw the Osages running desperately and shouting, trying to catch up their remaining horses. One man nocked an arrow and sent it flying after Jack, but Jack was already too far away for a good shot. He grinned as he rode, exulting in his triumph, loving the feel of the wind against his face, the sensation of a fast horse between his legs again. He figured it would take the Osages a while to catch up their five errant horses. Then they might follow him, or they might not. It didn't matter either way. He would be well away from them by that time.

He rode a little more easily once he was out of the Osage country, but he still had to remain alert. He was in the Cherokee Nation, and he was an outlaw there too, a fugitive from justice. Anyone who saw him and recognized him might try to take him in or kill him for the reward that was on his head. Of course, not everyone would recognize him. Still, he was not completely relaxed. He wanted a good meal, and he wanted to replace his lost guns, but he really had no idea where he was going to get either of those things.

He decided that he would not really be safe until he had traveled almost the entire distance across the Cherokee Nation from north to south to reach the area where most of his friends, the other former citizens of the Cherokee Nation West, had settled, the area around Webber's Falls along the Arkansas River just across the line west of Fort Smith. He still had quite a distance to travel without a friendly haven along the way. Even once he reached the area around Webber's Falls, he thought, many of his former friends and associates might not be so ready to welcome him into their homes because of his status as a wanted fugitive. He would have to be careful even there. That was when he remembered Tom Starr.

Like Jack, Tom Starr had been declared outlaw by the Cherokee Nation. Like Jack, Starr had a price on his head. The difference was that while Jack had brought outlawry on his own head by continuing to fight Osages after the peace had been made, Tom Starr was an outlaw because of his activities right at home in the Cherokee Nation. Starr's loyalties were with the treaty signers and their friends and families, known as the Treaty Party. Those loyalties had been transferred to the Cherokee Nation West, and with the Cherokee Nation West having been absorbed by the much larger Cherokee Nation, Starr had engaged in a variety of violent acts against the Cherokee Nation. Jack wasn't at all sure that he agreed with Starr's actions, but the Starr stronghold might be the only safe place in the Cherokee Nation for Jack to stop in. He made up his mind to search out Tom Starr.

With that decision made at last, Jack became impatient to find Starr and his gang of outlaws. The rest of his trip through most of the Cherokee Nation was slow and tiresome. He was weary and hungry. But he finally made it on the stolen Osage pony.

Arriving at last at the "outlaw stronghold" of Tom Starr, Jack moved slowly. There was a narrow trail through the thick woods, and Jack knew that Starr or some of his associates would be watching the trail and any other possible paths into his headquarters very carefully. Sure enough, he heard a voice come at him from somewhere.

"*Hlesdi*," it said in Cherokee, and then in English, "Stand where you are, stranger."

Jack halted the paint and held his hands well out to his sides.

"I'm unarmed," he said, "except for a knife and a war ax. I want to see Tom Starr."

There was a moment of silence before the voice came back again.

"Who are you and what's your business here?"

"I'm Jack Spaniard," Jack said. "They call me Spanish Jack."

"Stand patient," the voice said.

Jack waited in the trail for some minutes wondering just what was about to happen. At last a figure stepped out of the woods. A dark-skinned man with black hair cropped shoulder length, wearing a hunting jacket fashioned from a trade blanket and a flat-brimmed black hat walked toward Jack. He was carrying a rifle easily across his arms, and he was one of the biggest men Jack could ever recall having seen. He stopped a few feet away from Jack. Jack threw a leg over the paint and dropped to the ground.

"So you're Spanish Jack," the big man said.

"That's what they call me," Jack answered.

The tall man stuck out his right hand for Jack to take. "I'm Tom Starr," he said.

Sitting at a table in Tom Starr's comfortable log home, following a sumptuous meal and lots of coffee, Jack felt better than he had since his fight with the Osages on the narrow mountain trail. Starr, sitting across the table, offered Jack a pipe and tobacco. Jack accepted, filled the pipe and lit it. Starr did the same. They sat quietly and puffed their pipes for another moment. It was Starr who at last broke the silence.

"So, Jack," he said, "what brought you to these parts?"

"I'm through killing Osages," Jack said. "I couldn't think of anywhere else to go. I'm a wanted man in the Cherokee Nation."

"So am I," Starr said, "but you wouldn't be here if you didn't already know that. I notice that you're not packing any guns."

"I lost them," said Jack, and he decided to let it go at that. "I need to make some money and get some new ones."

"I'm a little short myself just now," Starr said. "How would you like to join me on a horse raid? We'll round up a small herd, drive them down to Texas and sell them for cash money."

"Where will we get them?" Jack asked.

Starr grinned and puffed his pipe.

"Down south," he said. "The Choctaw Nation. We'll already be halfway to Texas."

"When do we leave?"

"First thing in the morning," said Starr.

The next morning, riding a fresh horse and carrying a brace of pistols and a rifle, all furnished by Starr, Jack rode out with Tom Starr, his brothers and a couple of other men. All were Cherokees. Riding into the Choctaw Nation, they picked up horses where they found them. Some were grazing in pastures. Others were in unguarded corrals. By the time they reached the Red River, they had a fair-sized herd. Tom Starr knew exactly where he was going too. He had a buyer in mind ahead of time. Jack realized soon that Starr had a well-organized operation.

And Starr was generous. He split the money almost immediately, giving Jack an equal share with the others. Jack offered to pay Starr out of his share for the guns and horse, but Starr refused to accept the payment. "You're one of us now," he said, "for as long as you care to stick around." Before they left Texas, Jack found a store and bought himself a new suit of white man's clothes. He bought a pair of boots and a black hat, similar to the one worn by Starr. Dressed in his new clothes, he checked himself over in a mirror there in the store. The Spanish blood that coursed in his veins, though diluted by several generations, showed itself in his features.

He thought about some of the Frenchmen, Spaniards and Creoles he had seen in New Orleans on some of his own earlier trips to sell stolen Comanche horses. He could pass for one of them easily, he thought. Riding back to Starr's home, that same thought kept returning to his mind. He wasn't at all sure that he relished the idea of a life of outlawry among his own people, and the only way he could think of to get out of it was to clear out. To see if he could get himself lost in the general population. To try to blend in.

He was also outlawed by the United States, but outside of the Cherokee Nation, he doubted if anyone would notice him or think about him. Probably the only Americans who knew anything about him were the soldiers at Fort Gibson. And now that he had made his peace with the Osages, he would likely be soon forgotten. He made no hurried decision, but the thought stayed in the back of his mind.

He felt a sense of obligation to Tom Starr, though, and he could think of no graceful way to tell Starr that he was leaving. So he stayed. It was a couple of weeks later when he rode out with the Starr Gang to rob a country store operated in the Cherokee Nation by a white man. The white man and his wife were lucky to escape with their lives. The outlaws took all their money and a good stock of supplies. Then they set fire to the store and rode away whooping. Jack felt guilty. He felt sorry for the two whites. He had nothing against them.

They were riding back toward Starr's stronghold, when Starr's brother, Ellis, who had been taking up the rear, came riding hard to catch up with them.

"Light Horse," he said. "Coming at us."

The outlaws raced their horses toward a valley ahead. Bean Starr rode well ahead of the others. Suddenly, he reined in, turned and came back toward the group.

"Light Horse ahead," he said.

With Cherokee National Police both ahead and behind, it seemed that a big fight was coming, and the outlaws were out-numbered. Jack looked around quickly. There was a narrow passage just ahead to the right. He pointed it out quickly, then said, "All of you—take that way out. I'll lead them away from you."

Tom Starr started to protest, but Jack insisted.

"Go on," he said. "I'll be all right."

Tom Starr led the rest of the gang into the narrow passage. Jack looked around. The Light Horse was not yet upon him. If he could get them all together in one bunch, he might stand a chance of escaping from them. He turned his horse and rode hard up the steep side of a hill. Dismounting, he pulled the horse back out of sight. Then, taking his long rifle, he leaned into the side of a large

outcropping of rock and watched the valley below. The Light
Horsemen coming from the rear rode into view. A moment later
the other group of policemen rode up. The two groups stopped
when they came together and milled about talking until one of the
men pointed out the narrow passage that Starr and his men had
ridden through.

They knew that they'd had the gang between them, and so,
apparently, they figured out that the passage was the only way the
gang could have gone. Forming one bunch, they headed for the
passage. Jack waited for a moment, letting them get almost to
the entrance. Then he fired a shot, carefully calculated to miss its
mark. It accomplished his purpose though. The rider in front of
the group reined in. He was almost run over by those following.
The posse was a mass of confusion for a minute or two. At last,
they got their horses calmed down again. They talked among themselves again, and then one pointed to Jack's approximate location
as the place the shot had likely come from.

By that time, Jack had reloaded the long rifle. One more
shot should do it, he thought. He aimed the rifle just off to the
right of the riders below, and he fired again. Again the horses
jumped and stamped. The riders fought with their mounts, shouting and cursing. Jack turned and ran back for his own horse. He
jumped onto its back and rode hard across the top of the mountain. He was riding east.

The Light Horse at last started up the steep hill toward the
spot from which Jack had fired the two shots. Jack could see them
coming. He watched for a place where he could go back down the
side of the hill, and by the time the first Light Horseman was on
top, he had found one. He turned his horse and started down. It
was a steep decline, and Jack leaned so far back in the saddle, he
was almost lying on the horse's rump. The horse slid and neighed
and fought the slide. At last he made it to the bottom. Jack looked
up. He could see the policemen beginning to bunch up again up
on top. He rode hard toward the Arkansas border.

By the time the posse had managed to get back down from the
top of the hill, Jack was too far away to chase. Tom Starr and the
others were long gone. Jack was sure that he had eluded the Cherokee lawmen, and finally he slowed his horse, allowing it to walk
along the road. He leaned forward and patted its neck, talking to

it softly and telling it that it had done a good job. And it had. He had given it a hard ride.

Now and then, he looked back over his shoulder, just to make sure, but he was close to relaxed. He could see no pursuit, and he couldn't figure out how anyone could be pursuing after the chase he had led them. Ahead was the border between the Cherokee Nation and Arkansas. They could not follow him across that. Over there in the United States, he would be safe from pursuit by Cherokee lawmen. And he had found his graceful way out of Tom Starr's lawless gang. He felt good about that.

Jack felt as if he were riding into a new life. He had guns and a good horse. He had on a new suit of clothes and money in his pockets. He was riding away from his life as a fugitive and an outlaw. He felt free. But he also felt alone. Very much alone. He began to ask himself just what kind of life could a lone Cherokee lead, away from his own people, away from the only home he had ever known. What would he do with himself? How would he live? Would he ever find friends? A place to settle down? As he approached the borderline and rode across, these questions and others nagged at his brain.

4

Jack rode into Fort Smith, Arkansas. What had begun as an army outpost was developing into a bustling settlement with trading posts and inns outside the walls of the fort. He hoped that no soldier would recognize him in his new suit and hat. He had not plucked whiskers since the incident on the high trail, and he had grown a mustache and a scrawny beard. He had decided to keep that too. It helped his disguise. If he should run into anyone who had seen him before, that person would remember Spanish Jack as a Cherokee in buckskins and a turban with a smooth face. The new look might help keep him safe.

He found a livery stable and saw to it that his horse was well taken care of. Then he located an inn where he could have a good meal. Following the meal, he drank several more cups of hot coffee. He then went out to find a trading post where he bought himself two more suits of clothes and a valise in which to pack them. He also purchased more powder and shot, a short clay pipe and some tobacco. He went back to the inn, where there were tables and chairs outside, and he sat and smoked.

He was out of the Cherokee Nation, and, though he was wanted by the United States, he felt reasonably certain that no one would recognize him in Arkansas, or anyplace else outside of Cherokee or Osage country. But he had no purpose, and that fact bothered him. He did not want to remain in Fort Smith, but he had no idea where else he might go or why. It came into his mind that his share of the money from the stolen Choctaw horses would not last him forever. He would have to find a way to make some more money. He was thinking of that when a stranger in a box coat and a shiny black top hat walked over to his table and doffed his hat.

"May I join you, sir?" the stranger said.

Jack motioned to the chair across the table from himself, and the man sat down.

"Thank you, sir," the man said. "My name is Morgan Conrad. You seem to be a stranger in town."

Conrad reached across the table with his right hand, and Jack took it.

"Jack Spaniard," he said before thinking. Immediately, he chastised himself for not having come up with a phony name. Here he had been thinking of his appearance, and the first man he had spoken to, he had blurted out his own proper name.

"It's a pleasure, Mr. Spaniard," Conrad said. "May I buy you a cognac?"

Jack nodded. "Thank you," he said.

Conrad ordered two drinks. He lifted his, and said, "To your health, sir."

Jack picked up his own glass and responded appropriately. Both men took a sip of the strong, sweet liquor. Jack was not a hard drinker, but he had tasted whiskey before. He thought that he preferred it to this sweet stuff.

"It's a pleasure to encounter a gentleman," Conrad said. "I traveled out here from St. Louis, and all I've met are rough frontier types. Even the soldiers here are uncouth. The officers, of course, are gentlemen, but I've seen little of them."

Jack wondered what Conrad would have thought of him had he not changed into store clothes. He also wondered why a white man who thought of himself as a gentleman would travel from St. Louis to Fort Smith, but he kept the question to himself. Then, as if reading Jack's mind, Conrad said, "I'm a purchaser of furs for a company in St. Louis, and my business occasionally forces me to travel to these remote outposts. And you, sir, what is your business, if I may be so bold?"

"Horses," Jack said. "I buy and sell horses." It was only half a lie. Jack had never bought a horse in his life, but he had sold a good many.

"Ah," Conrad said. "Then you might be interested in the race tomorrow morning. They say it will be a big one—a good many horses will be running, and I dare say, there will be some heavy wagering."

"Tomorrow morning, you say?"

"Yes, sir," said Conrad. "Just beyond the east wall of the fort. Will you be there?"

"I just might," said Jack. He was a good judge of horses. With any luck, he could pick a winner. It was one way of increasing his cash. Jack bought a second round of drinks and sat for some time making small talk with Morgan Conrad. Then they parted company, declaring their intention to see one another in the morning at the racetrack, and Jack found himself a room for the night in an inn.

Jack was surprised at the size of the crowd gathered there outside the fort to watch the race. He was surprised as well at the number of horses and riders. It seemed as if the commander of the post had turned everyone out for the event, but there were civilians in attendance as well, outnumbering the military personnel. They had seemingly come out of the woods from every direction. Jack had not before considered just how many whites had moved so far west, so close to the new land of the Cherokee Nation. He located Morgan Conrad and exchanged greetings with the man, and then he noticed, across the track, a small contingent of Osages.

Near the Osages, the army officers were seated underneath a canvas awning. There were no other seats. The crowd stood. It was a loud and boisterous gathering with a pervasive holiday spirit. Whiskey flowed freely, and bets were being made openly all around. The track was straight, and Jack estimated it to be about a half mile in length. It was wide enough for four horses to run side by side. Jack and Conrad walked over close to the starting line. The horses and riders for the first race were taking their places. Jack looked them over and selected a long-legged roan with a scrawny white man on her back.

Nearby a white man in shirtsleeves and a black vest was taking bets. Jack counted out some of his money and placed a bet on the roan. Conrad followed Jack's lead. They moved to a better spot from which to watch the race. The horses lined up, and the jockeys had to fight them to hold them back. The crowd grew louder. The gun was fired, and the race was on. For a moment the roan was behind. Then with a sudden burst of speed, she moved out in front, and she stayed there, crossing the finish line well ahead of the horse that came in second. Jack and Conrad collected their winnings as the second group of horses were moving up to the line.

Jack looked them over carefully with Conrad standing close by his side. "The black," he said. They placed their bets again, and again they won. By the end of the day, Jack's pockets were well stuffed with money, as were Conrad's. The large crowd was beginning to break up. Jack noticed a group of four soldiers looking disgruntled. He thought they were looking at him. They had lost all their money, and they had seen him winning, he thought. He'd have to watch his back.

He was walking with Conrad back toward the inn to buy a meal, and then he glanced at the small band of Osages. He was sure that one of them looked at him directly. Then the Osage walked over to the awning and spoke to one of the officers there. Jack knew that he was the subject of the talk. Suddenly he felt very insecure at Fort Smith. It was too late in the day to start traveling, especially when he had no destination in mind, but he made up his mind to leave early the next morning.

He made it back to the inn with Conrad, and they ordered a meal and drinks. Jack declined the sweet cognac and had a whiskey instead. All the time they sat, even during the meal, Conrad carried on about Jack's knowledge of horses, and how they had bet on the right horse every time. Jack began to feel uncomfortable around the man. He was too loud, and he talked too much about the wrong things. Anyone within earshot who had not already known about their luck was hearing about it.

Finished with his meal, Jack leaned back to smoke a pipe and sip his whiskey. He turned his chair slightly in order to comfortably cross one leg over the other, and he found himself staring out at the river where a large steamboat was docked. Casually, he said to Conrad, "Is that what you came west on?"

"The very thing," Conrad said, "and I wish I was going back with it in the morning."

"It's leaving in the morning?" Jack asked. "Going back East?"

"That's right," Conrad said.

The plan came to him all at once. There were still Cherokees back East, not many, but a few had managed to avoid the massive roundup and removal. There was a place he could go. He had heard that no one was bothering those who had stayed behind. He could go find them and live with them. He had never even seen the old Cherokee country. He had been born in Missouri and grown to manhood in Arkansas. It was about time he saw the land of his fathers and mothers, the place of the beginnings. And the steamboat would take him almost all the way. The plan was so simple and made such good sense that he wondered why he had taken so long to come up with it. When it became convenient, he excused himself and parted company with Conrad. He walked down to the river and onto the boat, where he booked passage. He felt better now that he had a goal.

On his way back to the inn, he stopped by the livery stable and sold his horse to the liveryman. He didn't get what he thought it was worth, but that was all right. He wouldn't need a horse for a while, and he had plenty of cash. Back at the inn, he sat outside and drank coffee. Once he saw the four disgruntled soldiers walk by at a distance. He thought that they were looking his way. When suppertime came around, there was no way he could avoid Morgan Conrad. They sat together for their evening meal. Jack did not mention his plans.

He had been sleeping well in his room in the inn when a noise disturbed his sleep. From long habit, he came quickly awake. It was dark in the room, but he could see four dark shapes moving about as if they were searching all his belongings. He did not jump up at once. He took in the situation. There were four men. One was leaning over his valise and rummaging through the clothes in it. A second was digging hands into his coat pocket. A third was down on his knees looking at something on the floor, and the fourth was at the door, holding it open a crack and peeping out.

Jack moved his right hand slowly. He gripped his hunting knife by the blade, the leather of the sheath protecting his hand from the sharp cutting edge. Then he moved fast, sitting up and bashing the head of the man on the floor with the handle of the knife. The man fell forward stunned. The other three quickly turned on Jack. Jack again swung the knife like a club, slapping the man nearest him across the side of the face with the handle. The third man got hold of him by the throat, and the fourth one came in close to help. Jack pulled the knife from its sheath and drove the blade into the heart of the choker. The man gasped and gurgled horribly as he crumpled onto the floor.

"Let's get out of here," one said, and the three still living ran out the door.

Feeling around in the dark, Jack found all of his belongings. Even his money seemed to have been untouched. He had come awake in time and driven them off before they could find anything to steal. But he had killed one. He cleaned his knife blade on the shirt of the dead man, and then he got dressed. He packed his things, took them up and moved to the door. A bit of light came in through the door from the main room of the inn, and Jack glanced back at the body on the floor. It was one of the four disgruntled soldiers. He went out and shut the door.

Jack spent the rest of the night in the woods near the fort. When the sun came out, he took up his things and walked down to the riverboat. He walked calmly and casually as if nothing were wrong. Apparently the three soldiers had not yet sounded the alarm. He wondered how they would report the incident. They couldn't very well tell the truth about the way their comrade had been killed. Perhaps they were waiting, trying to concoct a good story, or perhaps they would just keep quiet and pretend to know nothing about it when the body of their friend was finally discovered.

And that could be a little while yet, Jack thought. The innkeeper would likely think that Jack was still asleep. The door was shut, and he had not told the man about his passage on the riverboat. He had paid for the lodging ahead of time, though, so he was not guilty of having defrauded an innkeeper. In spite of all this, he kept expecting to be confronted by angry soldiers or arresting officers or someone as he made his way to the boat. He was not. He did not feel quite safe, though, until the boat was well on its way down the river.

It was Jack's first ride on a steamboat, and he enjoyed it. The engines chuffed, the rear paddle wheel turned and black smoke billowed. His quarters on the boat were much nicer than his room at the Fort Smith inn, and the meals were good. Jack busied himself the first few days walking around the boat, looking everywhere he was allowed to look and taking in all the details. Sometimes he leaned on a rail and watched the water as the boat slid through the river. Other times he relaxed in a deck chair and enjoyed the passing scenery. He learned about the dangers of sandbars and sawyers, those fallen and submerged trees that lurked just under the surface of the water.

At the same time, they were passing through the part of Arkansas that had once been the Cherokee Nation West, and Jack was bitterly aware that he was looking at land that had been stolen from him and his people by the government of the United States. He was noticing all along the way, too, that his former country was being rapidly populated by whites. At each stop the riverboat made, more passengers boarded: one or a few.

One new passenger was a tall and gaunt white man in fancy clothes: a top hat and a long-tailed frock coat. One afternoon he approached Jack where he sat on deck smoking his pipe.

"Good afternoon, sir," he said. "Allow me to introduce myself. J. Worthington Jones."

Jack took the man's hand. "Jack Spaniard," he said. He had still not come up with an alias, and he had decided to just forget about it.

"Mr. Spaniard," said Jones, "are you a gambling man by chance?"

"I've been known to bet on the horses," Jack admitted.

"A worthy sport," Jones said. "The sport of kings, but I was referring to cards. Poker, sir. Do you play?"

"I've never played poker," said Jack. "I wouldn't know how."

"I could teach you the game," Jones said, "and I promise you that I won't take your money while you're learning."

So from then on, Jack spent his days at poker with J. Worthington Jones. In a matter of a few days, he had learned the game well enough that Jones had said, "You're on your own now, and if you play with me, I'll show no mercy."

"Do your worst," said Jack.

Other players joined their games, and Jones had taught Jack well enough that he won as often as he lost. He figured that he was staying pretty much even. He decided, though, that he would not make a professional gambler like Jones. In order to call it a profession, a man would have to stay ahead, not just stay even. Traveling along the river, though, it was a pleasant enough way to pass the time.

There were four of them playing one afternoon: Jack, Jones, a small, bald businessman named Wilson and a large, red-faced man called Striker. As usual, Jack was managing to break even. He won some and lost some. Wilson was losing, and so was Striker. Striker was losing the most. Finally, cleaned out, as Jones was raking in the pot, Striker grabbed his wrists. Jones looked him in the eyes.

"You're cheating," Striker said. "No one wins that much without cheating."

"Take your hands off of me," Jones said. "I'll forget that you said that."

"I'll say it again," Striker said. "You're a cheat."

Jones jerked his hands free, and Striker stood, reaching under his coat for a pistol. Quick as a flash, Jones came out with a small pocket pistol and fired, the ball tearing into Striker's chest. It was a small-caliber ball, but the shot was fired at close range, and the ball hit the heart. Striker fell dead. Jones raked his cash in and pocketed it. In a matter of a few minutes, the first mate and the captain were on deck.

"He called me a cheat," Jones explained, "and he went for a gun. I acted in self-defense."

The captain looked at Mr. Wilson, who was mopping his bald head with a handkerchief.

"It's true," Wilson said. "The man called him a cheat and pulled a gun."

The captain then turned to Jack. "How did you see it?" he asked.

"Just as you've heard," Jack said. "Striker was a bad player and a bad loser. He accused Mr. Jones of cheating. There was no cheating in this game. He tried to kill Mr. Jones, but Mr. Jones was faster. That's all."

"Then that's the way we'll report it," the captain said. "Even so, Mr. Jones, I'll ask you to leave this boat at the next stop."

Jones did not argue. At the next stop, he said his farewell to Jack.

"Don't be concerned," he said. "Another boat will come along."

Jack missed Jones at first. The poker games had helped to pass the time. The newness of river travel had worn off, and he was getting bored. He began thinking more about his destination. He was headed for the land of his origins, and there were still Cherokee people there, living where they had always lived, Cherokee people who had not been driven out by the greedy white men, living the way Cherokees had always lived. His mind conjured up images of ancient Cherokee villages, seemingly untouched by the white man. He saw hunters coming home with freshly killed deer to the smiling faces of happy women and children. He was anxious to join those people. He was anxious to wash away the stains the white men had left on his life.

Then one day the river trip was at an end. The boat stopped at a place called Ross's Landing, and Jack disembarked. He was in Tennessee, and he knew that all around him as far as he could see had once belonged to the Cherokees. He felt a swell of resentment rise up within, but he swallowed it and walked toward the settlement. Making inquiries, he discovered that the Cherokees were in North Carolina, several days' horseback ride to the east. He bought himself a good riding horse and a saddle, and everything he thought he would need for camping out along the way. It was late in the day, so he paid for a room at an inn. He would get an early start in the morning.

5

His first day of riding, Jack came to another settlement by the time he was hungry for a noon meal. These white men, he thought, pushed the Indians out of the eastern part of the country to make room for themselves, and now they were doing their best to fill up all the space they had taken. He kept his thoughts and his bitterness to himself and bought himself a meal. Then he rode on. He passed a few travelers along the road, and when he had ridden into evening, he came to a settler's house. He paid the settler and his wife for a home-cooked meal and a place to sleep the night. He resumed his journey the following morning, after paying the settler's wife for a breakfast.

Jack had begun to think that he had outfitted himself needlessly for the road trip. It was looking as if he would not have to camp at all. But by high noon, he found out that he had come to a hasty conclusion. There was nothing near. There was no sign of human habitation. The woods were thick and close on both sides of the road. He kept riding. In a while, he came to a wide spot at the side of the road that showed evidence of prior usage as a campsite. He stopped, unsaddled his horse and let it graze and built himself a fire. Checking back into the woods a bit away from the road, he discovered a clear-running creek. He led the horse to the creek and fetched some water for himself to the campsite. He fixed himself a meal and boiled some coffee.

When he had finished his meal, he relaxed for a while and

smoked a pipe. Then he cleaned up his campsite, saddled his horse
and resumed his travel. He saw few other people that day, and
that night he slept on the ground at a campsite. He was moving
into the mountains. Travelers and settlers were scarce, so whenever he did come across either one, he stopped and asked directions.

Jack marveled at the mountains. By comparison the mountains
he had known all his life in Missouri and Arkansas were foothills.
After a few days of travel, he found himself going down into a
deep, dark and cool valley. The vegetation was lush. He began to
feel a hatred for the men who had driven his people away from
this land; but he drove away the hatred by thinking of the idyllic
existence of the Cherokees who had remained secure in their an-
cestral homes, the people he was about to meet and visit.

And then he found them. And then he saw that they were
living in abject squalor. Their pitiful settlement was built on the
steep side of a high and rocky mountain. There were some crude
lean-tos, fewer small and primitive log houses, and nearby caves
were being used as homes for some. Their clothes were ragged,
and most had no shoes. They took him to be a rich white man,
but he held out his hands and rubbed his skin, saying, "Look. I'm
not a white man." He spoke to them in the Cherokee language,
and then when he told them his name, some of the older ones
slowly nodded their heads.

" 'Squan,' " they said. "Yes. The name of Spaniard goes way
back among us. There's a story about a man who was called that
because his father was a real Spaniard. This 'Squan' was only an
adopted Cherokee. His mother was an Indian from some other
tribe, but she married a Cherokee man, and they raised this boy.
'Squan' was what they called him. Spaniard."

"His friend killed him," said another one. "It was an accident."

"But before he was killed," said yet another, 'he had married
a Cherokee woman, and they had children. One was called Whirl-
wind, and she became a famous War Woman."

Having identified Jack as being descended from a long and
distinguished line of Cherokees, the mountain refugees accepted
him. He was still strange to them, though, dressed in his fine white
man's clothing and riding a fine horse with an expensive saddle.
They fed him, and he discovered that they did not have much to

eat. He started to ask if the hunting was not good in these mountains, but then he realized that he had seen no guns.

"Are there still deer in these mountains?" he asked finally.

They told him that the white men had hunted around them so much that they had killed off or driven away most of the animals.

"We get one now and then with our bows," a man said.

Jack asked their permission to hunt, and it was granted. He asked their advice on where to look and how far away he would have to go. He changed to his buckskins and saddled his horse. Then he went out with his long rifle. He was gone all night, but the next morning, he returned with a large buck. The people had a grand feast. For the next several days, Jack hunted, and he kept the people supplied with venison and with other game. But he was beginning to feel that he was a burden to this poor community, and he felt like a guest. He did not feel at home, as he had expected to feel.

He got up early one morning and spoke to one of the old men.

"I'm going down to see some white men," he said. "I'll come back in a few days."

Jack went back out on the same road he had used when he had first arrived at the settlement. He rode for two days before coming to a settlement of white people, and he found a man with a herd of cattle. Counting out a good portion of his cash, he purchased a dozen head. Tucking the bill of sale into his coat, he began herding the cattle back along the trail toward the Cherokee settlement. He had made up his mind that he was going to leave, but he was going to leave the people with more than they'd had when he found them.

Back at Ross's Landing, dressed again in one of his new suits, Jack sold his horse for a loss and purchased passage on a steamboat back to Fort Smith. That would put him near home. He could buy himself another horse and get back into the country and among the people he knew. As he boarded the boat to head west, he was surprised to see none other than J. Worthington Jones.

"I told you there would be another boat," Jones said. "There is always another boat."

"But how strange that I should come across you again like this," Jack said.

"Not strange at all," Jones said. "I ride this river all the time, plying my trade."

Jack found the expression interesting, and he asked himself, what was his own trade? Stealing horses to sell? It had been exciting enough when he was younger, but, after all, it was not a dignified trade except among Plains Indians. He was a Cherokee, and the white people called them "civilized." He had enjoyed playing poker with Jones, but he had already decided that he could not successfully follow that as a profession. He would leave that to Jones and others like him. Many Cherokees were farmers, but Jack found the idea of farming repugnant. The rich ones had large plantations that were worked by slaves; but Jack was not rich, and he did not own slaves. He did not want to own slaves. He had witnessed a slave auction once in New Orleans on a trip to sell Comanche ponies, and the entire proceedings had disgusted and saddened him.

So what else was there for him to follow as a trade? Nothing he could think of. He guessed that he would just wait until his money was almost gone, and then he would steal some more horses from the Comanches. It was what he knew best.

In the meantime, on the long boat ride back to Arkansas, he played poker with Jones and other passengers. As before, he won some, and he lost some. He sat for long hours on the deck smoking his pipe and drinking coffee. Now and then, he sipped whiskey. He spent a great deal of his time contemplating his future.

At the last stop before Fort Smith, Jack left the riverboat. He was not anxious to be seen around the fort, since he had left a dead soldier in his room the last time he was there. He bought himself a horse and saddle, changed again to his buckskins, and started riding toward the Cherokee Nation. It was a longer trail, skirting around Fort Smith as he did, but he thought that it was worth it to save his neck. Several days and several campsites later, he rode across the border, leaving Arkansas behind him. He was in the southern part of the Cherokee Nation, that part where his friends and neighbors from the former Cherokee Nation West lived. He wasn't too far from Tom Starr's place, but he didn't really want to get hooked up again with Starr.

He had a few friends he thought would make him welcome, though, and he decided that he would look for them. He was riding toward Webber's Falls when he saw a group of mounted men coming toward him. One of them shouted and pointed, and then he realized that he was facing a group of Light Horse Police. He thought about staying calm and trying to bluff his way past them, but they sped up their horses riding toward him. That was not a good sign. Then one of them pointed at him and shouted again.

"Spanish Jack," the man called out. "Stay where you are."

Jack turned his horse and raced back toward the Arkansas border. He knew, though, that he would not make it riding hard like that. He turned off the road onto a side trail that led up into the rugged hills. They had seen him, though, and were following, riding single file and more slowly now. Jack kept going until he spied a large outcropping of rock. He rode behind it and dismounted. Leveling his long rifle, he fired a shot into the dirt almost between the forelegs of the horse in front of the chase.

The rider shouted as his frightened horse reared and neighed. The man had a rifle in his hands, and trying not to drop it, he lost control of his fidgeting horse and fell backwards out of the saddle and right into the path of the next rider. That rider jerked back on the reins of his horse in an effort to keep from riding over his fallen companion. Those behind him did the same, but one or two of them did ride into the horse and man just ahead.

They shouted and cursed in their confusion. Jack jumped back on his horse and hurried along as much as he could on the steep and rugged trail. Reaching the top of the hill, he found it easier going, and so he ran the horse for a time. Then he found a way back down to the main road. He thought that he had lost the Light Horse men, but he couldn't be sure. So I'm an outlaw, he said to himself. I'll show them outlawry. He turned his horse north and headed for Tahlequah, the capital city of the Cherokee Nation.

On his way into Tahlequah, Jack could see that something was going on. Tremendous numbers of people crowded around the capital square. The square itself was occupied by a large arbor, underneath which as many people were gathered as it would hold. Up on a platform, a man stood behind a podium making a speech.

Jack wondered if it might have been the Principal Chief, John Ross. He had never seen Ross.

Two small log cabins were on the far side of the square. Jack knew that they had been erected to house government offices. Around the square a number of businesses had been established: mostly inns and eateries. They should be doing a brisk business, he thought. He moved slowly along one side of the square, avoiding pedestrians and other riders. He could see that on the far side, along Wolf Creek, many people had set up campsites. Finally, he found room to stop and hitch his horse in front of one of the inns. He dismounted and went inside. The place was almost empty. A sweaty man wearing a greasy apron stepped forward to greet him.

"You don't seem to be doing much business," Jack said.

"Been busy as hell," the man said. He looked to Jack like a white man, but he was likely one of those mixed-blood Cherokee citizens. "When the chief started talking most everyone went over there to listen to him."

"So you've had a good day then," Jack said. He pulled out both of his pistols and pointed them at the man. "Bring out your cash box," he said.

"Oh, hell," the man said.

"Be quick about it," said Jack, "or I'll put a hole in your belly."

The man moved behind a counter and leaned over.

"If you come up from there with a weapon," Jack said, "you're a dead man."

The man straightened up and put a box on the counter. Jack moved over to the counter. He tucked one pistol back into his belt and reached for the box. He told the man, "Back up," and as the man did so, Jack reached out with his left hand and opened the box. It was full of cash. Jack took a fistful and stuffed it into his jacket. He took a second grab and a third. He looked into the box.

"That's enough," he said. "I won't leave you broke. Now just stay where you are and keep quiet."

He backed to the door, and as he started to turn to open it, another man stepped in. He looked at Jack and saw the pistol. He looked at the man in the apron.

"What's going on?" he said.

Jack stepped quickly behind the man and shoved him on into the room. Then he went outside, closing the door behind himself.

He vaulted into the saddle and turned his horse. Ignoring the crowd, he rode hard, headed north. He shouted as he rode, and frightened citizens jumped left and right getting out of his way. Behind him, the two men came rushing out of the eatery, yelling, trying to get someone's attention.

"I've been robbed," the greasy proprietor called out.

"There he goes," shouted the other man.

"Who?" someone asked. "One of the Starrs?"

In a matter of minutes, a half dozen Light Horse were on Jack's trail, but Jack had a good head start on them. He turned east, headed again for the Arkansas border, but crossing from Tahlequah, he would be a good distance north of Fort Smith. He felt good. The Cherokee Nation had made him into an outlaw because of his continued fight against the Osages. Now that he had given up that fight, they still called him outlaw. He had plenty of money, but he had pulled the robbery in Tahlequah out of defiance. All right. Now he was a real outlaw.

Reaching a high point on the road, he turned to see the riders coming after him. They were still well behind him though. He continued on his way until he came to a cabin with a corral nearby. In the corral were several horses. Jack rode over to the corral and changed his saddle from his tired horse to one of the fresh ones in the corral. It was a fair trade, he thought. As he mounted the fresh horse, a Cherokee woman stepped out the front door of the cabin.

"What are you doing?" she asked in Cherokee.

"I'm trading horses with you," Jack said. "Mine is better than yours anyway. You're getting the best of the deal. Thank you."

He turned the fresh horse back onto the road and hurried it along. Now he would really extend the distance between himself and his pursuers. He soon lost sight of the six riders behind him, and by the time he reached the Arkansas border, he figured they had given up the chase some miles back. He stopped by the edge of a stream to rest and water the horse. Digging into his pockets, he brought out his pipe and tobacco. He filled the pipe, then he used the flint in one of his pistols and a piece of char cloth to light the tobacco.

As he smoked, he wondered just what he would do next and

where he would go. He thought about Missouri, but he didn't
know what he would do there. He wondered if he would be able
to ride the rivers like J. Worthington Jones, but he didn't really
think so. He finished his pipe, cleaned it and put it away. Then
he moved back over to his horse. He took hold of the saddle horn
and was about to mount up when he realized that there was someone behind him. He looked over his shoulder. Five Osage men had
managed to slip up on him. He was ashamed of himself.

He let go of the saddle horn and turned to face the Osages.
They were well armed with bows and arrows, spears, knives and
war axes. Even with his guns, he would not have much of a chance
against these five at such close range. Besides, he had sworn that
his war with the Osages was at an end. He greeted them in their
own language. The man standing nearest him gave him a suspicious look.

"So you speak our language," he said.

"Yes," Jack said.

"But you're not Osage," the man said. "You look like a that-
thing-on-their-heads person to me."

"I am a Cherokee," Jack admitted, "but the war between our
people is over now."

"Do you have coffee?" the Osage asked.

Jack nodded. "Yes," he said. "I have."

"Let's drink some of your coffee," the Osage said.

Soon they had a fire going and a pot of coffee boiling over the
fire. Jack was careful to make no sudden or suspicious moves. The
Osage men drank all the coffee they wanted, and then the man
who had spoken to him before said, "Where are you going? Your
country is over there." He nodded toward the west across the Arkansas line.

"I'm visiting over here," Jack said. "I have friends in Missouri."

"We're going to Fort Smith to see the soldiers there," the
Osage said. "Do you have friends at Fort Smith too?"

"I know some people there," Jack said.

"Why don't you ride with us," the Osage said. "Why don't you
go see your friends at Fort Smith?"

"I had other plans," Jack said.

The Osages closed in around him. One man had already

picked up Jack's long rifle. Another now pulled a pistol out of his belt, and yet another took the second pistol. Jack made no move to resist them.

"You can change your plans," the talking Osage said. "I think you should ride to Fort Smith with us."

"Why should I do so?" Jack asked.

"I think your friends the soldiers will be happy to see you," the Osage said. "I think they've been looking for you. I think that your name is Spanish Jack."

The man holding Jack's rifle stepped forward defiantly, and said, "I think we should kill him right here."

"No," said the other. "The soldiers want him. They'll pay us money for him."

"They'd pay money for his scalp," said the one with the rifle.

"Maybe," said the other, "but I think we should take him to the soldiers—alive. He was right. The war is over. If we kill him ourselves, that might get it started again. We don't want to be blamed for that. Come on. Let's ride to Fort Smith and take him with us."

6

J ack stood before the desk of Major Bradford at Fort Smith, his
Osage captors behind him and on both sides. Across the desk,
Bradford leaned back in his chair. His chin resting on his
chest, he looked up at Jack from underneath heavy eyebrows.

"We thought about just killing him ourselves," said an Osage,
"for all of our people he has killed."

"I'm pleased that you did not " Bradford said. "The war might
have started all over again."

"We considered that," said the Osage. "We did not want to be
the ones responsible for breaking the treaty. We also thought
about the money you promised to anyone who brought him in to
you."

"Uh, yes," said Bradford. These Osages would remember that
reward, he thought. He leaned forward in his chair, laid out a piece
of paper and took up the quill on his desk. Dipping the pen in an
inkwell, he wrote something on the paper. "Lieutenant," he called
out. A young officer stepped into the room and stood at attention.

"Yes sir?"

Bradford held the paper out toward the lieutenant. "Take this
note along with these Osage men to the paymaster and see to it
that they receive their money," he said. Then to the Osages, he
added, "You can leave Jack's guns here with me."

"Yes sir," said the lieutenant. He turned to the Osages. "Would you—gentlemen—follow me, please," he said. He left the office with the Osages right behind him.

"Sit down," Bradford said to Jack.

Jack sat in the nearest chair to the desk.

"I had hoped to never set eyes on you again," Bradford said.

"I admit that I wasn't looking forward to this meeting myself," said Jack. "Will you hang me or put me in front of a firing squad?"

"You've been a fugitive for some time now," Bradford said, ignoring Jack's question, "and there was a time when I wanted to get my hands on you very badly. You've been the source of a great deal of annoyance to me over the last few years. And quite a lot of frustration. Hence, the reward which I just had to pay."

Jack raised an eyebrow. Bradford was talking in the past tense. This was becoming interesting.

"You see," Bradford went on, "times have changed. Things have been quiet between the Cherokees and the Osages. We want to keep it that way. You were outlawed because you kept up the fighting after the peace had been made, but it seems that you've quit at last. Is that correct?"

"I made my peace with the Osages," Jack said.

"If I were to put you on trial for your past activities against the Osages," Bradford said, "it might heat things up again. We might find ourselves back in the middle of a war. I don't want to do that. So just now, I'm inclined to say that the war is finally over and just let it all go at that."

"I see," Jack said, but he was still cautious. What else did this white soldier have in mind, he wondered.

"There is another matter," said Bradford. "It's a serious matter. There's the matter of the body of a soldier that was discovered in a room which you had occupied at an inn here the very night of the killing. The body was discovered the next morning, and you had departed just hours earlier on a steamboat headed east."

"I killed the man," Jack said. "I was sleeping in that room. I woke up to find him and three others going through my things trying to rob me. I fought with them and killed that one. The others ran away."

"Do you know who they were?" Bradford asked.

"No," said Jack. He didn't bother telling Bradford that he thought he could recognize them though. He had not actually gotten a good look at the three men who had escaped his room that night, but he was reasonably sure they were the same ones he had seen watching him the day before. There had been four of them, disgruntled losers at the racetrack. The one he had killed in his room had been one of the four. He didn't lie to Bradford, though. He did not know their names.

"If the man had broken into your room and was trying to steal from you," Bradford said, "in the company of three other men, why did you not come in here and report the incident? Why did you slip away instead?"

"Because my name is Jack Spaniard," Jack said.

"Um, yes," Bradford said. "I see. Well, the body was discovered in the room you were occupying, and the incident did occur in the middle of the night. I see no reason to doubt your word. I, um, I knew the man too. He and three of his companions, probably the other three in your room that night, have long been scourges here.

"I strongly suspect that those three were the other three in your room that night, but I have no way of proving it." He heaved a sigh before continuing. "Now, I'm going to write this up as a hearing, and I'm going to say that the decree of outlawry placed on your head by the United States is hereby rescinded. I'm going to say further that the killing of the soldier was done in self-defense. There are your guns. You're free to go, Spaniard, and I hope that you find no more trouble in your life."

Jack walked back over to the inn where he had stayed before. His horse and his guns had all been returned to him, and he had left his horse at the livery stable along the way. He sat down at one of the inn's outside tables and ordered himself a whiskey. It seemed to him that he did have something to celebrate, but even so, he felt strange. The Osages had captured but not killed him, and they had accepted the reward from the United States. The trouble between Jack and the Osages seemed really to have come to an end. That in itself was a great change in Jack's life. Then Major Bradford had astonished Jack by declaring him to be a free man, no longer wanted by the United States.

The only place left where Jack was still an outlaw and a fugitive was back in his own country, the Cherokee Nation. Suddenly, he was free to roam at will anywhere he pleased except in his own home among his own people. Life had taken a surprising and ironic twist for Jack Spaniard. He sipped the whiskey and savored the burning sensation as it slid smoothly down his throat. There were some good things that the white man had brought to the Indians, he thought. Guns and horses and whiskey and the ability to curse vilely when it was called for. Those were all good things that Jack appreciated.

"Mr. Spaniard."

Jack looked over his shoulder to see Morgan Conrad approaching with a broad smile on his face and his right hand extended. Jack stood up and took Conrad's hand, and Conrad pumped vigorously.

"Join me for a drink," Jack said, genuinely glad for the man's company.

"Thank you, sir," said Conrad, and both men took their seats across the table from one another.

"I'm surprised to find you still here," Jack said.

"Oh, I'm afraid I'll be around for some time yet," said Conrad. "I haven't gathered the supply of furs I need before returning to St. Louis. So I sit around here and wait for more hunters to come in and offer me their wares. When I have enough, I'll take them back with me to St. Louis."

"I see," said Jack. "Well, in the meantime, I'm glad of your company."

"You've been away for quite a time," Conrad said.

"Yes," Jack said. "I've been to North Carolina and back. A long trip."

"Business?" Conrad asked.

"I bought some cattle," Jack said, "and disposed of them."

"Oh," said Conrad. "Profitably, I hope."

"Yes," said Jack. "Thank you. I believe the whole transaction was satisfactory to all parties."

"Good," Conrad said. "Good. I'm always happy to hear of a friend's successful business venture."

"I also visited some relatives," Jack said.

"Ah, mixing business and pleasure. By the way," Conrad said, "do you play cards?"

"A little," Jack said.

"A gambler got off the boat here yesterday," Conrad said. "A man named Jones."

"Not J. Worthington Jones?" said Jack.

"The very man," said Conrad. "You know him?"

"Yes. I spent some time with him on the steamboat going east."

"What a happy coincidence," said Conrad. "He's hosting a game of poker right here tonight. Perhaps you'll join us."

"I'd be delighted," said Jack. "It'll be good to see Mr. Jones again, and poker is always a pleasant diversion. Thank you very much."

Jack was indeed glad to see Jones again, and he welcomed the opportunity to pass away some time with the cards. After exchanging some pleasantries, they played a few hands, and, as usual, Jack managed to stay about even. Jones, of course, was the biggest winner. As the evening progressed, some players dropped out, and new ones joined the game. At last they declared a break and ordered a round of drinks. Jack lit his pipe, and they sat and made small talk. In the company of Conrad and Jones, Jack was about to decide that white men were not so bad after all. Then the three soldiers that Jack already knew too well came walking up. They approached the cardplayers at their table.

"Is this game open?" one asked.

"Yes indeed, sir," said Jones. The three soldiers dragged out chairs and sat down, giving Jack hard looks. He chose to ignore them. Jones dealt the cards, and they played a hand. Jack won, and the soldiers grumbled. They played another hand, and he won again. The looks of the three soldiers were getting harder. Jack sensed trouble ahead. Another hand was dealt, and Jack won the pot again. The soldiers threw down their cards in disgust and left the game mumbling to themselves.

"Well, Jack," Jones said, "either your luck or your skill has improved."

Jack shrugged. "If it's skill," he said, "then you deserve all the credit for having taught me."

Soon after that, Conrad excused himself to go to bed. The sun was low in the sky. Jack and Jones sat up a while longer. They had themselves another whiskey, and Jack smoked another pipe. When darkness set in, Jones said good night and went on his way. Jack sat alone to finish his pipe.

At last, finished with whiskey and pipe, Jack was about to stand up to go inside, when he felt a hard smack across the back of his head. It stunned him, but he did not lose consciousness. He put both his hands on the table and tried to get up. Someone jerked the chair out from under him, and someone kicked his legs just above his ankles, and he fell to the ground. Then someone kicked him in the side again and again, and he knew that at least two were kicking. He covered his face with his arms.

He felt rough hands grab the front of his jacket and pull him to his feet, and he was being held up on his feet by two men behind him. A third, in front of him, drove his fists repeatedly into Jack's midsection. Fighting for his breath, Jack raised his head just enough to get a look at the man in front of him. It was one of the three hard-luck soldiers. Then the man dealt him a smashing blow across the side of his face, and then another, and Jack drooped as if he had passed out.

"Let's get him out of here," he heard one say.

He felt himself being dragged, and then he felt himself being lifted and thrown roughly across the back of a horse. He heard the voices of the three soldiers as they mounted horses and started to ride. The horse under him moved along with them. It was a rough ride for Jack, slung like a sack of grain across a saddle, and it seemed like a long ride. He was in pain, and he was barely conscious. Then he felt himself slipping, but there was nothing he could do about it. In another few feet, he hit the ground headfirst.

"Corbin," he heard someone say. "He fell off."

"Hell," came the answer. "We're far enough out anyhow. We'll let him lay here. Let's get off and get his cash."

He was aware of their movements. He felt them pulling at his coat and shoving their hands into his pockets. He felt a final kick to his ribs, and then he heard them mounting up and riding away. He thought that he was lying in the middle of a road, but he did not know where the road was. They had ridden out from Fort Smith, but he had no idea in what direction. He had no idea how far they had taken him. He thought that he should try to get himself out of the way of any traffic that might come along, but he lacked the strength to crawl to the side of the road. He felt himself relaxing, and he tried to fight it, but slowly his consciousness faded away into dark oblivion.

The next morning, J. Worthington Jones and Morgan Conrad hurried into the office of Major Bradford, both wearing concerned looks on their faces. Bradford stood up to shake their hands.

"Sit down, gentlemen," he said.

The two men took seats across the desk from Bradford.

"What is it that's so urgent?" Bradford asked.

"Jack Spaniard has disappeared," Conrad said.

"Oh," said Bradford, "is that all? Jack Spaniard has had a way of disappearing for years now. When he takes it into his head to go somewhere, he goes. He doesn't tell anyone about it. I wouldn't worry about Jack Spaniard."

"But his horse is still in the livery," Jones said. "We just came from there."

"And his belongings are still in his room at the inn," Conrad said.

"We were playing cards late last evening," said Jones. "Poker. Mr. Spaniard was the big winner. There were three soldiers in the game. They lost heavily, and they were looking rather surly when they departed."

"One of the three was seen already this morning with quite a roll of bills in his possession," Conrad added.

"I see," said Bradford, suddenly serious. "Did you happen to get the names of these soldiers?"

"One of them was called Walker," said Conrad. "His friends were, let's see, Fitch. Yes, Fitch was one."

"The other was Norton," said Jones. "I'm sure of it."

"Walker, Fitch and Norton," said Bradford with a sigh. "I figured as much. I'll have them arrested and see what I can find out, but, gentlemen, if those three have gotten Jack Spaniard's money, then I fear they've killed him for it. He wouldn't hand it over to them without a fight, and Spanish Jack wouldn't give up a fight until he was dead."

"Empty your pockets," Bradford ordered.

Walker, Fitch and Norton, heavily guarded, complied, throwing bills onto the table there in front of them.

"And where did three privates in the U.S. Army get their hands on so much cash?" Bradford asked.

"We won it in a poker game last night," Walker said.

"You won it?" Bradford said.

"Yes sir," said Fitch.

"That's right, sir," said Norton. "We won it, all right."

"That's not the story I heard from two witnesses to the game," said Bradford. "What I heard was that you lost. All three of you. You lost heavily. A man by the name of Jack Spaniard won, and Spaniard is nowhere around this morning. He hasn't been seen. I believe that you jumped Spaniard and overcame him somehow. I believe that you robbed him and left him dead somewhere."

"No sir," said Walker, "We did not. We won this money, just like we said. We never seen that Spaniard again after the game was over. You say you got two witnesses against us? Well, there's three of us. That's our word against theirs, and it's three to two. Besides, if you think that there Spaniard's been killed, then where's the body?"

"I have men out looking," Bradford said. "We'll find it. In the meantime, I'll let you three cool off for a while in the stockade. We'll see if that changes your story any."

As the three were being led away under armed guard, Walker looked back over his shoulder.

"Hey," he said. "What about our money?"

"It'll be safe enough with me," Bradford said.

He sat down with a heavy sigh. He did not like those three. He'd had trouble with them before. He was convinced that they had been the ones in Jack Spaniard's room the night Spaniard had killed their unfortunate companion. He was equally convinced that somehow they had killed Spaniard the night before and stolen his money. But he was afraid that Walker had been right. At a trial it would be the word of three soldiers against the word of one respectable citizen and one professional gambler, whose reputation was at best unsavory. And without a body, it would be almost impossible to convict the men of murder.

He could have them cashiered out of the army on a string of lesser complaints, general disciplinary problems, bad attitudes, conduct unbecoming a soldier in the U.S. Army, that sort of thing, but what about the money? He hated the thought of letting them have it. He thought that maybe he could hold on to it, at least for a while, claiming it as evidence in an ongoing investigation.

Funny, he thought, that he had become so concerned about the fate of Spanish Jack. Not too long ago, he would have welcomed news of the man's death, but the situation in Arkansas and the Cherokee Nation and the Osage country had changed dramatically since then. And he had actually sat and talked with Jack since then, and he liked the man. Now it seemed that Jack Spaniard was no more, and now Major Bradford was going to miss him.

7

Lorn Upbate sat on the wagon box and held the reins, but the old horses mostly knew what they were doing. Upbate didn't really feel like he was driving. He was just giving the horses the courtesy of seeming to do his share of the work. His wife, Leta, sat on the box beside him, and in the back of the wagon their two sons, Abry and Ish, lounged. The boys were almost grown, and both Lorn and Leta thought with mixed feelings of the time, probably not too long in the future, when the boys would be thinking of going out on their own, finding their own homesteads, and taking wives likely. They didn't talk about it much, though, but they both knew the time would be coming soon.

They were on their way from the "lick log," the gathering place for the prayer meetings every Sunday. The God-fearing folks from miles around found their way each Sunday morning to the "lick log," where crude benches had been fashioned from logs and a large arbor had been erected to gather under and listen to the itinerant preacher and sing the hymns they all knew so well. It was just about the only social occasion in the lives of the Upbates and most of the other frontier folk who met there.

Lorn Upbate and his family had moved into western Arkansas not long after the Cherokees had been forced into their new western home, and the Western Cherokees had been forced out of Arkansas to be reabsorbed by the Cherokee Nation. That had freed up the former Arkansas lands of the Cherokee Nation West for more white folks, and the Upbates had been among the early im-migrants to that area. They had left behind land in West Virginia that had been in the Upbate family for three generations, land that had been farmed by Lorn's father and his grandfather, land that was worn out from overuse.

Riding their slow way home following the meeting, Lorn and Leta talked about the fellowship, about the good singing and about the rousing message delivered by the preacher. In the back of the wagon, the boys talked of other things: the good food they had shared with the others following the meeting, the fine-looking young Higgins girl, who had stayed right close to her mother's side the whole time, other things of interest to growing young men. They were surprised when they heard their mother's warning.

"Dad," she said to Lorn, "look out ahead."

"What is it, Mother?" Lorn said. The two boys were on their feet looking over the shoulders of their parents.

The warning had been unnecessary, for the horses came to a stop on their own.

"Up there in the road," Leta said. "It looks like a man. He's either dead or hurt."

Lorn tied up the reins and climbed down off the wagon bench. He hurried ahead to see what he could discover. The two boys jumped out of the wagon to follow him, and Leta came down from her perch a little more slowly, encumbered by her long, loose dress. Lorn found the man lying facedown in the road and care-fully rolled him over on his back. He was beaten and bloody.

"This looks like the work of road agents," he said. He leaned over, placing the side of his head close to the man's face. In an-other few seconds, he laid his head on the man's chest. He straightened up.

"He's alive," he said. "Boys, let's load him in the wagon. Care-ful now."

Jack Spaniard woke up in a strange bed. He had been undressed and washed. His wounds had been cleaned and bandaged. He could recall having been dumped somewhere on a road outside of Fort Smith, but he remembered nothing after that. Someone had picked him up and taken him in. Whoever had done it, he was grateful. He tried to sit up, but the pain in his side stopped him.

Broken ribs, he thought. He'd felt that sensation before. He could tell that he would be laid up for a spell.

He thought about the three soldiers who had done this to him. They had caught him by surprise from behind. He felt like a fool. Well, he vowed, he would meet up with them again, and it would be a very different story. Plenty of Osages had felt the wrath of Spanish Jack in the past. These three soldiers would feel it sometime in the future.

He looked around the room he was in. It was a clean and well-built log house, much like a hundred other such houses. It was furnished with chairs, tables and beds hewn by hand from materials provided by the abundant woods around. He made another effort to sit up, and in spite of the intense pain, he managed it on this second try. He could not, however, reach around to adjust the pillows behind his back. He leaned against the hard headboard to catch his breath.

The front door opened, and a woman came in. She was a white woman, Jack guessed, in her mid-forties. She was carrying a towel, which he guessed she had taken outside to shake. Almost immediately, she saw Jack sitting up and walked over to the side of the bed.

"You're awake," she said. "Good. How are you feeling?"

"I'm sore," Jack said, "but I feel like I'll live."

"I'm Leta Upbate," the woman said. "My man and our two sons are out working, but they'll be back in right soon now. It's about time to eat. I reckon you'll have a pretty good appetite about now."

"Yes, ma'am," said Jack. "How did I—

"We was coming home from the church meeting," Leta said, "and we found you laying in the road. Looked like you'd been set on by road agents. We loaded you in the wagon and brung you home with us. I done what I could for you."

"Oh, you did just fine," said Jack, "and I'll be eternally grateful to you."

"Weren't no more than any good Christian would do," Leta said.

The door opened again, and Lorn came in, followed by Abry and Ish. They all moved across the room to join Leta there by the bed.

"Howdy, stranger," Lorn said. "You're looking some better."

"I'm feeling much better," Jack said, "thanks to you and your family."

Lorn stuck out a hand for Jack to shake. "We're glad to have been able to help," he said. "I'm Lorn Upbate. This here is Abry, my oldest, and his brother here is Ish. I reckon you've done met my wife, Leta."

"Yes," said Jack. "It's a pleasure meeting all of you. My name is Jack Spaniard."

"Well, Mr. Spaniard," Lorn said, "we're going to take our places at the table over there to have ourselves a feed. I reckon that Mother here will fetch you something."

"I surely will," Leta said.

"You're very kind," said Jack.

Jack felt a strange mixture of feelings toward this family of whites. He had always thought of whites as the enemy. He had especially thought of these settlers as the land thieves. They were the ones who came into the Cherokees' country to carve out their own homes and were then followed by an army to protect them against any action by the rightful landowners. And this family of Upbates was living on former Cherokee land. But they had picked him up from the road and taken him in. They had cared for him. Likely, they had saved his life.

Having dished out food for her husband and two sons at the table, Leta Upbate brought a bowl of stew over to Jack in the bed. She put the dish down on a side table and helped him into a comfortable position. Then she handed him the bowl and spoon. The stew had a delicious smell. Jack tied into it like he had not eaten in days, and he found that it was indeed delicious. When he finished it, Leta dished it full again, and he ate a second bowlful. Then she brought him coffee. Finished with their meal, the Upbates all dragged chairs over and gathered around Jack.

"Mr. Spaniard," said Lorn, "tell us, was I right about how come you came to be out on that road the way you was? Was it road agents?"

"In a way," Jack said. "Actually, they jumped me back at Fort Smith, and after they had pounded me into near unconsciousness, they took me out on the road to dump me. I guess I'm luckier than if they had caught me on the road. My horse is in a livery stable at Fort Smith, and my guns and most of my other belongings are in a room at the inn there. They did steal all my money though."

"Ruffians," said Leta. "There are too many of them out on the frontier."

"Will your things be safe enough there at Fort Smith?" Lorn asked.

"I don't know," Jack said. "I'll be owing the liveryman and the innkeeper, and now I have no money to pay the bills."

"Me and Abry will take the wagon in there first thing in the morning," Lorn said. "We'll see what we can find out. Likely you got friends there who'll be glad to hear that you're all right."

"The post commander," Jack said. "Major Bradford. He might be interested. And if they're still around, there's a Mr. Morgan Conrad and a Mr. J. Worthington Jones."

"We'll be looking them up for you," said Lorn.

"Dad," said Ish, "how come I can't go in with you?"

"We can't be leaving Mother here alone," Lorn said. He looked at Jack. "No offense, Mr. Spaniard. I didn't mean to imply that you ain't here, but if there was any problem to come up, you ain't in no shape to have to deal with it. That's all I meant."

"I understand," Jack said, "and Mr. Upbate, please call me Jack."

"I'll do that, Jack," Lorn said, "if you'll return the favor by calling us all by our given names."

Lorn and Abry drove their wagon into Fort Smith just before noon the next day. They came to the inn before the fort, so they stopped. Lorn got out of the wagon and went inside where he introduced himself to the innkeeper and explained his mission.

"I'm glad to hear that Spaniard's all right," the innkeeper said, "but I still can't let you take his stuff to him. I got to be paid first."

J. Worthington Jones happened to be passing through just then, and he overheard part of the conversation. "Excuse me, sir," he said. "Did I understand you to be speaking of Mr. Jack Spaniard?"

"That's right, mister," Lorn said. "Jack Spaniard is out at my house all laid up from a bad beating he took at the hands of some road agents. He ain't fit to travel none yet, so I come in here to see if I could maybe fetch his stuff out for him."

"Innkeeper," said Jones, "I'll pay Mr. Spaniard's bill. Let this gentleman take his things." Then he turned to Lorn again. "His horse is at the stable," he said. "He'll have a bill there too. I'll go along with you and take care of that. Then we should go see Major Bradford and inform him of the situation. He'll be very interested."

Jones paid the innkeeper, then rode the wagon with Lorn and Abry to the stable, where he paid Jack's bill. They threw Jack's saddle and tack into the wagon and tied the horse on behind. From there, they drove on into the fort. Jones showed Lorn where to pull up to the commander's office. They got out of the wagon and went inside.

A lieutenant sat at a desk just outside the major's office. He stood up when the three civilians stepped inside.

"May I help you?" he asked them.

"We've come to see Major Bradford," Jones said. "These gentlemen have news of Jack Spaniard."

The lieutenant opened the door to the major's office and stepped inside. He was back out in a few seconds, opening the door wide and stepping aside.

"Go right in," he said.

As the three stepped into the office, Bradford came out from behind his desk.

"Mr. Jones," he said. "You have news about Spaniard?"

"Not me, Major," Jones said. "These gentleman. Mr. Lorn Upbate and his son Abry."

Bradford shook their hands hurriedly, and then he said, "What's the news?"

"Me and my family come across him laying on the road all beat-up," said Lorn.

"Alive?" Bradford asked.

"Yes sir," said Lorn. "He's out at our house right now trying to heal up."

"Thank God," Bradford said. "We had feared the worst. Tell me, did he say who it was that beat him and robbed him?"

"No sir," Lorn said. "He never. He did say that they done it to him right here at the fort, and then they took him out on the road and dumped him there where we found him."

"Damn," said Bradford. "I'm sure that I know the guilty parties, but I needed Jack's testimony to make a charge stick. I let them go this morning. I had to let them take the money they stole from him too. I had no proof that they were lying to me about having won it at poker. Damn it all."

"May I ask whom you suspect?" Jones said. "Those same three soldiers?"

"Yes. The same. I just dismissed them from the army," Bradford said. "Jack knows them well, I think. Their names are Walker, Fitch and Norton."

"I'll inform him," Jones said. "That is, if Mr. Upbate will be kind enough to allow me to accompany him back to his home."

"Why, sure I will," Lorn said. "I expect that Jack will be glad to see a friend."

"Now that I know Jack's alive and well," Bradford said, "I'll issue a warrant for the arrest of those three. With Jack as a witness, we can put them on trial."

"If they ever show themselves around here again," Jones said. "If they have a brain among them, they'll be getting as far away from here as they can."

Jones found Conrad and told him the news. He also told Conrad that he'd be accompanying Upbate back to his home to pay Jack a visit.

"Please tell him how glad I am to hear the news," Conrad said.

Jones assured Conrad that he would do that. Then he mounted a rented horse and rode alongside the Upbate wagon. Some distance out from the fort, Upbate pointed ahead.

"Right up yonder's where we found him laying," he said.

They traveled the rest of the way to the Upbate cabin mostly in silence. When they arrived there, Abry took Jack's belongings in his arms. Upbate led Jones to the door and opened it. As they stepped inside, Jack saw them.

"Jones," he said. "What a surprise."

Leta walked toward her surprised houseguest wiping her hands on her apron.

"My wife Leta, Mr. Jones," Lorn said.

Jones took the hat off his head and gave a slight bow.

"A great pleasure, madam," he said. He walked over to Jack's bedside. "What a relief to find out that you hadn't been murdered."

"I think they tried to beat me to death," Jack said, "but my skull's too thick. I'll mend all right, with the fine care of Mrs. Upbate here."

"Leta," Leta corrected him.

"Yes," Jack said. "Leta has been my nurse, and she's a fine one too."

"Well," said Jones, "we've brought your horse and your things from the inn, so that you'll have them when you're ready to be up and about again. We're pretty sure that we know who it was that attacked you and robbed you, but unfortunately, they've escaped with your money."

"Those three soldiers," Jack said.

"They're no longer soldiers," said Jones. "Bradford was unable to place them on trial, he said, lacking sufficient evidence. For the same reason, he could not take the cash away from them. They swore that they had won it at cards. There were three of them and only two of us, Conrad and myself, to challenge their claims. At any rate, the major tossed them out of the army for general bad behavior, and they've left the fort. Who knows where they've gone?"

"I see," Jack said, and to himself, I'll meet them again somewhere. Then aloud, he added, "Good riddance to them."

"And to your money," Jones said. He reached into his pocket and withdrew a wallet. "Do you need any—

"No," said Jack. "Please. Keep your money. I've no place to spend it just now anyway."

Jones glanced from Jack to Lorn to Leta. "But perhaps the Upbates need some help with their expenses in taking care—

"Oh, no sir," Leta said. "We don't need to be paid for helping out a body in trouble."

"It wouldn't be right to take money for being a good neighbor," Lorn said, "but we thank you just the same."

Jones heaved a heavy sigh as he put back his wallet. "Well then," he said to Jack, "is there anything I can do for you?"

"You've done more than enough already," Jack said. "I daresay I owe you for my stable and room expenses."

"Well," Jones began, but Jack interrupted him.

"I'll repay you in time," he said, "and then I'll do my best to win it back from you at poker."

Both the Upbates looked at the floor trying not to show their disapproval. Just then Abry came back in. "I put away the horse and tack," he said.

"Thank you, Abry," said Jack.

"Right now," Leta said, "you can go out to the field and help your brother."

"Yes, ma'am," Abry said.

"I'll go with you, son," said Lorn. "I've done whiled away enough of the day. Mr. Jones, it's been a pleasure meeting you. Stick around as long as you like."

Leta went back to her work, and Jones took a seat next to the bed. He leaned in close to Jack and spoke in a low voice.

"It's too bad those soldiers got away," he said, "but Bradford has issued warrants for their arrest. Perhaps they'll be caught and brought to justice."

"I hope not," Jack said.

"What?" said Jones. "What do you mean by that?"

"I mean to find them myself," said Jack, "and when I find them, I mean to kill them."

8

For the next several days, Jack stayed in bed being nursed by Leta. He could feel his strength returning slowly and steadily. As soon as he could do so, he got out of bed and dressed, and he began helping around the house a little at a time. In a few more days, he was working outside with Lorn and the boys.

"You been a big help around here lately, Jack," Lorn said one afternoon, "but you ain't no hired hand, and I can't afford to pay you."

"You're right, Lorn," Jack said "I'm no hired hand, so there's no need to think about paying me. If anything, I'm repaying you and your family for all the help and hospitality you've given me."

"Ain't no need to repay us," Lorn said.

"I know that," said Jack. "It looks to me like you'll have a good corn crop this year."

"It does at that," Lorn said.

The next morning, with the work around the place pretty well caught up, Jack saddled his horse and took his rifle. He was gone all day, but when evening came, he rode back up to the Upbate cabin bringing along with him a fresh-killed buck. They had plenty of venison for a while. Jack was beginning to feel restless though. And he felt like, even though he had begun to do his share around the place, he was in the way. He was one more mouth to feed. He was thinking about leaving soon, and he had nothing in mind to do except kill three ex-soldiers. But it would take money to go out looking for them. He had about decided that he would go west first and steal some more horses from the Comanches. After driving the horses to New Orleans to sell, with money in his pockets again, he would go on the trail of the three robbers.

He had planned for it to be his last day with the Upbates. He went out to the fields with the men and worked alongside them. At the end of the day, they were ready to head for the house and a well-deserved meal when the temperature dropped and the sky turned dark. Jack looked up at the clouds that were rolling in.

"Could be a bad storm moving in," he said.

As if in response to his comment, there was a long, low rumble of distant thunder.

"Let's get back to the house," Lorn said.

It started raining before they reached the house, and by the time they had put everything away and taken care of the animals, they were all drenched. They walked into the house dripping water on the dirt floor.

"Get out of those wet clothes," Leta ordered. "All of you."

When they were all dried and changed, Leta sat them all at the table and served them hot stew and biscuits. When they had finished, she poured coffee all around. Outside the claps of thunder sounded closer. One shook the house. Flashes of lightning caused strange flickering lights in the cabin. The howling of the wind and the pounding of the rain made it difficult for the people in the house to hear one another. They had to shout to communicate. And the driving storm kept up all through the night. About daylight, it was over.

Without waiting for his breakfast, Lorn Upbate went outside. Jack was right behind him, and then the two Upbate boys followed. Leta stepped outside the door wringing her hands. The whole ground around them was a large mudhole. Branches were broken out of trees and lying around here and there. Part of Upbate's pole fencing was down. The animals were all right, but everything around was a mess. Upbate headed for the cornfield, again followed by Jack and the boys. At the edge of the field they stopped. No one said a word at first. Finally, Lorn spoke.

"It's ruined," he said. "All ruined. All that work."

Jack thought about Walker, Fitch and Norton out there somewhere spending his money. He wished that he had some of it. The

Upbates could sure use some help just at that point. He recalled again just how distasteful was farming to his mind, and he had before him a vivid illustration of one of the main reasons. The farmer was utterly at the mercy of the whims of the weather. He wondered how the Upbates would make it now. It was too late to put in another crop. A whole year of their lives was shot by one storm. One quick flash had wiped out all that labor of three men, for a short while, four. Jack had never felt so helpless, and he knew that Lorn Upbate and his two boys were feeling the same.

"Well," said Lorn, "the Lord giveth and the Lord taketh away."

He turned and led the way back to the house. As they walked back in, Leta was looking at Lorn with frightened eyes. Lorn shook his head.

"It's all gone, Mother," he said.

"All?" she said.

"Gone," he said.

She caught her breath and steeled her emotions. "Well," she said, "all of you sit down to eat."

"There's a lot of cleaning up to be did out there, Mother," Lorn said. "The sight of it all like to took away my appetite."

"Storm or no," Leta said, "you got to eat. Sit down."

They ate in silence. When they were done, Leta poured one more round of coffee.

"What will you do, Lorn?" Jack asked.

"Got to go out somewhere and make some money," Lorn said.

"Where'll you go for that?" Leta asked. "Our neighbors'll all be in the same fix we're in. Even if they still got crops to work, ain't none of them got cash to pay help."

"Me and Ish might could go out somewheres and find jobs," said Abry.

"I heard some fellers talking over to the fort the other day," Lorn said. "Seems there's money to be made in furs. If we could gather up a good supply and sell them, likely we could last till time for our next crop."

"That's right," Jack said. "My friend Conrad is staying at the fort right now. He's a buyer of furs for a St. Louis company. We can talk to him."

Lorn looked up at Leta, who was standing across the table from him. "Likely we'll have to go off a ways and stay gone a while," he said. "The hunting's pretty slim around these parts. Too many folks has moved in and drove the creatures out."

"I hear it's still pretty good down around the Red River," said Jack. "I know that country pretty well."

"You mean you'd go along with us?" Lorn said.

"It would be a pleasant diversion for me," Jack said, lying to the Upbates. He had other things he wanted to do, but he felt a need to help these people who had done so much for him. "I have some powder and shot," he went on, "but not enough. We'll need rifles for all of us. And we'll need traps."

"I have one rifle gun," Lorn said. "A little powder and shot."

"I'll ride into Fort Smith and have a talk with Conrad," Jack said. "Maybe we can work something out."

There was more discussion, and at last it was decided that Ish would stay at home with Leta. Jack, Lorn and Abry would make the trip to the Red River. But first they had to be properly outfitted. The next morning, Jack, Lorn and Abry headed for Fort Smith. Jack rode his horse. Lorn drove the wagon with Abry sitting on the box beside him.

Jack found Morgan Conrad at the outside tables of the inn, having a drink with J. Worthington Jones. Jones had, of course, met the Upbates. He shook their hands and introduced them to Conrad.

"Please join us here, gentlemen," he said. They all sat down. "May I order you a drink?"

"Just God's pure water," Lorn said.

"Me too," said Abry.

Jones looked at Jack. "A whiskey?" he asked.

"You know my money has all been stolen," Jack said. "I won't be able to return the favor."

"Tut tut," said Jones. "Not today perhaps, but another day." He turned in his chair and waved a hand and called out for the waiter. Soon the two Upbates had glasses of water in front of them, and Jack had a whiskey.

"We actually came in here to talk to you, Conrad," Jack said. "The Upbates lost their entire crop in the recent storm. Trying to come up with a way to make some money, we thought of the fur business."

"You're going after furs?" Conrad asked.

"That's what we came to see you about," said Jack. "How long will you be here buying? How much are you paying and for what?"

"I represent a small company," Conrad said. "Our larger competitors have staked out all the northern territories. That's why I'm here. But even though we're small, we pay top dollar for beaver, marten and fox. But are you properly outfitted for such an expedition? You know the creatures cannot be shot. It spoils the value of the fur."

"Yes, I know that," Jack said, "and no, we are not properly outfitted. I'm thinking of selling my horse and saddle."

"I won't hear of that, my friend," Jones said. "I'll stake you. You can pay me back from the proceeds."

"That's very kind of you, sir," Lorn said.

"Jack," Conrad said, "I'm leaving for St. Louis tomorrow morning, but I'll be back here by the time you have what you need." He looked over where Lorn had parked the wagon. "If you bring that wagon back loaded with pelts," he said, "I would estimate that you'll earn around five hundred dollars."

"We can last better'n a year on that," said Abry, wide-eyed. Lorn gave him a stern look.

"Well then," said Jones, "is it settled? Shall we go shopping?"

Conrad went along to help make the selections so that Jack and the two Upbates would have everything they needed. Jones took care of the bill, and Lorn insisted on signing a paper that showed just how much he was in debt to Jones. When the Upbate wagon rolled out of Fort Smith it was loaded full. Lorn drove it back home to unload a few supplies that Leta and Ish would need while they were gone. They slept the night there at the house and got an early start the next day.

Lorn took the wagon across the river into the Cherokee Nation. Jack was a little nervous, but he kept his feelings to himself. He did tie his horse to the back of the wagon and climb up on the wagon box with Lorn and Abry, thinking that if they happened across any Cherokee Light Horsemen, he might not be quite as noticeable to them that way. They would not be in the Cherokee Nation long, but it wouldn't take long if the national police spotted him. They made it through and passed over the line into the Choctaw Nation, however, without incident, and Jack breathed a sigh of relief. He climbed down from the wagon and remounted his horse.

Moving around the wagon, he told Lorn and Abry that he would ride a little ahead. Their route was the old military road that led from Fort Gibson all the way down to the Red River. Jack knew that there could be outlaws lurking along the way, and he did not want to be caught by surprise. About high noon, he rode back to rejoin the Upbates in the wagon. They pulled off the road and stopped to fix themselves a meal. Sitting there sharing a fire and food with the two Upbates, Jack considered again the ironies of life. Under different circumstances, these two white men might have been found searching for him over the barrels of their long rifles. And it would not have been that many years ago.

Their meal done, they set about the business of cleaning up their campsite. Abry wondered aloud about the length of the journey and the time it would take them to get there. "It's the wagon that makes it seem slow," Jack said. "But we'll get there all right." Soon the wagon was rolling again, and once again, Jack was riding out ahead. He met some Choctaw travelers who were riding north and passed the time of day with them. Then when they rode on, he waited a bit, doubled back and watched them to make sure there would be no trouble between them and the Upbates. There was none, and Jack turned south again.

The sun was low in the western sky, and Jack was beginning to look out for a good camping spot for the night when he saw two riders coming his direction from the south. He rode on to meet them, and as they drew closer, he saw that they were two white men, dirty and ragged, but well armed. They came closer and stopped their horses. Jack stopped his.

"Hello there," said the tallest of the two gaunt men. "Riding south?"

"It looks that way," Jack said.

The man gave a nervous laugh, but his partner sat still with an unmoving expression on his dirty face.

"Traveling alone?" the tall one asked.

Jack looked around himself. "I don't see anyone else," he said.

"That's a nice horse you got there," the man said. "Nice rifle too."

"You buying?" Jack asked.

The man laughed again, and said, "No. No, just making conversation. I'm wondering what a man alone like you is headed south for. Hunting trip? Planning to settle in Texas? Ain't no civilization in that direction."

"I'm riding away from the law," Jack said. "They want me for some killings."

"Some killings?" the tall man said. "How many you done?"

"I lost count sometime back," Jack said. "Now I think I'll be riding on."

"Yeah," the tall man said, "well, watch out for them wild Indians down south. Come on along, Ezra. Come on."

The two men rode past Jack, and as they did, he backed his horse and turned it so that they did not ride behind him. He watched them until they were well on their way. Then he saw them turn off the road onto a trail that went east. He stayed right where he was and waited for the Upbate wagon. In a few minutes it appeared. Jack watched as it rolled past the turnoff where the two wretched-looking riders had gone. The two did not make another appearance, and the wagon moved on slowly in Jack's direction. He waited for it, then rode alongside it until they came to a campsite. As they set up camp for the night, Jack kept watching their back trail.

"Something wrong?" Lorn asked.

"Maybe not," said Jack. "Just go on like everything's all right. I may fade back into the dark now and then. Don't worry about it."

"What is it?" Abry asked.

"Get the cooking started, Abry," Lorn said.

It was full dark, and Jack was nowhere to be seen. The meal was almost ready when the tall man and Ezra appeared in the light of the fire seemingly out of nowhere. Each held a long rifle in a relaxed position.

"Can a couple of weary travelers find hospitality at this fire?" the tall man asked.

Abry jumped, startled, and Ezra laughed.

"I never turn away a man in need," said Lorn. "Sit yourselves down. Food'll be ready in just a minute. Abry, pour our guests some coffee."

Abry did as Lorn had told him to do, but he was nervous, and it showed. The tall man looked in the direction of the loaded wagon sitting off to one side of the fire.

"You got a passel of goods there," he said.

"Supplies," said Lorn.

"What kind of supplies you hauling, friend?" the tall man asked.

"Supplies for trapping," Abry said. "We're going for furs."

Lorn shot a hard glance at Abry, but in the flickering light around the campfire, it was lost.

"You're out to get rich, are you?" the tall man said.

"We're just trying to make an honest living," said Lorn. "That's all."

"Bet a man could sell all them goods for a pretty penny," the tall man said.

"It would be foolish of me to sell them," Lorn said. "I just bought them. And on credit. It'll take me a whole season to pay for them and make myself a profit."

"A man like me," the tall man said, "who never paid for them in the first place could make a hell of a nice profit on them goods."

"What're you talking about?" Abry said.

"Keep still, son," said Lorn.

"Mind your pappy, now, son," the tall man said. "How about pouring me another cup of that coffee?"

Abry looked at Lorn.

"Go on ahead and do it," Lorn said. Then he looked at the tall man. "You and your friend can eat your fill," he said, "and then you can go on your way."

"You can't send us out in the middle of the night like that," the tall man said. "It ain't hospitable."

"Eat and be on your way," Lorn said.

"Well now, I don't think so," the tall man said, raising the barrel of his rifle to point at Lorn. At the same time, Ezra raised his rifle and aimed it at Abry. As the tall man began to pull back the hammer of his long rifle with his dirty thumb, Spanish Jack stepped out of the darkness with a pistol in each hand. As the two surprised outlaws opened their eyes wide in astonishment, he pulled the first trigger sending a ball into the chest of the tall man. He fired the second pistol and blew a hole in Ezra's forehead.

Jack shoved the pistols into his belt and walked over to the fire. He looked down and saw that Ezra was dead. He moved over to check the tall man and found him gurgling. Jack pulled out his knife and knelt to slit the man's throat. Then he wiped his blade on the dirty shirt that the tall man wore. He looked back over his shoulder to see Abry staring in wide-eyed disbelief. Lorn was looking stern.

"I'll get rid of them," Jack said, and he started to drag Ezra's body into the darkness.

9

Both Upbates were shocked. They were shocked first that they had been threatened. Then they had been shocked by Jack's surprise rescue. Finally, they had been shocked at Jack's casual handling of the corpses of the two men he had killed. Lorn insisted that the men be given decent burials, even though they had been reprobates, and he recited some scripture over their graves. Abry, on the other hand, was fascinated at the cold and efficient way in which Jack had taken care of the dangerous situation. He was afraid to say anything out loud in front of his father, but he thought that he would like to be able to take care of problems that way himself. He had never seen anything like it before in his life. He would like to be the kind of man that could do that. When Jack and the two Upbates were back at their campfire, they sat for a while in silence. At last Jack spoke.

"Lorn, Abry, I didn't invite those men in here," he said. "And I sure didn't ask them to try to kill you and steal our supplies. They came, and I did what I had to do, and that's all there is to it. Now, we've got food hot and ready to eat. We don't want to waste it, and we'll all need our strength, so I suggest we get at it."

They ate in silence, and then they sat over coffee. At last Lorn cleared his throat, preparing to speak.

"Jack," he said, "I apologize for my attitude. I know that you saved our lives, and I'm grateful. Believe me I am. It's just that

I've never been a man of violence. I'm not angry at you. I'm just angry, no, disturbed, I guess, at the ways of the world."

"The world is what it is," said Jack. "We're the ones that have to learn to live in it. Let's all turn in and try to get us an early start in the morning."

After several more days of slow travel, much of it through mountainous terrain, they reached the Red River. Searching its northern bank, they located a suitable spot and settled into a camp. In short order, they had their traps out. Things went well. In a matter of some weeks, they had a good supply of pelts, all processed and bundled. The Upbates were pleased, but they were also anxious to get back home. Lorn had not been away from Leta since their marriage, and Abry had never been away from home in his life. Jack could tell that the separation of their family was wearing hard on them. He felt sorry for them, but he was glad that they would have the money they needed to get through the year and get their next crop out. Another week, he thought, the way things were going, and they could head back. Conrad would be waiting for them at Fort Smith. He would pay them for the furs. Jack would pay J. Worthington Jones. He would give the rest of the money to the Upbates, and then he would go after some Comanche horses to sell in order to line his own pockets. It was a line of work he was good at.

They had just finished a noon meal and were busy cleaning up their dishes. Abry stood up suddenly with wide eyes. Lorn saw him, and said, "What is it, son?" Jack looked over to where the boy was standing, and he turned his own gaze in the direction of Abry's stare. Across the river and up on a knoll were a number of Indians sitting horseback and looking in their direction.

"Indians," Abry said.

"I'm an Indian," said Jack.

"Do you know them?" Lorn asked.

"Just stay easy," Jack said. "Go on about your business. Act like nothing's wrong. I'll ride over and have a talk with them."

"What if they decide to fight you?" Abry said. "There's too many of them. Even for you."

"If they kill me," Jack said, "then you get the guns. All of them, and get ready for a big fight. I'm leaving my guns here. I don't think I'll have any trouble with them."

Jack pulled the pistols out of his belt and laid them beside the long rifle. Then he took his horse by the reins. He didn't waste time putting on the saddle. He threw a blanket over its back and hopped on. Then he rode slowly toward the river, his eyes on the Indians across the way.

"Be careful," Abry said.

"God be with you," said Lorn.

The Upbates watched wide-eyed as Jack rode slowly to the river's edge and stopped. He looked across at the Indians, who were still just sitting there in the same spot, who had not moved. They were looking back at him, watching his approach. He urged his horse forward into the water. He knew that the river was shallow just there. He had already crossed it a time or two. Keeping his eyes on the Texas Indians, he forded the river. Then he rode toward the knoll and on up to the waiting warriors.

"*¿Habla Espanol?*" he asked them.

"*Sí, yo hablo,*" one answered. He was sitting about in the center of the line of Indians. He was a man of perhaps thirty years. He wore moccasins and a breechcloth, but other than that, he was naked. His head was mostly shaved, and he wore a bright red porcupine tail roach on top. Designs were painted on his body and on that of his white war pony. He carried a long lance. The others were similarly attired, painted and armed. Jack continued speaking to the man in Spanish.

"I'm a Cherokee from north of here," he said. "My name is Spanish Jack. Have my friends and I come into your territory?"

"All of this is ours," the man said, "on both sides of the river. What are you and your friends doing here?"

"My friends are white men," said Jack. "They're farmers. A big storm destroyed all their crop. I brought them here to trap for furs, so they can sell them for money to live on until time to plant their next crop. We won't take too many. Only a few more. We're almost done. In a few days, we'll go home."

"I've heard of you from our Osage friends, Spanish Jack," the other man said. "Many of them would like to kill you. They say you have killed more of their people than they can count. It would make my friends very happy if I were to kill you for them."

"I killed Osages in war. If you've seen your friends recently," Jack said, "you'd know that we have made our peace. It was a long war, but it's over. I'd like to make my peace with you right now. I rode over here unarmed."

"When we saw you coming over here without your weapons, we thought that maybe you were crazy."

"I came without weapons, because I came to talk. Not to fight." But Jack thought, I might be crazy too. It won't take this bunch long to kill me, if they decide to do it.

"The animals you're killing for their furs belong to us," the man said. "Maybe we should kill you for that reason, and then go across the river and kill your friends."

"If you heard of me from the Osages," Jack said, "you know that I won't be easy to kill. A few of you will die too."

"But you're unarmed."

"I can kill with my hands. Then when you've finally killed me, the ones who are left alive will be killed by my friends. They have long rifles that can kill you from over there. You have only lances. You would all die. Let's not fight. We'll leave you a share of the furs to pay you for what we take."

The man turned to his companions and spoke to them in their native tongue. Jack did not recognize it. He knew some of the tribes south of the Red River, but he did not know them well. He guessed these to be Tonkawas, but he wasn't sure. He waited while they conversed a while. Then the Spanish-speaking one looked back at him.

"We'll leave you alone for now, Spanish Jack," he said. "When you're ready to leave our country, we'll come back and see how many furs you are willing to pay us."

They turned and rode away fast without another word. Jack sat and watched them go for a while. Then he turned his own horse and rode back down the knoll, across the river and into his camp.

"What did they say?" Abry asked.

"They won't fight us," said Jack. "At least not for a while. I promised to leave them some furs for payment."

"What do we have to pay them for?" asked Abry.

"They say that we're on their land," said Jack, "and we're killing their animals."

"Are we?"

Jack shrugged. "I didn't choose to argue the point," he said.

"We'll pay and gladly to avoid any trouble," Lorn said. "And I'm pleased to discover, Jack, that you can negotiate as well as you can fight."

"It's all part of staying alive in this country," Jack said.

They worked a few more days, and they were talking about the trip home. They set aside bundled furs for the local Indians. The time for the return journey was just about on them. In another few days they were packed and ready.

"Do you mean to just leave those furs stacked out here like that?" Lorn asked, referring to the bundles set aside for the Texas Indians.

"That's what I said I'd do," Jack answered.

"Someone else might come along and take them," Lorn said. "I'd feel much better about it if you were to locate the rightful owners and tell them that we're leaving and that their furs are here."

Jack hesitated a moment, then with a sigh, he said, "I'll see what I can do." He mounted up, rode across the river and made a turn to the east, the direction in which he had seen the riders go. There was no guarantee that they had been riding toward their village, but that possibility was really all he had to go on. They had not been seen again since that first and only visit. After a while of riding, he realized that he had ridden half the morning away. By the time he could get back to the Upbates, half the day would be gone—wasted. It wasn't worth it. He would just tell them that he had been unsuccessful. He was about to turn around and go back when he saw the smoke ahead. He rode on some more and came to a walled village of grass houses built alongside the river. He rode down toward the entrance

Drawing close to the opening in the wall, Jack was not totally surprised to find the Spanish-speaking Indian standing in his way and smiling. "So, Spanish Jack, you came to see me," the man said. "Why?"

"We're finished with our work," said Jack. "We're ready to go home now. I came looking for you to tell you that your furs are stacked there where we had our camp. They'll be waiting for you there anytime you want to get them."

"That's not good," the man said, shaking his head. "We'll ride back there with you now. That way, we'll see if you left enough for us, and there will be no chance of the wrong people coming along to pick up our furs."

Jack had been afraid of that. He chastised himself for having listened to Upbate. He should have, he thought, ridden out a ways and then gone back to report that everything was all right. A white lie wouldn't have hurt Upbate at all. Now the Indians would ride back with him, and almost for sure, they would demand more furs than Jack had stacked aside for them. Well, it was done. He gave a shrug.

"Whatever you say," he said.

The Spanish-speaking Indian made Jack get off his horse and accompany him into the village. He took Jack to his house and had him sit down. People gathered around to look at this strange visitor, and they asked questions about him in their language, and the Spanish-speaking Indian talked to them. Now and then, he could hear his name spoken. A woman at the house brought Jack some food in a bowl, and he took it and thanked her, and he ate. There was nothing else to do. It was well past the middle of the day before Jack rode out of the village with the Spanish-speaking Indian and six others riding along with him. And they did not ride fast. Jack figured this travel day was lost. He would not stay the night in the same camp though. He would insist that they ride ahead for as far as the daylight held out. He had already told these Texas Indians that they were leaving.

When at last they arrived at the river crossing, Jack was anticipating some dickering with the Spanish-speaking Indian over the amount of the payment. But as he rode into the water, and looked across, he could see that something was wrong over there. He should have been able to see the wagon right there where the camp had been. Perhaps the Upbates had decided to move on ahead rather than just sit and wait. That would have been a wise thing for them to do. Jack could easily catch up with the slow wagon riding horseback, and they would have a better start on the day than if they had waited so long at the campsite. He was a little surprised, though, to think that Lorn had made such a decision on his own. Jack led the way on through the shallow, red water of the river, the seven Indians right behind him. He rode on into the camp. He stopped. The bundles of furs were not there where he had left them. The wagon was gone. Something was wrong. Jack swung a leg over his horse and dropped from the saddle. He pointed to a spot.

"Your furs were there," he said in Spanish. "I left them there. And I left my friends here in their wagon. Something's happened here."

The Spanish-speaking Indian, still sitting on his horse, looked around. "Over there," he said, "I see some blood on the ground."

Jack looked where the man indicated, and then he walked over there to a spot where blood had soaked into the ground. There was no mistake about it. He looked around himself some more, and he saw unfamiliar footprints. Shoes or boots. White men. Several of them. And not the Upbates. These prints were unfamiliar. The Spanish-speaking Indian rode slowly around the edge of the camp, looking carefully all the way. About halfway around, he stopped, looking off to his right in the thick brush.

"Over here," he said. "I've found something."

Jack hurried over to the man's aide, and he looked into the brush. There he saw the thing he had been trying not to think about. He saw the bloody body of Abry Upbate. Jack took hold of the ankles and dragged the body out into the open. Young Abry's throat had been cut, and his skull had been crushed. Such a sight was not new to Jack. He had seen brutal death before. He had even caused more than his share of it. But the sight of Abry sickened him. He knew this boy, even liked him, and he had appointed himself the protector of this boy and his father. He forced himself to look away, and he stood up to go searching for Lorn. One of the other Indians found him first. Leaning over from his horse's back, the Indian took hold of a trouser leg and dragged Lorn's bloody body unceremoniously out of the brush. Jack looked and saw that Lorn had been shot in the chest. His throat had been cut too.

"White men did this," said the Spanish-speaking Indian.

"Yes, I know," Jack said. "The worst kind of white men. And they've just killed the best kind."

Two other of the Indians studied the ground all around closely and spoke with one another and with the Spanish-speaking one, pointing out different things that they saw. Then the Spanish-speaking one turned to Jack. "Six white men came here," he said. "There are six different sets of footprints. They rode in here on horses, and they killed these two. Then they tried to hide them in the bushes. They took the wagon and all of the animals and all of the furs. My furs too."

"I'm going to find those six white men and kill them," Jack said. "But first I have to bury my friends."

The Texas Indians did not help Jack. They sat quietly while he dug two graves and buried the two Upbates. The sad chore done, Jack stood beside the two fresh mounds of earth. He took the hat off his head.

"If I knew the words you use from your Bible," he said in English, "I'd speak them for you, but I don't know them. So I'll just say, Lorn and Abry Upbate, I mean to find and kill the men that did this to you. And I mean to see that the furs get sold and the money goes to Mrs. Upbate and the boy. I make both of you those two promises."

Jack heaved a deep sigh, put the hat back on his head, turned and walked to his horse.

"Are you going after those white men?" the Spanish-speaking Indian said.

"Yes, I am," Jack answered. "I mean to kill them and get my furs back."

"And mine," the other said.

"And yours," said Jack.

"We'll ride along with you for a while. We'd like to kill some white men. You've given us a good reason now."

Riding out of the campsite with the seven Texas Indians right behind him, Jack was thinking of many things. He was mourning for the murdered Upbates, and he was still reacting to the recent discovery of their grisly deaths. He was angry, and he was thirsting for vengeance on the wretched vermin who had done the cold-blooded deed, and at the same time, he was also thinking of Leta

Upbate and young Ish. He tried to think of how he would tell them what had happened. He tried to come up with words he could use. And he tried to think of a way to convince himself that their untimely deaths had not been his fault.

How would they take the news, he wondered. They had been such a close and happy family. Good people too. There was no reason at all for a such a thing to have happened. No reason except that there were men walking this earth who had no right to do so. There were men who needed to be killed in order to make the world a better place. What was it that Lorn had said to him after he had killed the two would-be road agents on the trip south? He'd said that he was angry and disturbed at the ways of the world. Well, Jack meant to do his part to clean it up, at least a little.

I O

hey moved along at a pretty good clip, thinking that, even
though the murdering thieves ahead had a few hours' start
on them, they would not be making very good time with the
wagon. It was easy enough to stay on their trail, too, because of
the wagon tracks. The tracks indicated that the six men had stolen
the wagon and were driving it along the road, and it was accompanied by six riding horses. So Jack figured that at least one of the
men was in the wagon, and his riderless horse was tied on behind.
He also figured that he and the Texas Indians would be plenty
enough to handle the six renegade whites when they finally caught
up with them.

Jack and the six Texas Indians rode the afternoon away, and
the sun was low in the western sky. They had not yet spotted the
six men with the wagon. Jack had hoped to catch up with them
before nightfall, but the cutthroats must have had a bigger lead
than he had originally thought. Jack turned to the Spanish-
speaking Indian who was riding along beside him just to his right.

"Shall we keep riding?" he asked. "Or do you want to stop and
camp somewhere for the night?"

"Our horses are tired," the man said. "And we are hungry. Let's
stop and make a camp."

They rode on a little farther until they came to a suitable place,
a clearing in the woods beside a stream, one that had obviously
been used for such purposes before, and there they stopped and

made their camp. They built a small fire. Jack thought about the coffee that was with the supplies in the stolen wagon, and he felt a craving for it. Some of the Texas Indians went out hunting, and they came back with a small deer. It was plenty for all of them, and they cooked and ate it. They drank water from the clear stream, and then they slept. They were up and on the trail again early the following morning. It was midday when the Spanish-speaking Indian stopped, and his companions stopped right behind him. Jack pulled in his own horse and turned to face the man.

"What is it?" he asked.

"This is as far as we go," the man said. He offered no further explanation. Jack figured that they were about to get out of their accustomed territory, or they had just decided that the effort was too much for the value of the furs and the fun of killing the white men. He'd be sorry to lose their company, and he would have to change his plans regarding the cutthroats he was chasing, but he kept all those thoughts to himself.

"I'll keep after them. If I find them," he said, "I'll bring your share of the furs back to you."

The Texas Indians turned their horses around and headed back west. Jack continued alone on the trail of the stolen wagon. He realized, of course, now that he was alone, he could not simply ride up on the thieves and start shooting. When he came across them, he would have to come up with some other kind of plan. He would be one man against six. Maybe he could pick them off one at a time from a distance. Hit and run until he had them all. He would have to study the situation when he finally caught up with them. But he rode on the rest of that day without seeming to get any closer to the fleeing wagon.

When Jack finally arrived at the point where he and the two Up-bates had turned west, he stopped and studied the wagon and horse tracks. They had not turned north to head for Fort Smith. They had turned south. There wasn't much of Arkansas left south of them, no place to stop and do any business, so they must be planning to sell the goods somewhere in Louisiana, he thought. There were several places along the river down that way. Probably the best bet would be Natchitoches. With U.S. troops quartered there, a sizable community had developed. Business was thriving.

The market was probably better in New Orleans, but the distance was much greater, and Jack figured that these scum would want to turn their ill-gotten gain into cash as soon as they could. Of course, they could load it all onto a riverboat and get all the way to New Orleans in relative comfort and pretty good time. At Natchitoches, though, after a few more days of traveling, he found the answer.

The wagon was easy to spot. It was sitting unhitched and unloaded in front of a trading post. Jack tied his horse to a hitching rail and went inside. A burly, bald-headed white man with hairy arms was stacking and counting furs. He glanced up as Jack walked in, made a quick note, then said, "What can I do for you?"

"Is that your wagon out front?" Jack asked.

"I just bought it off some trappers," the man said.

"They sell you some furs too?"

"They did, and a mess of other stuff too. All their supplies. All their horses. Like they're going out of the business. What's this all about?"

"That wagon belonged to my partners," Jack said. "Lorn Upbate and his son Abry. We'd laid in a good supply of furs. We were just getting ready to pull out. I was away from camp for a while. When I got back, the wagon was gone. I found my partners murdered. I tracked that wagon here."

The man shook his head.

"I never should have trusted that Peek Eder," he said, "but I got a policy here. I buy quality goods and don't ask questions."

"You say Peek Eder?" Jack asked.

"Yeah. That's who it was. Peek Eder and his brother Sug. They run with a man called Fermel. This time, though, they had three more with them. I never seen the three new ones before, and I only caught one name. Fitch it was."

Fitch, Jack thought. He wondered if it could be the same Fitch he knew. Could he be so lucky? Three new men were with this Eder, and one of them was named Fitch. Could the other two have been Norton and Walker? If so, then the men he was after for having beaten and robbed him back at Fort Smith, and the men who had murdered the Upbates were now all together in one gang. He might be able to get them all at once.

"You said they sold their horses," Jack said. "All of them?"

"That's right. They caught the steamboat right out here and headed for New Orleans. Pretty well heeled too. I guess they're looking for a real good time in the city."

"Thanks," said Jack. He turned to leave, but the man's voice stopped him. He turned back around.

"Peek Eder's a bad one. Watch yourself."

"I will," said Jack. "Thanks for the warning."

He left the trading post and mounted up. He would have to follow the Eder gang on horseback. He had no cash to finance a river trip. He hoped that the men he was after had enough cash on them now to last a few days, to play around with long enough in New Orleans to allow him to catch up with them there.

He would move along as fast as he safely could. He was traveling light, and he would eat what he could find along the way. If he found nothing, that would be all right too. He could last several days without eating. He had done so before. Jack was comfortable heading into New Orleans. He knew people there. He had taken his stolen Comanche horses into New Orleans on several occasions, so he knew the men who bought and sold horses. He knew his way around the town. He knew the parts of town where one could relax, and he knew the places where one could get himself killed. If Eder and the other five men were there, he would find them.

Jack approached the outskirts of New Orleans on a busy day. The traffic going into the city was heavy, and there was not much coming out. Most of it was wagons and buggies, but there were a few horseback riders, and even fewer pedestrians. Soon Jack made his way through the crowds to the stables of Herman Nye, a man with whom he had dealt on several occasions. He saw Nye dickering with another man over the price of a horse. At last, the man paid him and led the horse away. Jack rode up close to Nye's back.

"That horse wasn't worth what you charged the man," he said.

Nye turned around fast, ready to defend himself, but when he saw Jack, his expression changed from one of belligerence to a broad smile.

"Jack Spaniard," he said. "What brings you to town? I don't

believe I've ever seen you without a herd of horses in front of you."

"I've got one good horse under me," Jack said. "What'll you give me for it?"

He swung a leg over the saddle and dropped to the ground. Nye hurried over to meet him, his right hand extended in greeting. His left still clutched the bills he had received for the horse. Jack took Nye's right in his own.

"It's been a long time, Jack," Nye said.

"Yes, it has been," Jack agreed. His mind wandered back to the last herd of stolen horses he had driven to New Orleans. It had been quite an adventure. "But you got the best of me on that deal," he said.

Nye looked hurt. "I gave you the best price you could have got anywhere in town," he said. "And you know it. I'm a fair man, Spaniard."

Jack nodded toward the horse he had just been riding. "How much?" he asked.

"You're serious?" Nye said. "You want to sell that horse? Your riding horse?"

"That's why I'm asking," Jack said.

"You'll be on foot."

"I'll be around town for a spell. I'm looking for someone."

Nye shrugged and counted out some of the money from his left hand and held it out toward Jack. Jack stood still and expressionless. Nye pulled another bill from his left hand. He held the money out again. Still Jack did not move.

"You including the saddle?" Nye asked.

"The saddle won't be any good to me without the horse," Jack said. "Give me one price for the horse and saddle."

Nye took one more bill from his left hand, and Jack reached out and took the money from Nye's right hand. "Sold," he said.

"You drive a hard bargain," said Nye. "You say you're looking for someone. Can I help?"

"Maybe. Maybe we'll talk about it later. What's going on here anyway? Why all the people coming into town?"

"Oh, there's a big slave auction tonight."

Jack's displeasure showed in his face. "I'll try to avoid that unpleasant spectacle," he said.

"Well," Nye said, "just watch where the crowds are headed and don't follow them."

"Where can I get into a card game tonight?" Jack asked.

"I didn't know you were a cardplayer."

"There're likely a few other things about me you don't know. What about the game?"

"Poker?" Nye asked.

Jack nodded.

"Well, my friend, there just happens to be a big game tonight that I will be sitting in on, and I'd be most pleased to take you along and win that money back from you."

"Maybe I'll use it to get some more out of you."

"We'll see about that."

When the game was over, Jack Spaniard was the big winner. The players were all gentlemen and took their losses well. As the others rose from their chairs, Jack counted out some money and handed it to Nye.

"What's this?" Nye asked.

"I'll need my horse and saddle back," Jack said.

Nye counted the money and looked up at Jack sternly from under heavy eyebrows.

"I gave you more than this," he said.

"The horse is older than he was when I sold him to you," said Jack. "Besides, you're broke now. You need the money."

Nye scowled darkly at Jack and shoved the money into his pocket. "Buy me a drink then, and it's a deal," he said.

They stood up and Nye led the way out of the back room where they'd been playing cards into the larger saloon and over to the bar. He ordered a cognac, and Jack a shot of whiskey. Jack paid for the drinks.

"What are you doing here, Jack?" Nye said. "You rode in and sold one horse, the one you were riding. Then you got into this card game and cleaned me out and bought your horse back. You came a long way to play a game of cards."

"I had no money when I hit town," Jack said.

"What if you'd lost at cards? Then you'd be broke again and on foot."

Jack shrugged.

"Oh, yeah," said Nye. "You said something about looking for someone. Are you going to tell me about that?"

"I'm looking for six men," Jack said. "A gang of thieves and cutthroats. Their leader is a man called Peek Eder."

"That's a dangerous bunch, Jack," said Nye, dropping his voice down low. "They're well-known around here, and they're not well liked. They are the prime suspects in a whole series of robberies and murders, but so far the law has not been able to prove anything against them. Some who have been on their trail have been discovered with their throats slit—and worse. They've been haunting the old Natchez Trace now for some time, so most of their activity is north of us here."

"They made their way out west along the Red River recently," said Jack. "They murdered two friends of mine."

"My God," Nye said. "Are you sure of it?"

"I'm sure."

"If you have proof of that, you should report it to the law," Nye said. "Don't go after them yourself, Jack. Don't try it. You could wind up at the bottom of the river with a belly full of sand."

"I don't have either the time or the inclination to establish the kind of proof necessary for a court of law," Jack said, staring straight ahead. "I know they did it, and that's enough. I mean to make them pay."

Nye tossed down what was left of his cognac and ordered another. Jack still had most of his whiskey, but he paid for Nye's second drink.

"Well," said Nye, "they've been here all right. Peek Eder, his brother Sug, Fermel, and three new additions to their gang by the names of Walker, Fitch and Norton."

Jack's heart thrilled. So the three ex-soldiers he wanted to get were with Eder. If he found one of them, he would find them all. He was suddenly anxious to be on their trail again. He was anxious to have them in his sights. He was ready to do some killing.

"You said they've been here," Jack said. "Does that mean they're gone now?"

"They came roaring into town, stayed a few days, drinking, gambling, whoring. They got into a couple of fights, but Peek stopped them before they went too far. He sees this as a safe playground, I think, and he doesn't want any trouble from the local law. He wants to be able to come back when he's ready for another good time. I don't know if they spent all their money or lost it gambling or what, but they came to me and bought six horses and saddles, they had just about enough left for that, and then they rode out of town. My guess is that they're headed back for the Trace. They'll waylay some unlucky travelers and steal their money until they have enough for another fling."

"Why would they go back up to the Natchez Trace," Jack asked, "if they're so well-known up there?"

"They know the road and every hiding place along the way," Nye said. "It's a long stretch of highway, but it's like home to them. They know every mile. The Trace has a long and bloody history of land pirates: Big and Little Harpe, Joe Hare, Sam Mason, John Murrell, they all ran wild. Most of them are dead and gone, but this Eder gang, they're about as bad as any of them. Jack, if you're damn fool enough to go after them, all alone, then go on up to the Trace. Go on. That's where you'll find them for sure. Sooner or later. But be careful, Jack. Keep all your guns loaded. Keep your powder dry. Sleep with your eyes open."

At Nye's insistence, Jack spent the night as his guest. In the morning, he had a good breakfast of eggs and ham and biscuits, and he drank lots of fresh-brewed coffee. He relaxed for a bit and smoked a pipe. Then he walked out to the stable and saddled his horse. He mounted up and rode to a nearby store, where he outfitted himself well for a long trip on horseback. He made especially sure that he had plenty of powder and shot, and he had bought two extra pistols. He would keep all four loaded and ready. With his long rifle, that would give him five shots before he would have to reload. He left the store and rode back past Nye's stable on his way out of town. Nye, his face wearing a worried expression, saw him coming and walked out to meet him to say his farewells.

"Spaniard," he said, "it's been a pleasure to see you again. Have a safe journey, my friend."

Jack reached into a pocket and pulled out a couple of bills. He reached down to hand them to Nye.

"What's this for?" Nye asked him.

"That's the rest of what you gave me for the horse and saddle," said Jack. "I was only funning with you."

He started riding and did not look back.

"Jack," Nye shouted after him, "be careful. Remember what I told you about that bunch. Be careful."

I I

The old Natchez Trace ran from Natchez, Mississippi, to Nashville, Tennessee, at which point, its name changed, and it became known as the Wilderness Road. From Nashville, the Wilderness Road continued northeast halfway across Kentucky, then made a turn south going down into Knoxville. Jack had to ride from New Orleans to Natchez to reach the southernmost end of the Trace. When he started his journey, he was going only on the word of Herman Nye that, once out of money, the scoundrels he was looking for would return to the Trace to pursue their chosen, nefarious profession. But Jack kept thinking that there was no guarantee. They had recently altered their habits by attacking and murdering the Upbates along the Red River just north of Spanish Texas.

He did not have to ride far, though, before Nye's wisdom was confirmed. He had not yet reached Natchez when he stopped at an inn beside the road. The innkeeper had seen six men who matched the general descriptions given by Jack. His descriptions of the two Eders and of Fermel were just what he had heard from others, but he had seen the three ex-soldiers up close himself. He was pretty sure that the innkeeper had seen the six men he was trailing. He rode on.

In Natchez at last, his suspicions were absolutely confirmed by the owner of a tavern. The Eder gang had been there, the man said. He knew them personally. They had come in for a meal and some drinks, and they had been loud and boisterous, but they had stopped short of any actual rowdiness. They had gone on their way after a few hours' rest and recreation. He suspected that they had gone north along the Trace. Jack thanked the man and went on his way.

When Jack reached the town of Livingston, he decided to stop for the night. He bought himself a hot meal and drank a little whiskey in a tavern. Then he went out to look up an inn with a stable where he could find lodging for both himself and his horse. He spent a restful night and was up early in the morning. The innkeeper's wife prepared a fine breakfast, and Jack ate his fill, following the meal with two extra cups of coffee. He had saddled his horse and was about to mount up and ride on when he noticed a small crowd across the way. There was some kind of excitement. His curiosity got the better of him, so he rode over to join the crowd. He found them gathered around the bodies of two dead men lying in the bed of a hay wagon. Dismounting, Jack worked his way into the crowd.

"I found them just beside the road," a man was saying. "They was shot and their heads was bashed in. Just as ye can see. I checked their pockets and found them empty. Road agents it was."

"I'll bet it was that Eder gang," someone called out.

"Eders or whoever," another voice said, "we'll go after them. Get your weapons and your horses, men. Gather up right back here, and be quick about it."

Most of the crowd scattered, leaving the old man with his hay wagon and its grisly load and the man who had shouted the orders at the last. Jack stepped over to join them.

"You think this is the work of the Eder gang?" he asked.

"There's no proof," the man said, "but it's as likely as not. Who might you be?"

"Jack Spaniard's my name. The Eder gang murdered my two partners out west. I'm trailing them."

"I'm the constable here, Spaniard. My name is Caleb Marsh. You're welcome to join us in our chase. I can see you're well armed."

"I'll ride with you," Jack said.

It wasn't long before a sizable posse had gathered there, and finally Marsh called for them to all mount up and follow him. The wagon driver was riding alongside Marsh to show him exactly where he had discovered the bodies. They rode out north of Livingston for about an hour before the old man stopped them. He pointed to a spot just off the right side of the road.

"Right there," he said. "That's where I found them. Right there."

Marsh dismounted and walked over to the spot. He knelt to study it.

"This is right where it happened too," he said. "Their lifeblood spilled out on the ground right here."

"Mind if I take a look?" Jack asked.

"Help yourself," said Marsh. "I've seen all I can see."

Jack climbed down out of his saddle and walked over to the bloody spot. He studied it closely, then began to look around. Standing up, he faced Marsh.

"How heavily traveled is this road?" he asked.

"Not much anymore," Marsh said. "The traffic is light. Especially this time of year. It's not like in the old days."

"I think there were six of them then," said Jack. "Six men with horses. I know there are six in the Eder gang, and I've seen their work before. I believe that this was their doing. I also believe that they headed north from here after they finished their bloody business."

"You've had some experience at this sort of work," Marsh said.

"Some," said Jack. "We'd better get going. They're some hours ahead of us."

Jack and Marsh remounted their horses. The old wagon driver said, "I'm going back to Livingston. You don't need me no more."

"Go on," Marsh said, "and thanks for your help."

As the old man turned his horse south, Jack, Marsh and the rest of the posse rode north. Jack felt the blood thrill through his veins. He was closing in on the kill. He kept a close watch on the road though, and after riding along for a ways, he held up a hand.

"Hold up," he yelled.

He stopped his horse. Marsh hauled up beside him and the rest of the riders stopped behind them. "What is it?" Marsh asked. Jack pointed to a narrow trail leading off to the right through the woods.

"They turned in there," he said. Without waiting for comment

from Marsh, Jack rode into the darkness of the thick woods. Marsh
was right behind him, and the remainder rode along single file
after him. The trail was too narrow to do otherwise, and the woods
were too thick to move off the trail, especially on horseback. They
rode for thirty minutes or so before Jack stopped again. He dismounted, keeping quiet. Marsh got down from his horse and
walked up to stand close to Jack. Jack pointed ahead.

"Campsite in the clearing," he whispered.

Marsh, with silent gestures, scattered the possemen through-
out the woods on both sides of the trail. Slowly they closed in on
the campsite. The smell of burning wood caught their nostrils. Jack
had faded into the woods just to the right of the trail. As he eased
his way closer to the camp, he heard the sound of voices ahead.
Someone was there all right. Then he heard the sound of a man
crashing clumsily through the woods, and the men in the camp
ahead heard it too.

"Someone's coming," a man shouted from up ahead.

"They're onto us," Marsh yelled. "Charge them."

The possemen crashed through the woods yelling, perhaps for
their charge, perhaps because the thick tangle was tearing at their
faces and bodies. Gunshots sounded from the campsite, and fire
was returned from the posse. Jack moved back onto the trail and
ran forward. As the clearing opened up ahead, he raised his rifle
and aimed too hastily. He could see three men fleeing into the
woods on the other side of the camp. The other three had already
vanished. He fired. One of the three men yelped and hopped,
but he kept running. Jack moved on into the clearing, and Marsh
came up beside him. Soon the rest of the posse was with them.
Some of the men were scratched and bloody from tearing through
the woods. No one had been shot.

"Where are their horses?" someone asked.

"They must have hid them somewhere nearby," Jack said.

"They all got away, damn it," another man said.

"They're not far," Marsh said. "Let's scatter through the woods
and search them out."

Some of the men began to show signs of faintheartedness at
Marsh's suggestion, but no one said anything. They fanned out
and started moving in cautious pursuit. Jack found a hint of a trail
and followed it. Soon he found himself in another clearing. Look-

ing around closely, he could see that the six horses had been pick-eted there. He studied the clearing some more.

"Marsh," he called out. "Over here."

Marsh managed to locate Jack in a couple of minutes. As he stepped into the clearing, Jack said, "Here's where their horses were waiting. They rode out that way." He indicated a trail leading off through the woods. It was about as wide as the one that had brought them in from the Trace. Marsh followed Jack's gesture with his eyes.

"Is that blood on the ground there?" he asked.

"I hit one of them back at their camp," Jack said. "Let's go back and get our horses."

In a short time, they were again riding single file through the woods. They had gone along this second trail only for about a quarter of a mile when a voice came from the rear of the line.

"Hey, Elmer's turned around and headed home."

"We'll never find them in here," another voice said. "I say we give it up."

"Go on back if you want to," Marsh said, exasperated. "I can't keep you here."

Jack rode on quietly. In a few more minutes, Marsh said from behind him, "There are just four of us still here. The rest of the cowards have all turned back."

All of a sudden, Jack heard and felt his horse step into soft, wet ground. He looked down to see that they had ridden into a marsh. He eased the animal ahead a few more steps, then stopped. The path widened a bit, and Marsh came alongside.

"How wide is this bog?" Jack asked him.

"Several miles," Marsh said. "There's few who know the way across. Some have got themselves lost out there and never been seen again."

"Damn it," said Jack. "There's no way to track them in there."

"We've lost them for sure," Marsh said.

"For now," said Jack.

Marsh and the three remaining possemen rode back to Liv-ingston, and Jack went north along the Trace. He saw no point in returning to Livingston. It was unlikely that the Eder gang would do so. They might show themselves again, though, up ahead somewhere. They would be thinking that they had successfully eluded the pursuit from Livingston by running into the bog, and so when they decided to reemerge, they would most probably hit the Trace going north again. Jack rode until dark, but there was no place to stop for the night. He kept riding. It was well after dark when he saw the lights of a roadside tavern ahead. He rode up to the front door, dismounted and tied his horse to the rail there. He went inside. A fire was burning in a fireplace. A sleepy or drunk man sat at a table, his head down on the tabletop. Another groggy man looked up from behind a counter.

"Traveling late, ain't you?" he said.

"It was not by choice," said Jack. "Do you have a room for me?"

"If you have the price I do," the man said.

"A stall and some oats for my horse?"

"Just around back. You'll have to see to it yourself."

Jack paid the man and went back outside to tend to his horse. When he had taken care of that, he went back inside. Inquiring about food, he was told that there was still cold meat from supper. He paid for a helping of that and some hard biscuits. There was no coffee, so he had a glass of whiskey. He considered asking the man about the Eder gang, but decided that it could wait for morning. He went on to his room and to bed.

Lying in the strange bed, Jack contemplated the events of the day. He had been close enough to the Eder gang to wing one of them, but they had gotten away. They had escaped, because some blundering fool in the posse had given them away by crashing through the woods. Jack thought that he would have been much better off had he gone in pursuit of the gang alone. He had been a fool, he thought, to agree to ride with the posse. He could have ridden out alone while Marsh sat and waited for the posse to gather. He could have tracked the gang as easily alone as he had with the posse tagging along. He could have come up on their camp silently and unknown. He would have had five shots without stopping to reload. With a little luck, he could have killed them all. Even if he had not done so well, he could have gotten some of them and gotten himself away from the others. He'd have at least part of the job done. As things had turned out, he still had it all to do, and he did not know where they had gone. He swore that he would not join another posse. Disgusted with himself and his day, he drifted off to sleep.

The next morning Jack had himself a hot breakfast and some fresh, hot coffee, then he got on the road as quickly as he could. It was around noon when he saw the tracks of six horses. He couldn't be sure, but he thought that the tracks were those of the Eder gang's horses returning to the Trace from the woods. If he was right, they were ahead of him on the road again. A little farther up the road, he came to another wayside inn. He and the horse could both use some food and rest. He stopped at the inn.

He took care of his horse first, then sat down for his own meal. A few other people were in the inn, and most of them were also getting themselves a meal. A woman and her husband made small talk with Jack, and Jack was polite but noncommittal. One man sat off in a dark corner alone, drinking rum. Now and then he yelled at the innkeeper for service. Often he moaned or grumbled aloud to himself. The woman exchanged disapproving glances with her husband. Jack finished his meal and was about ready to get back on the road, but he wanted a word with the innkeeper first. He was watching for an opportunity to catch the man in private. At last the man headed back to the kitchen. Jack pushed back his chair, stood up and hurried over to catch him just before he went through the door.

"I'd like a word in private," he said.

The innkeeper pushed the door open and nodded. Jack followed him to just inside the next room.

"What is it?" the innkeeper said.

"I don't want to alarm the ladies," Jack said, "but I'm following some bandits. Six of them. The notorious Eder gang. I know they're somewhere ahead of me on this road. Did they come by here?"

"They came and left," the man said. "Most of them."

"Most of them?" said Jack. "What does that mean?"

"That means, they came, and then most of them left. They left one behind. They got to fussing with one another, and this one finally said to them, go on then, and he cursed them some, and they left him. I think he's got a slight hurt. I don't know if that had anything to do with why he stayed behind or not."

"Well," said Jack, his blood racing, "where is he then?"

The innkeeper opened the door slightly and nodded toward the rude man in the dark corner.

"That's him there," he said, keeping his voice low. "They call him Fermel."

Just then Fermel shouted.

"I'm out of rum. God damn it, innkeeper, fetch me a bottle of rum."

The innkeeper hurried to get a bottle, but Jack took it from him. He got himself a glass and walked over to the table where Fermel sat. As he placed the bottle on the table, Fermel looked up at him and squinted.

"Who the hell are you?" he asked.

Jack pulled out a chair and sat down. He poured Fermel's and his own glass full of rum.

"I don't like to see a man drinking alone," he said. "Have one on me."

Fermel looked at Jack suspiciously, but he picked up the glass. The other diners were casting strange and curious looks in the direction of Fermel and Jack, but Jack's total attention was on Fermel. He saw that Fermel's left arm was bloody from a wound to the shoulder. That must have been from Jack's shot.

"I see you've been hurt," Jack said. "Bandits?"

"Yeah," Fermel said. "Bandits."

"I hear they're bad along the Trace."

"The worst in the world. They shot me from ambush, robbed me and left me for dead."

"But they didn't get all your money. You must have had some hidden away. A very intelligent thing for you to do."

"Huh?" said Fermel, and he looked at Jack with blurred vision.

"Well," said Jack, "you managed to buy yourself a bottle of rum."

"Oh, yeah. That. They did miss a little that I had tucked down into my boot."

"That was lucky for you. I had two friends, a man and his young son. They were farmers, but a bad storm ruined their crop.

They made a trip down to the Red River where it runs north of Spanish Texas to gather some furs. They needed the money to feed their family until they could bring in another crop. Bandits came down on them just as they were ready to head back home. They murdered them both. Father and son. Murdered them in cold blood. Shot them and cut their throats. Bashed their heads in. They rode away with the whole wagonload of furs and sold them in Louisiana. You're lucky you escaped with your life and with some cash—in your boot."

Fermel squinted at Jack. He was puzzled. The story he had just heard was familiar, but why was this stranger telling it to him? He couldn't figure it out. There was something about this man that bothered him.

"I followed those men," said Jack. "I tracked them all the way to New Orleans. There were six of them. I trailed them up here to the Trace, and I joined a posse at Livingston that rode out after them after they had murdered two men along the road. We found them at their camp, but a fool in the posse gave us away, and they ran for the swamp. Just as they were running into the woods, I managed to shoot one of them. I think I hit him—in the left shoulder."

12

Fermel roared like a cornered wild animal. With both hands he flung the table hard up into Jack's face as he, himself, came to his feet. The suddenness and the weight and force of the table threw Jack over backwards in his chair, and before he could scramble to his feet, Fermel was upon him. The hurt to Fermel's left shoulder did not seem to bother the burly man, as he grabbed Jack's coat lapels with both his hands and pulled Jack to his feet. Jack raised a knee sharply up to Fermel's crotch, and an instant later, slapped both his open palms hard against Fermel's ears. Fermel yowled in pain, but he did not loose his grip. Instead, he ran toward the nearest wall, shoving Jack along ahead of him until he had run Jack hard against the wall. Then he bounced Jack back and forth, hammering him into the hard logs of the wall.

With his left hand, Jack grabbed a handful of Fermel's hair and pulled his head back. Then he smashed his right fist into Fermel's nose. Blood squirted in all directions as Fermel's nose was splattered into a spongy mass against his face. He howled again. This time he lost his grip on Jack's coat and staggered back a few steps, rubbing desperately at his bloody face. Jack moved to Fermel's side while recovering from the pounding he had just taken. As soon as Fermel had wiped the blood from his eyes, he reached for a tomahawk at his belt. Jerking it loose, he raised it high, stepped forward and took a violent swing at Jack.

But this was Jack's kind of fighting. He dodged Fermel's blow neatly and pulled the war ax from his own belt. Fermel took another wild swing. Jack blocked this one with the handle of his ax, then kicked Fermel in the belly. Fermel expelled some air with a whuff and stepped back, sucking deeply for more air. He growled low in his throat like a wounded bear.

The other diners in the tavern got up from their seats and huddled together against the far wall with frightened and fascinated looks on their faces. The innkeeper still stood in the doorway to the kitchen, the door held open so he could move either way. He watched closely, not wanting to miss anything.

"Come on, you cowardly murderer," Jack said. "Come on. Try me again."

Raising his weapon high for an overhead blow calculated to split Jack's skull, Fermel ran forward, swinging hard. Jack easily sidestepped the blow. Using the blunt side of his own war ax, he tapped the big man on the back of the head. The blow stunned Fermel, but it did not knock him down. He stood still for a moment and shook his head as if to clear it. Then he looked up again through eyes now bleary with blood.

"That could easily have been your deathblow," said Jack, "but I'm not quite ready for that. Try me again."

"I'll kill you slow," Fermel said. "I'll peel your skin off while you're still alive."

"You won't kill me at all," said Jack. "You're like a clumsy ox."

Again Fermel ran swinging, and again Jack stepped out of the way. This time he used the sharp edge of his ax and sliced into Fermel's right shoulder. Fermel roared in pain and anger and dropped his tomahawk. In spite of his fresh wound, he bent to retrieve his weapon, but as his hand neared the floor, Jack took another swing that chopped the fingers off Fermels's right hand. Fermel howled in rage, and with his left hand, he fumbled for a pistol at his belt. Dropping his ax, Jack stepped in close and grabbed Fermel's left wrist with both his hands. The gun was still tucked in the belt. Jack slipped one hand down over Fermel's hand, which clutched the pistol. He cocked the pistol and forced Fermel's own finger to pull the trigger. The ball went into the inner thigh of Fermel's right leg.

Now Fermel fought like a dying and enraged animal. Swinging his nearly useless arms like clubs and slinging blood from the stumps where his fingers had been, he bellowed. But he staggered from the bullet wound in his thigh, and he drooped as he weakened from loss of blood. Jack stepped back as Fermel fought the air, blinded from blood and rage. A sword hung on the wall behind the counter of the tavern, and Jack went over to get it. Moving back close to the wild dying man, Jack wielded the sword.

"Fermel," he said, "can you hear me? For once in my life, I hope your preachers are right, because if they are, I'm sending your soul to the flames of hell."

Then with one mighty stroke, he lopped the head off the shoulders of the wretched land pirate. The lady in the small crowd across the room fainted. The head bounced and rolled on the floor. The headless body staggered and drooped, then finally crumpled.

"Now there are but five," Jack said.

"Great work, sir," the innkeeper shouted.

Jack picked up the head from the floor and went outside. One of the men was busy fanning the fainted woman. Another stepped toward the innkeeper. "My God, sir," he said, "what was that all about?"

"That man just killed one of the worst ruffians in these parts," the innkeeper said. "The dead man was Fermel, one of the villainous Eder gang. They've murdered and robbed countless travelers along this road. Why, they're worse than Big and Little Harpe. They're bloodier than John Murrel."

"Then when he said just now that there are but five left—"

"He was referring to the rest of the Eder gang," the innkeeper said. "Those that are still alive and on the loose. And from what we've just seen, I'll wager he gets them all. Every last one."

Outside, Jack looked up and down the sides of the road for a suitable tree. He found one not far from the tavern and across the road with a fork in it just higher than his head, and there he planted the head of Fermel for all who passed by to see. He walked back over to the tavern and went inside. The fainted lady had recovered somewhat and was sitting up with the chivalrous man still fanning her vigorously.

"Is the lady all right?" Jack asked. "I'm sorry that scene had to develop in your presence."

"Oh, sir," said the man with the fan, "no apologies are necessary. Doubtless we all owe you great thanks for making the road a bit safer for everyone. Why, judging from what we just learned, we may owe you our very lives."

Jack walked over to the headless body and took hold of the jacket.

"I'll get this out of here," he said, and he dragged it out the front door, across the road and into the woods. He went through all the pockets and took all the money he found there, figuring it to be a share of what the Eder gang had stolen from the Upbates. Tucking it into his own pockets, he walked back over to the tavern and went inside. He was met by the innkeeper handing him a glass of whiskey.

"Allow me, sir," the innkeeper said.

Jack thanked the man and took the drink.

"If anyone should ask who did this deed," he said, "you may tell them that it was Jack Spaniard."

He finished the whiskey and put the glass down.

"If you'll give me some water and rags," he said, "I'll clean up the mess I made."

"Oh, no," said the innkeeper. "I'll take care of that." He was already wiping the blade of the sword clean. Finished, he got its belt and sheath and slipped the sword back in place. Then he held the sword out toward Jack. "And you take this along with my gratitude."

"What's it going to be like in Arkansas, Paw?" the lanky boy asked, as he walked alongside the too-loaded wagon.

The driver, Keeps Tuckow, his wife Rae and daughter Mey seated beside him, gave a flick of the reins.

"Green and rich, Ram," he said. "I guess it ain't a whole lot different from this here. Only thing is there's good farmland that ain't yet been too much used. Rich, black earth. They just cleared a bunch of Indians out of there to make room for folks like us. Lots of good land to be had."

"Where'd the Indians go?" Mey asked.

"Oh, I don't rightly know," Keeps said. "Moved them west, I guess. There's lots of room out West."

"When we get there," Ram said, "can we just pick us out a place and build our house? Just like that?"

"Lord, you young'uns are full of questions," said Rae. "Can't you leave your paw's brain to rest a little?"

Keeps laughed out loud. "That's all right, Mother," he said. "They're just natural curious. Why, we're going on a mighty adventure here. I expect we're all some anxious to plant our roots and see the new country and build our new home and watch our crops grow. Yes, indeed. It's a mighty adventure."

"Well then?" said Ram.

"Well what, son?"

"Do we just look around till we find what we want and then just take it?"

"Oh, I suppose there'll be a land office of some kind or other to deal with. We got to make sure we ain't planting ourselves where someone else has already got a claim. But other than that, I reckon that it'll be might near the way you said it."

"I'll be glad when we get there, Keeps," Rae said. "This has been a mighty long road. I'll admit that I'm a getting weary."

"Yes it has, Mother. Mighty long. But we'll get to the end of it. Don't you worry about that. We'll get to the end of it before you know it."

"Paw?" said Mey. "It seems like we ain't going nowhere. I mean, Arkansas is west of us, ain't it?"

"That's right, gal."

"Seems to me like we just keep on going south."

"We go where the roads take us." Keeps said. "This road here'll take us down south to Natchez. Once we get there, we can turn west."

Word spread quickly about the fight in the tavern, and people showed up seemingly out of the woods from every direction. They came to see the bloody trophy in the tree, and they came to see the man who had done the deed. They listened over and again to the innkeeper tell the tale of the fight, and they all wanted to buy whiskey for Jack Spaniard, the man who had killed the notorious Fermel and who was also known to be on the trail of the rest of the infamous Eder gang. With the blessing of the innkeeper, one man painted a new sign to hang outside, and changed the name of the tavern to "Fermel's Head Inn." They ate and drank and talked far into the night, and when Jack said that he could take no more and had to find a bed, the grateful innkeeper insisted on giving him a room for the night at no charge. When Jack asked directions to the room, a buxom young doe-eyed lass jumped up from her seat among the cheerful crowd.

"I'll show him the way," she said, giving the innkeeper a wink. He smiled back at her, handed her a lit candle, and let her take over.

"My name's Dolly," she said to Jack as she took his arm. Jack took up his long rifle, his bundle and his newly acquired sword and allowed her to lead him up the stairs and down the hall to a dark room. She opened the door, went in and set the candle on a small table against the wall. "How's this?" she asked.

Jack looked at the bed. It was all that really interested him at the moment.

"It will do nicely," he said. "Thank you."

He turned away from her and found places around the room to stash his belongings.

"You don't want me to go away, do you?" she said.

He turned back and looked at her, and he did not.

It was morning, and Keeps Tuckow had gotten his family off to an early start. There was still a damp chill in the air from the night before. The Tuckows were travel-weary, but their spirits were still high. They had all caught the sense of adventure from old Keeps, so they were anxious each morning to get on the road to Arkansas. They had driven maybe two hours down the Trace from the last wayside inn when they rounded a curve to find themselves suddenly facing five men standing in a line across the road, blocking their way. Each of the five men had a rough and dirty look about him, and each was heavily armed. Each held a long rifle across his chest. Keeps pulled back on the reins to stop the wagon.

"Good morning to you," he said. He received no response, only sullen looks. "I'd be obliged if you'd step aside."

"Where might you folks be traveling to?" asked Peek Eder.

"Arkansas," said Keeps. "And we need to be moving along, if you'll be kind enough to clear the way."

"Let's visit a spell first," Eder said. "We ain't seen many travelers along this road lately. We're getting tired of each other's boring conversation. Ain't talked to no womenfolks in a while neither. Climb on down and set a spell."

"We really ought to be moving on, Keeps," Rae said. She did not miss the way the wretched-looking men were leering at fourteen-year-old Mey.

"I'm asking you kindly to let us pass," Keeps said.

Sug Eder raised his rifle and shot Keeps through the chest.

"Paw!" shouted Ram. His mother and sister both screamed in horrified disbelief.

"You hadn't ought to a done that, Sug," Peek said. "Now we got to kill them all."

Ram started pulling an old gun out of the wagon, and Corbin Walker shot him through the middle. The lanky youngster doubled over in pain. Fitch and Norton raced over to him and bashed his head in with their pistol butts. Mey was still screaming, as Rae tried to get her down from the wagon seat.

"We got to run, baby," she said. "We got to run."

Just then Walker grabbed her from behind by the hair and pounded her head with his gun butt. Mey could not run. She stood frozen to the spot, screaming hysterically. Peek Eder raised his own rifle and aimed at the girl, but Walker stepped in front of her.

"We ain't got to kill her," he said. "Not for a while at least."

Jack did not get as early a start as he had hoped to. He'd had a night of carousing and slept late. When he did get out of bed, the innkeeper insisted on feeding him a big breakfast, and he still refused to accept any payment from Jack. At last, Jack, well fed, mounted his horse and rode north in pursuit of the Eder gang. He felt like he was getting closer, but all he actually knew was that they had been at the tavern where they left Fermel behind. He knew they had not gone south on the Trace. If they had, he'd have seen them. He did not think that they'd have gone into the woods or the marshes, at least not for any distance away from the road. Surely, he thought, if he continued north on the Trace, sooner or later, he would come across them or evidence of their nearness. He had almost ridden away the day before he found that evidence.

It was not the kind of evidence he had hoped to find. Three bodies. An old man and woman and a boy not quite grown. They had been brutally murdered. A wagon with some goods in it, and other goods strewn about on the road. The killers had gone through the family's belongings searching for anything that might be of use to them and flinging everything else out of the wagon. The old mare that was hitched to the wagon had not been attractive enough for the robbers to bother with. It was still hitched, just standing there unconcerned.

Jack couldn't help himself. He thought of the Upbates, looking at these more recent victims of the same vermin, and he felt sick. He thought about burying the bodies but decided against it. There should be a settlement or at least a tavern or something not far ahead. It was about time for one to appear. He decided to load the bodies in the wagon and take them there to report the incident. There were blankets and quilts scattered in the road, and Jack wrapped each body and placed it in the wagon bed. He tied his horse to the back of the wagon, climbed onto the box, turned the wagon north and drove ahead. He drove for about two hours before he came to the inn. He stopped in front of the door, climbed down and went inside. A friendly-looking man with a round, red face greeted him.

"Hello, stranger," he said. "I'm Vernon Braxton, owner of this establishment. How may I serve you?"

"I have a sad mission," Jack said. "I found some murdered travelers on the road south of here. I put the bodies in their wagon and brought them along. Is there a constable or a magistrate anywhere near?"

"Oh, no," Braxton said. "How terrible."

He went to the door and stepped outside. Looking in the back of the wagon, he uncovered the faces.

"My God," he said. "It's the Tuckows. They just left here this morning. They were going to Arkansas to start a farm. Real nice folks. They were planning to start a whole new life out West. But wait. Where's the girl?"

"There were only the three bodies," Jack said.

"They had a pretty little daughter about fourteen years old," Braxton said. "Oh no. Oh my God. If you didn't find her, or her body—

"Then the outlaws took her along with them," said Jack.

"I hate to think what they'll do to her."

"There's no time to lose," Jack said. "I'm going after them."

He hurried to his horse, jerked loose the reins and mounted up, turning it sharply back south. As he rode away, Braxton shouted after him, "I'll take care of things here. I'll fetch the constable over right away."

13

The Eder gang was not very far from the spot on the Trace where they had murdered the three unfortunate Tuckows. They had run off into the woods on the west side of the road, Corbin Walker dragging the hysterical Mey along behind him by the hair of her head. They did not follow a trail. Instead they forced their way through tangles and brambles that ripped at Mey's dress and her skin. When they came to a small clearing, Walker stopped. He took hold of Mey by her shoulders and looked her in the face and shook her hard. She shrieked and trembled.

"Shut up," he shouted into her face. She shrieked more wildly, and he shouted again. "Shut up, you little bitch." Still she shrieked, and he slapped her hard across the face, and again and again. At last she stopped. She stood trembling almost to the point of convulsions. Blood trickled from her nose and from a corner of her mouth.

"That god damn little gal's going to slow us up considerable," Sug Eder said. "You only saved her for just one reason. We ought to go on ahead and take our turns with her right now and get it all over with and done. Then we can kill her and leave her here."

"We got no time for that now," Peek Eder said. "When folks find her family out there, what we done to them, they'll know we got her. They'll be hot on our trail. We need to get going. We need to get to our hideout fast as we can. I shoulda killed her back yonder on the road like I started to do."

"You ain't killing her yet," Walker said. "I'm keeping her for a while."

"Well, you ain't diddling her yet neither," said Peek. He faced his brother. "Nor you neither. Come on now. Let's get. All of you. And you keep her quiet."

"I don't want to wait no longer," Sug said. "Looky here what I got on me." He reached down to his crotch and grabbed a handful of erection through his trousers. "I mean to do something about this right now. I don't care what you say. You're my brother. You ain't my daddy."

"Later," Peek said.

"Let me have her, Corbin," Sug said, ignoring Peek. He reached out and took hold of Mey's arm and pulled. Mey started screaming again. Peek pulled a pistol out of his belt and fired a shot into the brain of his brother. Sug dropped like a sack of grain. Walker stared unbelieving at the body.

"You shot your own brother," he said. "You shot his brains out. You killed him just like that, deader'n hell."

"Shut up. And shut her up and bring her along," said Peek, "or I'll shoot her too."

Walker smacked Mey again until she stopped screaming.

"Now looky here," he said. "You keep quiet. He'll kill you, just like he said he'd do. Come along with me now and do just what I tell you to do, and I'll keep you alive—at least for a while."

When Jack returned to the place where he had discovered the bodies of the three Tuckows, it didn't take him long to find where the Eder gang had crashed into the woods. He had not bothered to look for them before. He had been much too concerned at that time with the bodies of their unfortunate victims. Now with time to look, he saw that the gang had moved into the woods going west, and they were on foot. The woods were too thick for traveling through on horseback. So Jack tied his own horse there beside the road and followed their trail into the thick bramble. They had been in a hurry and had not even tried to cover their tracks. That much was good. The girl might still be unharmed. But Jack was determined to waste no time.

Once because of a tangle of brush, he lost the trail, but looking around, he quickly found it again and hurried on his way. Still, he did not crash through the woods, the way the clumsy posseman had done before. He did not want to alert the gang members that he was behind them. Somewhere along the way, they would stop and rest. Sometime they would feel like they had gone far enough to have eluded any pursuit. Then they would stop, and then he would catch up with them. He kept going. Now and then he came across a piece of material torn from a dress by wild-rose thorns. They had the girl with them. He was sure of it.

After some twenty minutes or so, the tracks led Jack to a small clearing. He readied his rifle and eased himself to the edge of the woods. There was no sign of life in the clearing. He stepped out cautiously, and then he saw the body. He moved on out into the clearing. There was still no sign of anyone around. He walked on out to the body to examine it. He did not recognize the man, but he knew that it must be one of the Eders. There were only five of the gang, and Jack felt sure that he would recognize any of the three ex-soldiers.

He wondered what had happened to this Eder though. If one of the ex-soldiers had killed him, would not there be trouble with the surviving brother? What if brother had killed brother? There was no telling with this kind of inhuman, savage scum. Well, he had no time to worry about it, no time for philosophy. He made a quick search of the pockets and found a little money, which he pocketed. They must be in a hurry, he thought. Then he searched the edges of the clearing until he found where the remaining four members of the gang had made their way into the woods again. They still had the girl.

He plunged ahead. He did not think they were too far ahead of him, but he knew that farther west, he would run into the marshes. If the outlaws knew a way through there, he would not be able to track them. He considered that they were going into that mire by design. He would have to catch up to them before they had gone that far. He hurried on, careful to keep watching for sign that he was still on the right trail. The woods grew darker.

And then he felt the ground beneath his feet growing soft. In a few more steps, it was soppy and muddy. Soon he was walking in shallow, black water. "Damn," he said out loud. Still he moved ahead. Then he realized that he could no longer tell if he was following the trail of the gang or not. He stopped. He had to consider what to do. They could have gone in any direction from there.

He stood quiet, listening for any telltale sounds, but he heard none. At last he decided that since they had been moving pretty much straight west through the woods, they might continue straight west through the marsh. He moved ahead but with less confidence than before. Now and then he stopped to listen and, hearing nothing, continued west. Then he found himself in water up to his waist. He stopped and backed out of it. If the outlaws knew this marsh, he thought, they wouldn't go through that way. Working his way back to lower water, he moved south for a while, then tried west again. This time he managed to get farther out. He thought that perhaps he had found their trail through the fen.

Then he thought he heard voices. He stopped still and listened. He heard it again. It was definitely the sound of human voices, but he couldn't be sure from which direction the voices were coming. The dank surroundings played tricks with sound. He couldn't determine the direction, but he was certain that they were not moving. They were somewhere not too far away from him, and they had stopped. That was both good and bad. It was good that he was that close to them, and they were no longer moving. But if they were settled in somewhere, it could be very bad for the girl if he didn't move in on them quickly enough. Desperately, Jack looked around. If they had stopped, perhaps they had built a fire. But the trees were too tall and too thick for him to spy any plumes of smoke.

He found a tall tree that he thought he could climb, and he propped his long rifle in the crotch of another nearby tree to keep it safe from the green and brackish water which covered the ground. Then he tackled the climbing tree. He had to hug the trunk and shinny up for a distance before he came to a branch. After that, the climbing was easy. He moved around the trunk from branch to branch going higher and higher until he found himself where he could look out over the tops of most of the trees. The forest appeared from there as a thick green carpet over the earth, and then he saw a wisp of smoke.

Knowing that his vantage point would be very different back on the ground, he took careful note of the direction, and he made sure that he knew what side of the tree he was on in descending. Back on the mushy ground, he calculated the direction. He retrieved his rifle and began moving through the bog as quickly as he dared. Even easy, cautious steps made sloshing noises, and he couldn't afford to give himself away.

And then he saw it. A swell in the ground that rose above the water level. It had been mostly cleared, and in its center, at the top of the mound, so to speak, was a crude lean-to. At the front edge of the lean-to a fire was burning. Underneath the shabby shelter were four men and a girl. The girl sat alone on the ground, hugging her knees to her breasts. Even from that distance, Jack could tell that she was terrified. At the moment, no one was molesting her. Jack hoped that they had not already done so. He hoped that he had caught up with them in time. He recognized the three ex-soldiers, and he knew that the fourth man was the surviving Eder. He did not know which Eder it was. He did not really care.

The question now for Jack was how to go about attacking the four outlaws without further endangering the Tuckow girl. He could easily get one of the men with a long rifle shot, but the distance was far too great for his pistols. And it would be very difficult, if not impossible, to slush his way through the swamp to get closer to them without revealing his presence. He told himself not to get too anxious, not to make any foolish mistakes. He told himself to stay calm, that he had plenty of time to think. The girl was safe enough for now. He would have to figure this just right to make it work. Then the voices on the island grew louder, and the gestures of the two men who stood facing one another grew more animated. Jack watched carefully and strained to understand the words.

"It was me what saved her life in the first damn place," Corbin Walker was saying, pointing a finger at Fitch and jabbing the air. "That means she's mine. If anyone gets to go first, it's me."

"But I said it first," Fitch spoke out. "You was talking about food. Said you was hungry. Said you could eat a horse. So go on and eat while I try out the little gal for you. I'll tell you how she was after I'm done, and you can have her back after you've et."

"You stay away from her," Walker yelled.

"Shut up," Peek Eder said. "The both of you. I'm still the god damn boss of this scurvy outfit. What we'll do is we'll draw straws. The short straw goes first. Then the next shortest and so on. Ever'one'll get a fair chance, and ever'one'll get a turn. That's my decision, and it's final."

He took up some pieces of straw from the bed on which he was stretched out, broke them, then held them up toward Walker, their lengths hidden in his hand. Scowling, Walker took a straw. Eder moved his hand toward Fitch, and Fitch pulled one. He held it over close to the one Walker had pulled, and they saw that Fitch's straw was shorter. Fitch laughed, and Walker angrily turned his back, crossing his arms over his chest. Then Norton pulled a straw. Eder held up the last one as his own. Fitch's straw was the shortest of all. He turned leering toward Mey, and he started unhitching his breeches.

"Come on, little gal," he said, drooling. "Get up."

Mey hugged her knees tighter

"Get your ass up from there," Fitch said, "and take off that dress."

Mey tried to squeeze herself into a tight ball.

"Then I'll just take it off of you," Fitch said. He reached out with both hands, taking Mey by the shoulders and pulled her to her feet. Mey screamed and clawed Fitch's face with both hands. Fitch yowled in pain and dropped her, both his hands going instinctively to his wounded face. Norton and Peek laughed, and Walker cursed. Mey fell back to the ground. Fitch took his hands away from his face and glared at Mey. He pulled a knife from his belt.

"Bet if I cut your hands off," he said, "you won't do that again."

Spanish Jack could see what was happening. There was no time for planning now. It was time for action. He raised his long rifle to his shoulder, took quick but careful aim, and fired. There was a poof and a fizz, followed by a loud boom as the kick of the rifle rocked Jack backwards. Fitch screamed in agony and dropped to his knees. Jack dropped his rifle and pulled out a pistol in each hand. He ran toward the island as fast as he could go, splashing through the marsh. Eder fired a rifle at him and missed. Then he ran across the lean-to, grabbed Mey by an arm, and ran into the swamp pulling her behind him.

Norton grabbed up a rifle and raised it to fire, but Jack had made half the distance to the island by then. The distance was better for a pistol shot. He raised his right hand as he ran, and he fired. The pistol ball struck Norton in the face. Norton howled and fell to the ground rolling about and whining. Walker, undecided, looked after Eder and Mey. Then he looked at Jack running hard toward the island. Finally, he turned and ran desperately into the murky water, fleeing for his life. Jack saw that neither Fitch nor Norton was in any condition for him to worry about. He saw that Walker and Eder had fled in different directions, but he knew that Eder had the girl. When he reached the island hideout, he ran across it and into the swamp on the other side in the direction of Eder's flight.

Peek Eder realized that dragging Mey along with him through the mire was slowing him down, and he knew that he was running for his life. He had grabbed Mey on impulse, without thinking, but he was thinking now. It was a shame and a waste, he thought, but his life was more important. He stopped running, and Mey fell into the ooze. Eder turned to face her. He pulled a pistol from his belt and raised his arm to fire.

Jack saw what Eder was about to do. It was a long shot, but he had no choice. He snapped off a quick shot from his second pistol, and he could see that it tore at Eder's coat sleeve. Eder roared and swung the barrel of his own pistol from Mey to Jack. As Eder fired, Jack moved to his left. The shot was wide to the right. Jack kept running. Eder turned to flee again as Jack pulled out his third pistol. He ran past Mey and stopped. He wanted Eder badly, but Mey's safety was more important. Jack fired a last shot at the escaping Eder, and he heard Eder yelp like a dog, and saw him flinch, but the brute did not slow down. Peek Eder disappeared into the black, steamy swamp ahead. Jack turned and sloshed his way back to Mey where she huddled against the slimy bark of a cypress tree. He put his guns away and held out a hand.

"I'm Jack Spaniard," he said, "I've come to take you back."

Mey pressed herself against the tree and shuddered.

"I'm not going to hurt you. I'm not one of those other men. They're all gone now, and you're all right. Please, come with me."

"Where?" she said in a weak and trembling voice.

"Back to Braxton's Inn. Do you remember the Braxtons? It was they who told me about you. What's your name?"

"Mey," she said.

"Will you come with me, Mey?"

Slowly she relented. She raised a trembling hand and stretched out her arm. Jack took her hand and helped her to her feet. They started walking back together. When they reached the island, Jack walked her past it to the place where he had dropped his rifle. He stood her against the same big tree he had leaned against.

"Wait for me here," he said. "I'll be right back."

He ran back over to the island.

Norton was still rolling around in pain, holding his bloody face. Fitch was lying still and breathing heavily. Calmly, Jack slit both their throats. Quickly he went through all their pockets. Both men had money on them. Jack took it all and stuffed it into his own pockets. He picked up their rifles one at a time and broke them against a tree trunk. Then he tossed their pistols into the mire. He made his way back over to where Mey waited, and he took her hand again. This time she did not shrink from him.

"All right now," he said. "Let's go."

They made it back to the road, where Jack was more than a little surprised to find his patient horse still waiting right where he had left it. He helped Mey into the saddle and jumped on behind her.

Back at Braxton's Inn, Braxton and his wife were overjoyed to see Jack riding up with the girl. Mrs. Braxton took Mey into a back room to give her a bath and some clean clothes. Braxton gave Jack a whiskey and waited while Jack drank it to hear the particulars. Jack drank the whiskey and put the glass down.

"Well," he said, "there are but two left alive. One is Walker, the ex-soldier. The other is one of the Eders. I don't know which one."

"It'd be Peek," Braxton said. "The older one and the leader of the gang. After you left here, I got the constable and some other men. We took a posse out after you. We made it to the clearing where we found the body of the younger Eder, Sug. We tried to keep up with you after that, but we were baffled by the mire. We had to give it up and come back. So you killed three of them yourself."

"Not this trip," said Jack. "I found the one you called Sug just the way you found him. He was killed by one of his own."

Braxton offered a hot meal, but Jack asked for a bath first. When the meal was finally laid out on the table, Jack and Mey were both cleaned up and wearing fresh clothes. Mey looked down at the table.

"Poor child," said Mrs. Braxton, "she's gone through a terrible ordeal."

"Mr. Spaniard," Mey said, her voice barely audible. "I owe you my life. I'm very grateful to you."

"I'm glad to have been of service," Jack said.

They ate, mostly in silence. They made some small talk. When the meal was done, Mrs. Braxton poured coffee around.

"Do you have anyplace to go, Mey?" Jack asked. "Relatives somewhere?"

Mey shook her head.

"An inn on the Natchez Trace is no place to raise a young girl," Mrs. Braxton said, "but she's welcome to stay with us until something can be done."

"We were going to Arkansas," said Mey.

"I know a very nice lady with a young son in Arkansas," Jack said. "They lost the father and another son recently. I know they'd welcome you in their home. I'll be glad to take you to them."

14

And so the decision was made. Jack would take Mey with him back to Arkansas to leave her with the surviving Upbates, Leta and Ish. In the back of his mind was the annoying thought that perhaps the Upbates would not want her, but he thought that it would really be all right with them. If it turned out that he was wrong about that, well, he would just deal with that problem when the time came. He decided that he would buy an extra horse for Mey to ride, and they would travel the Trace on horseback to Natchez, where they could book passage on a riverboat. They could then travel the rest of the way to Fort Smith by that faster and more comfortable method, and then it would be just a short horseback ride from Fort Smith on to the Upbate home.

But there was another annoying thought in Jack Spaniard's mind: he had not yet informed the Upbates of the fate that had befallen the rest of their family. That unpleasant chore was not something he was looking forward to, but it was something that had to be done. He had thought often that perhaps he should have gone directly back to the Upbate home and told them what had happened down on the Red River, but two things had prevented that. First of all, he had been in pursuit of the murderers, and he had not anticipated that they would lead him on such a long chase. He had hoped to catch up with them quickly, before the turn back north to Fort Smith, kill them and retrieve the stolen goods or their value in cash, then get on to the Upbate home, relate the sad news and give them the money. It just hadn't worked out that way. Jack had not caught up with them by the time he reached the turn, and then they had not turned north. Instead they had continued east.

Jack had plenty of time to think all these things over, for the Braxtons had insisted that he and Mey stay over for at least a couple of days.

"The poor girl needs some rest," Mrs. Braxton had said. "She needs time to, well, to get over the shock of what happened, to start to, you know, to start to heal. And you could use some rest, too, Jack Spaniard, from all the fighting and killing."

Jack had agreed without arguing, and then the next morning, the constable arrived. Braxton had already filled him in on the details, but he asked to see Jack. They sat at a table in the main room of the inn.

"It's not that I doubt your word, Jack," the constable had said, "but we require the physical proof. We require it for our records and for the comfort of the good people around here and of the travelers along the Trace. I hope you understand."

"Perfectly," Jack said. "I'll be glad to take you to the place."

The constable wanted the heads of the dead outlaws. He had already secured the head of Sug Eder from the clearing and stuck it on a pole on the side of the road as a gruesome warning to would-be road agents. Jack led the lawman and four other men to the hideout in the swamp. There they cut off the heads of Norton and Fitch. They would post them along the Trace as well.

"It's a great comfort to wayfarers," the constable said, "and it's an object lesson to wild young men."

Jack and Mey rested a second day at the inn, and then, the Braxtons having outfitted them well for travel, and Jack having purchased a second horse and saddle, they said their farewells to the Braxtons, mounted up and headed south. They rode quietly most of the first day. The second day, Mey began to talk a little. She talked about her parents and her brother. She talked some about the horror she had suffered, and she talked about how grateful she was to Spanish Jack. Their second night out, they stopped at the recently named Fermel's Head Inn. The innkeeper was having a good night with the place almost full of happily tipsy customers, but when he spotted Jack, he rushed over to greet him.

"Jack Spaniard," he said. "Welcome back."

"Hello, my friend," Jack said. "Do you have a couple of rooms for the night?"

"You want two rooms?" the innkeeper said, looking from Jack to Mey.

"Yes. One for me and one for the young lady."

"Well, yes," the man said. "I can accommodate you. But you won't want to retire right away, will you? The boys will want to drink some toasts to your health. Word has reached us, by the way, of your two new scalps. Hearty congratulations."

"I don't take scalps," said Jack. "I cut off heads."

The innkeeper laughed. "Yes," he said. "Of course. It was just a figure of speech."

"It's more civilized that way," Jack said. "May I please have the rooms? I'd like to see the young lady settled in for the night. Then I may rejoin you for a short while."

Jack saw Mey locked safely in her room. Then he went back downstairs. He didn't mind all the attention and the accolades. He rather enjoyed it. If these people wanted to make him into some kind of a hero, well, let them. And he had not failed to notice that there were some advantages to that role. The innkeeper met him this time with a glass of whiskey in his hand.

"It's on the house," he said. "You're my honored guest."

"Thank you," Jack said, "but I have to see to my horses first."

"We'll take care of that chore for you," the innkeeper said. Jack took the glass, and the innkeeper snapped his fingers at a young man who came running up to him. "See to the gentleman's horses, and be especially good to them," the innkeeper said. As the young man went out to obey his orders, the innkeeper called everyone in the house to attention. "I want to make sure that all of you are acquainted with our honored guest," he said. "This is none other than Jack Spaniard, the brave man who has single-handedly slain four members of the notorious Eder gang. One of them has given my inn its new name, and the deed was done in this very room right before my eyes."

There were cheers and hurrahs around the room. There were

hearty congratulations, expressions of appreciation, slaps on the back and several offers of drinks. A man got up and offered his chair, and Jack sat down at a table with three other men.

"Mr. Spaniard," one of the men said, "are you looking for the last two members of the Eder gang?"

"I hope to meet up with them one day," Jack said.

"Is it then your personal mission to see that this scourge is erased from our territory?"

"You could say that," said Jack.

"Do you think you'll find them then?"

"I sincerely hope so."

"But not tonight," said another man, with a sly wink.

"I beg your pardon," said Jack.

"Well, sir, I saw her when you came in. You have a lovely young thing with you tonight. No time to be bothering with outlaws. And I noticed that you've already tucked her away, keeping her safely to yourself."

Jack stood up. Looking down sternly at the man, he said, "The young lady is a child. She's orphaned—by that same gang of murderers we've been discussing. I'm taking her to a respectable home where she'll be properly looked after. I don't want to hear any more aspersions cast on her character—or mine as it involves her. I killed the last man who insulted her."

"I beg your pardon, sir," the man said, his face turning pale. "I had no idea. Really I didn't. Please resume your seat and allow me to buy your next whiskey."

Jack accepted the man's apology and sat down again.

"Jack Spaniard," said the fourth man at the table. He had been silent up until then. "Might you also be sometimes called— Spanish Jack?"

"I've often been called that."

"I've spent some time out in Arkansas," the man said, "and I heard of a man out that way, a man notorious for the killing of Osage Indians. Could it be—

"I am that same Spanish Jack."

"But they say that he, himself, is, uh, rumored to be a Cherokee Indian."

"It's much more than a rumor, sir," Jack said. "I am Cherokee."

"Oh. I see. How interesting."

"Do you still want to share your table with me? Do you still want to buy me whiskey?"

"Yes," said the man who had offered both drink and apology. He waved a hand, and the innkeeper came running over to the table. "A whiskey for Mr. Spaniard," the man said.

The innkeeper soon brought a fresh glass and put it on the table in front of Jack.

"There's no charge," he said.

"This gentleman offered to buy me a drink," Jack said. "Please allow him to do so."

The innkeeper took the man's money, and Jack drank the whiskey, stood up and excused himself.

"I have a long journey still ahead of me, gentlemen," he said.

The next morning, the innkeeper fed them breakfast, and Jack and Mey got back on the road. They had not gone far from the inn when Mey began to talk.

"You didn't tell me you were an Indian," she said.

"If I didn't tell you," said Jack, "then how do you know?"

"I heard you tell those men last night," she said. "I was listening at the top of the stairs. I also heard you tell that one that you'd killed the last man who insulted me."

"Mey," said Jack, "I told you to stay in your room with the door locked."

"I know," she said, "but it was just all too exciting. I couldn't help myself."

"You might have gotten yourself into trouble at that place," he said.

"I'm not afraid when you're with me," she said. "Jack?"

"What?"

"If you're really an Indian, why are you helping me? I remember my father saying that we were moving to land in Arkansas where some Indians had just been forced to move away."

"He was talking about my people," said Jack. "You were moving to what used to be my home. In fact, you're still moving there. The Upbates live on some of that land."

"Don't you hate us for that?"

"I don't hate you. I don't think I hate anyone anymore—except for cutthroat road agents."

"But they made people like you move to make room for people like me. That isn't fair, is it?"

"No, it's not fair, but I don't believe that you or me had much to do with making that decision."

"I'm just amazed that you would actually want to help me."

"We're all just people, Mey," said Jack. "When everyone realizes that, it will be a better world. You needed help, and I was there. That's all."

They rode on, and in a few days, they had reached Natchez. Jack knew Natchez well. He knew that the town was sharply divided into the respectable Natchez above the Bluff, with its beautiful public square, and new, brick buildings that housed various businesses, law offices and banks; and Natchez Under the Hill, a mudflat that ran down to the water's edge. Its two narrow streets and numerous dark alleys were lined with bars and brothels and gambling dens. It was a known hangout for ruffians of all kinds, and it was place where they knew that "anything goes." It was wide-open.

And the ruffians knew to stay "under the hill." Natchez above the Bluff was as safe a town as could be found in the frontier. Ladies and gentlemen strolled casually through the lovely city park, and businessmen made their deals. Money was spent freely in the shops and stores. All rowdiness stayed under the hill. They knew it above and they knew it below. Jack rode with Mey into Natchez above the Bluff, and he rode straight to the big front doors of Parker's Hotel. Mey stared wide-eyed. She had never seen such opulence. Jack hitched the horses, then helped Mey down from the saddle. He took her by the arm and led her into the luxurious lobby. He seated her in an easy chair, then walked over to the counter where he secured a room for her for the night.

He took what few things she had with her up to her room, and then he took her out shopping. He bought her a few new dresses, shoes and other things. And he bought himself a new suit of clothes. He found a restaurant, and they had themselves a fine meal. Then Jack took Mey back to her room. He told her to stay in the room with the door locked until he called for her in the morning, told her good night, went back downstairs and left the hotel.

It was a little early for going to bed, but Mey wasn't bored. She did not feel like Jack had left her prisoner in the lavish hotel room. She walked around checking every detail of the walls and the furniture. She felt the texture of the wallpaper. She rubbed the upholstered chairs. She tried each chair until she had selected her very favorite, and she flung herself onto the beautiful bed. She had never in her life seen such things. She had never dreamed that she ever would. She was saddened, of course, by the tragic loss of her family, but Jack Spaniard had begun to take their place in her young heart. She thought that the most fortunate day of her life had been the day that Jack Spaniard had come walking into it. She had heard tales of knights of old in shining armor riding to the rescue of ladies in distress. Jack Spaniard, Cherokee Indian, was her knight, and she was in love.

Jack left the hotel and took both horses. It did not take him long to find a buyer, and he got a good price for the two horses and two saddles. He pocketed the money and went to find the offices for the steamboat company. He was pleased to learn that a riverboat would be headed west first thing in the morning, and he booked passage for himself and for Mey. Pocketing the tickets, he left the office and headed for Natchez Under the Hill.

It was a world of difference. The air was filled with foul odors and raucous noises. The streets were mud. Men staggered from one bar to another. Here a man lay in the mud either dead or unconscious. There a man came flying headlong out of a dive, having just been thus ejected by someone for some reason. Whores stood in doorways or leaned out of windows beckoning to passersby. Jack went from one rowdy bar to another. He looked over the crowds of ugly, drunken faces He wondered if he would even recognize Peek Eder if he saw him. He knew he would recognize Walker.

"Jack Spaniard, as I live and breathe."

Jack looked over his shoulder to see none other than J. Worthington Jones.

"Jones," he said, as they pumped one another's hand. "What a surprise."

"We'd been wondering about you, Jack. Where have you been and what are you doing here?"

"Let's sit down where we can talk," said Jack, "and I'll tell you all about it."

"Well, that won't happen in this place," Jones said. "Follow me."

He led Jack outside and down the road a few doors. Then he went inside another dingy establishment. It was dark and smoky inside, but most of the customers were passed out, their heads on the tables.

"They're mostly opium smokers," Jones explained. He slowed down just long enough to order two whiskeys, then he took the two drinks to a table, and he and Jack sat down. Jack told Jones about the trip to the Red River with the Upbates and about his subsequent travels in pursuit of the outlaws. Bringing the story right up to the present, he told about Mey over in Parker's Hotel. Jones expelled a long breath.

"And what will you do with the girl?" he asked.

"I mean to see if Mrs. Upbate will take her in," said Jack.

"I see. I take it from your tale that Mrs. Upbate does not yet know the fate of her husband and her oldest son."

"No," said Jack. "She doesn't."

"And you'll give her the sad news and ask her to take on a new daughter all at once?"

"I—well, yes," said Jack. "I guess so, although the way you said it makes it sound—

"Callous?"

"Yes."

"Perhaps you'll find a way to smooth it out."

"I hope so. But now you tell me, what are you doing in this place, and why aren't you in a card game?"

"Never get in a card game in Natchez Under the Hill," said Jones. "They're all crooked, and chances are you'll get yourself killed. Anyway, I'm just passing time, waiting for the morning riverboat to take me back out West again."

"Are you taking the boat to Fort Smith?"

"Yes, I am."

"So am I—with Mey."

"It will be a pleasure to have your company again," Jones said, "and you'll never guess who else will be with us on the trip?"

"If I'll never guess, then you might as well go ahead and tell me."

"Mr. Conrad," said Jones. "He's been at his company's offices in St. Louis, and he's returning now to Fort Smith."

"I'll be glad to see him," Jack said.

"But there's one thing you haven't yet explained to me."

"Oh, what's that?"

"Why are you down here with the ruffians tonight?"

"I'd hoped that I might find one or both of the remaining outlaws down here," Jack said. "So far I haven't had any luck."

"Peek Eder and that one soldier?" said Jones.

"Yes."

"Well, I know nothing of the soldier, but Peek Eder is indeed here."

15

Where?" said Jack. "Where is the scoundrel?" He leaned across the table and clutched Jones's arm. Jones put his hand on Jack's.

"Relax," he said. "He's not going anywhere."

"Take me to the murdering bastard."

Jones pushed back his chair and stood up.

"Come along with me," he said.

Jack stood, and J. Worthington Jones walked toward the back of the room. Jack followed, thinking that perhaps Jones would lead him out a back door and into an alley, but he did not. He walked instead to the farthest table away from the front door and stopped. Like others in the room, a man was seated at the table, his head lying on the tabletop. He seemed to be in a drunken stupor. His breathing was heavy and loud. He was a large man, and he was filthy. Smoke was thick in the dimly lit room. The whole atmosphere was oppressive. Jack wanted to get out.

"Well?" he said.

Jones reached down and took a handful of the nasty man's black, greasy hair. He lifted the head from the table so that Jack could see the ugly scarred face. The drowsy man was seemingly oblivious to that fact.

"This is the notorious Peek Eder," Jones said. "Delivered right into your hands."

"That?" said Jack. "Is he drunk?"

"He's in an opium stupor," Jones said. "You could cut his throat right here and now, and no one would know the difference. He wouldn't even feel it himself."

"I'd like for him to feel it," said Jack. "I'd like for him to know who does it. And I want to make him tell me about Corbin Walker."

Jones shrugged. "Let's take him along to a nice, secluded place," he said. "Take an arm, and we'll bring him along."

Jones took hold of Eder's right arm, and Jack grabbed the left. Together they pulled the wretch to his feet. He was heavy and sodden, and his own rubbery legs did not help much in holding his nearly dead weight up.

"Come along, Peek," Jones said.

"Where?" Eder mumbled.

"We'll get you a nice pipe," Jones said. "Come along now."

They walked out the front door, practically dragging Eder between them. No one in the room seemed to care or even notice. Eventually his feet moved a little, shuffling along, and slowly he began to hold up a little more of his own weight. Still, Jones and Jack held up most of it. They sloshed their way through the muddy street past noisy bars and gambling dens, past staggering drunks and beckoning whores, past one knife fight, past a body or two, dead or drunk.

"Where are we going?" Jack asked.

"A nice pipe," Eder mouthed.

"A little farther," said Jones.

They walked until they were at last away from the buildings and the noise and the action, and then Jones turned them toward the water, black in the dark night. They walked straight into the shallow, muddy river water.

"Let go," Jones said.

They released his arms, and Eder fell straight forward into the murky water. As soon as he hit, Jones was sitting on the small of his back holding him down. He took a fistful of hair and pulled the head back. Eder sputtered and gagged.

"My friend has a question to ask you," Jones said.

Eder coughed, and Jones shoved his face back under the dank

water. He held it a moment as bubbles roiled up around the big head. Then he jerked it back again, and again Eder choked and gagged and coughed.

"Are you listening now?" Jones said.

"Uh-huh," Eder managed between hacks and splutters.

"He's listening to you now," Jones said.

Jack leaned over close to Eder's ear.

"Where's Walker?" he said.

"Walker?" said Eder, and Jones plunged his face into the water again. When he pulled back the head, Eder coughed and choked like a dying man.

"You're going to kill him like that," Jack said.

"Walker," said Jones. "Yes, Walker. You heard right. Now where is he?"

"I—I don't know," Eder said.

Jones pushed Eder's face into the shallow water with both hands so hard that he was mashing it into the muddy bottom. Eder's body convulsed.

"Bring him up," said Jack, and Jones did. Eder's face was caked with mud, and as he gagged and coughed, he spit wads of the goo out of his mouth. "Just hold him still," Jack said. "Eder, I am Jack Spaniard. Do you know me?"

"I—I know. Son of a bitch. Killed everyone."

"I did not kill your brother."

"No. I did."

"And I've not killed you—not yet."

"Not yet."

"Where's Walker?"

"I don't know. You seen him—as recent as me. I ran. He ran. You was shooting. Ain't seen him since."

"Then I have no more use for you alive."

Jack pulled his knife and touched the sharp edge to Eder's throat.

"This is for Lorn Upbate," he said, "and for Lorn's young son. It's for Mr. and Mrs. Tuckow and their son, and for all the other innocent people you've murdered in cold blood. And it's for the ones who've been left behind to mourn, for the widows and orphans. It's to clean this world up just a little bit, Eder. I want you to know that."

He was about to press the blade and slice, but suddenly he stopped. He saw himself just then, dressed like a gentleman, kneeling in the river mud ruining a new suit of clothes, about to bathe his hands in the slimy blood of the nastiest of human beings. He stopped. He stood up. Slowly, he backed away.

"What's wrong, Jack?" Jones asked.

"I can't do it," said Jack, as puzzled at his own words as was Jones.

"Why not, man?"

"They've made me into one of their own. I have become as bloody a monster as they."

"There's a price on his head, man," said Jones. "Give me the knife, and I'll slice it off his shoulders for you."

"No," Jack said. "We'll take him to the authorities. They can give him a trial and hang him."

Astonished, and somewhat disgusted, Jones let go of Eder's hair and stood up facing Jack. Eder rolled over in the water like a wounded otter. Suddenly he came roaring to his feet, a war ax in his hand. He ran toward Jones's back with the ax held high. Jack pulled a pistol from his belt and fired, the quick shot tearing the nose off Eder's face. Eder howled and spun away from the impact of the shot. He put a hand to his bloody face. Then, growling, he turned toward Jack. He lifted his ax again, screamed and ran, and Jack pulled a second pistol and fired a ball into Eder's chest. Eder still ran toward him. Jack stepped aside. Eder ran a few more steps, then pitched forward dead.

"May I take his head now?" Jones asked calmly.

"Do as you wish," said Jack. He turned away and started walking toward the path that would take him back up to clean, fresh air.

Jack did not sleep well that night. He rehearsed his own life over and over again. It had been a violent life, a bloody one. He had killed more men than he could count. All those years, he had told himself that it was all justified, that he'd had ample reason. He was not just seeking vengeance. He was administering justice. The Osages had murdered his young wife, and so he had killed Osages, as many as he could, and he would be killing them still had it not been for the fall down the cliffside. That had opened his eyes a little. The Osage he had been fighting was a man. Like himself. He had given up his mission to rid the world of Osages.

But then the soldiers had beaten him brutally, and he'd wanted his revenge. He had postponed it for a while to help the Upbates, and then Eder had come along, and though Jack had not known it until sometime afterward, he'd had those same soldiers with him. They murdered Lorn and Abry, and Jack had seen the bodies. Murdered them for a wagonload of furs. Jack had convinced himself that if he did not exact justice on the heads of those outlaws, no one else would do it. He'd had to hunt them down and kill them. It was for the Upbates, and then for the Tuckows.

Always there was justification. Always a reason. An excuse. But suddenly he saw himself as what he had become: a cold, calculating killer. A man who could cut the head off another human being without giving it a second thought, who could butcher a human body as he could a hog's. A man with the shadow and the stench of death hovering round him like a low-lying fog: bloody, brutal, violent death. And he saw that his soul was not pure, for he was a man. He was not an avenging angel sent down from the white man's heaven by an angry God. He was a man with blood on his hands and dark stains on his soul.

And he was seized by a sudden and urgent desire to be home among his own people, away from strangers, or rather, away from a land in which he was a stranger. His mind conjured visions of a Cherokee family at their home, the father returning with a deer to feed the family, the mother greeting him with a smile and open arms, grandparents sitting in chairs in front of the log house, and children running and playing barefoot.

But then, he had no family waiting for him to come home. No such domestic scene awaited him. And he really had no place to call home. Missouri? He and his people had left that behind. Arkansas? They had been forced to leave their homes there. The people he knew as his people were living on land that he had never called home. And even if he were to go there to try to make a new home among his friends and relatives, he was an outlaw there. He would find no peace.

And so he saw himself doomed to a sad and lonely fate. He had a choice. He could live his life as a stranger among white people, or he could live it as a wanted fugitive among his own

kind. And he knew that there was no one to blame but himself.
Who had made him continue a private war against the Osage Nation after all other Cherokees had called it quits? Who had appointed him a one-man posse to clean up the Natchez Trace?
Spanish Jack saw what he had made of himself, and he did not
like what he saw.

Jack's spirits were a little lighter with the morning light of the sun
after a few hours' sleep, and after a bath had washed away some
of the grime of the night before. In a fresh suit of clothes, and in
the company of Mey, walking to the wharf, he did not appear to
be a man of sullen spirits. At the same time, his realizations of the
night before were still with him. He was a changed man, but he
did his best to conceal the gloom that was in him.

On board the boat, he met J. Worthington Jones and introduced Mey. Jones pulled out a wad of bills and handed them to
Jack.

"What's this?" Jack asked.

"Well," said Jones, glancing at the young girl, "it's—for that
business of last night. I, uh, made the proper presentation and
collected the bill. It's yours."

"I did not apply for it," said Jack. "You keep it."

"I will not," said Jones. "I insist."

Not wanting to argue the matter, Jack said, "Give me half, and
we'll call it square."

Jones counted out half the money, and Jack counted out a
sum and handed that portion back to Jones.

"Now what is this?" Jones asked.

"That's the amount of the stake you provided for me and Lorn
Upbate back in Fort Smith," said Jack. "Now we are square." He
tucked the rest of the money into a pocket. After all, it would help
the Upbates and Mey. "Thank you," he said.

"Say. Look who's coming," said Jones.

Jack turned to see Morgan Conrad hurrying in their direction.
The three friends greeted one another warmly, and Jack introduced Mey to Conrad. In a few minutes, they found deck chairs
for themselves, and they sat and ordered lemonade. They made
small talk for a while. Mey finished her drink and grew restless.
She asked Jack if she could walk around the deck, and he said

that of course she could. She strolled off on her way. Jones watched her for a moment, then gave Jack a serious look.

"She's a lovely young woman," he said.

"Yes," Jack agreed. "She's suffered a great deal for one so young."

"She's enamored of you, Jack," Jones said.

"She's grateful to me," said Jack. "Nothing more."

"Even I can see it, Jack," said Conrad. "I believe that Jones is right."

"She's a child," Jack protested. "She's but fourteen years old. Even if you're right, she'll soon get over it."

"Younger than she are happy mothers made," said Jones.

"Ah, the Bard," said Conrad.

"I'll get her settled with the Upbates in Arkansas," Jack said, "and she'll soon meet a young man close to her own age, and that will be that."

The topic of conversation was beginning to annoy Jack. He had thought of Mey as an unfortunate child and himself as her rescuer. He had not thought of her in that other way. Not once. Not for a second. But she was lovely, and this unwelcome conversation was forcing him to think of her as, well, as a young woman. He tried not to. He did not want to. But now the thought was in his head, and he couldn't get it out. He would have to just get her delivered into the hands of Lena Upbate and ride away. Absence would soon get her out of his mind and him out of hers. He was suddenly very anxious for this journey to come to an end.

"I think I'll stretch my legs," said Conrad. "You don't mind if I visit with the young lady?"

"Not at all," said Jack. "I expect she's bored."

When Conrad was out of earshot, Jones said, "Jack, I can't help but notice that you're somewhat subdued. Is it because of the bloody business last night?"

"I'm all right."

"I remember hearing you say something that, well, was not all right. I remember hearing you disparage your own character."

"What I said was true enough. I have to live with it. That's all."

"You shot Peek and prevented him from burying an ax in my head. Do you regret that?"

"Not that. But what I was about to do before that. What else I've done. The others before him."

"Jack, had you not killed those men, where might they be to-day? What might they be doing, and to whom? Would Mey be on her way to a new home had you not killed? Think about it, man. Have you ever done a cold-blooded murder on an innocent human being? Have you killed women and children?"

Jack thought, I have never killed women and children, not even when I was killing Osages, but he said nothing.

"My friend, you've gone through some violent times, and what you have done was done because it was called for, and you have always done it with honor as far as I am aware. I can't bear to think of you tormenting yourself over what I can only describe as deeds of bravery and chivalry done by a man of honor."

Standing at the railing looking over into the water, Mey asked Conrad, "Have you known Jack long?"

"Actually, I only knew him for a few days at Fort Smith, but we spent quite a lot of time together and got pretty well ac-quainted. That was some months ago, and I've not seen him again till just today. I consider him a good friend, though, and I hope he feels the same way about me."

"I'm sure he does," Mey said. "He's a wonderful man."

"Why, uh, yes, I dare say."

"He saved my life, you know. He rescued me from a band of murderers. There's no telling what they would have done to me had he not come along just in time. He's the bravest man alive, and he has no fear. He killed two of them right off, and the other two ran for their lives."

"That must have been quite an experience," Conrad said.

"It was amazing," she said.

"I, uh, I understand that Jack is taking you to live with a family in Arkansas."

Mey frowned into the water.

"I might not like them," she said. "I might not want to live there. I think I'm tired of living on farms. I like the city. Have you ever been in the Parker Hotel in Natchez? It's so luxurious and everything in it is just beautiful. Jack got me a room there, and we ate supper there, and the next morning we had breakfast there. The food was delicious."

"Yes, I—I do know the Parker. It is a nice hotel. But perhaps if you actually lived in the city, you'd see it differently after a while. You might begin to long for the country life again."

"I don't think so," she said. "These clothes Jack bought me— I can't wear them on a farm. And they're so pretty."

"And you look lovely in them," Conrad said. "A pretty girl like you deserves to wear nice dresses sometimes. But—"

"I want to wear them all the time. I don't want to be frumpy again. Not ever. Jack has changed my life, Mr. Conrad. Forever."

Poor Jack, Conrad thought. Jones was so completely right. This young girl is madly in love. Jack Spaniard is her Romeo. Her Lancelot. In her eyes, he is perfection. He can do no wrong. And beside him, any other man is a worm. I wonder how poor Jack will deal with this situation when the time comes to leave her off. He will have only two choices that I can see. Be stone-hearted and cruel and walk away from her—or marry her.

16

Jack whiled away some of his idle time at games of cards with J. Worthington Jones and Morgan Conrad and anyone else who might want to join their games. He played conservatively, though, for he had told himself that most of the money he was carrying belonged to Lena Upbate. He won some and he lost some. Mey, on the other hand, spent her time the first two days on the river examining every detail of the steamboat. She found it fascinating. She had never been on board a riverboat before. She was full of wonder at the way her life had opened up because of Jack Spaniard. She had seen things and had experiences with Jack that she would never have seen and experienced had he not come into her life. Then she would find herself feeling guilty, because, had not the Eder gang slaughtered her family, she would never have met Jack. She found herself wrestling with a matter of conscience that was way beyond her philosophical reach. When that happened, she tried to shove the whole controversy out of her mind.

But after a couple of days of examining the boat, she grew bored with it, and to help her pass the journey more pleasantly, Jones suggested that they teach her to play cards. They played without betting until Mey had learned the intricacies of the game, and then Jack gave her a small amount of cash, and they played for low stakes. Mey took to the game with eagerness and delight, and soon she was winning almost every hand. J. Worthington Jones said with a frown that he had never seen anything like it.

Following an afternoon game, Jack excused himself and walked over to lean on the rail and stare down at the water. Mey soon moved over to stand beside him.

"I've won a bunch of money," she said.

"Yes, you have."

"Isn't it wonderful?"

"I suppose it is."

"Of course, you gave me the money to play with, so I guess it's really all yours."

"The money is for Mrs. Upbate," Jack said. "If you should wind up staying with her and her son, then it will also be for you. Their crop was ruined, and they have next to nothing. They'll need cash to survive on."

Mey frowned and stared into the water.

"Jack?"

"What, Mey?"

"Do I have to stay with the Upbates?"

"Where else would you go?"

"If I could win enough money," she said, "I could move to the city."

"You're not old enough to live alone in the city," he said. "If you still feel that way in a few years, you can do whatever you like."

"I might not be alone."

"Oh? And who would be with you?"

"I don't know. I might find a husband."

"I hope you don't find a husband yet," Jack said. "You're only fourteen years old."

"I had a cousin back home got married when she was just thirteen."

"I still hope you wait a while," he said.

"Jack?"

"What?"

"How old are you?"

"I'm way older than fourteen," he said.

"Oh," she said, "you're not so old."

"I'm old enough to be your father," he said, scowling at her. He suddenly felt very uncomfortable. There was a passion stirring inside him, in spite of himself, and he did not like it. He wanted to get himself away from this young white girl. Just then Morgan Conrad walked up, and Jack felt somewhat relieved.

"Do you two mind some company?" Conrad asked.

"Welcome," Jack said. "Please do join us."

"Well, were you two talking about important matters?" Conrad asked.

"Yes," Mey said.

"No," said Jack.

"I see," Conrad said. "Well, there's a gentleman over there who would like to get into a game of cards. Tommy Tompkins, I believe he called himself. Would either or both of you be interested?"

Jack shook his head. "Not now, Conrad," he said.

Mey looked at Jack, then at Conrad. "I'd be delighted," she said.

Mey walked with Conrad back over to the deck chairs where Jones was visiting with a stranger, a young man, well dressed. As she approached, the two men stood up.

"Miss Tuckow," said Jones, "may I present Mr. Tommy Tompkins?"

"How do you do?" Mey said.

Tompkins gave a slight bow. "It's a pleasure, ma'am," he said.

"Mr. Conrad said that you were interested in a game of cards," said Mey.

"It's a way to pass the afternoon," he said.

"I agree," she said. "Shall we, gentlemen?"

Jack watched as the four players went inside. He was glad to be rid of Mey's company, but he had a feeling that he was supposed to be somehow jealous. Why? He could not imagine. But there was something in the haughty way she had tossed her head as she walked away from him to join the other three men in a poker game. She had meant for him to be jealous. She had meant for him to not want her to play with them. She had meant—What did he care what she had meant?

"Damn," he said.

Inside, the players took over a table and chairs and got themselves a new deck of cards. Jones broke open the deck and passed it to Mey.

"Ladies first," he said.

Mey shuffled the cards and dealt them expertly. She won the

first game. The deck was passed to Conrad, and he dealt the next hand. This time Mey raised the stakes, and she won again. Tompkins frowned as the cards were placed in front of him on the table.

"Well," he said, "perhaps my luck will take a change now."

He shuffled, Jones cut, and Tompkins dealt. Mey raised the stakes, and again she won.

"You either have remarkable luck or remarkable skill," said Tompkins.

"The lady is a natural," said Jones. "We only taught her to play the game a few days ago. She's a natural."

"Or else she's played you two for fools," said Tompkins.

"What was that?" said Jones.

"Nothing," said Tompkins. "Nothing at all. Let's get on with it."

Spanish Jack decided that he wanted a whiskey. He went inside to the bar in the same room in which the card game was in progress. Conrad and Jones each gave him a nod. Tompkins did not, but of course; Tompkins and Jack had not been introduced. Mey did not look in Jack's direction. Jack walked straight to the bar and ordered his whiskey. The bartender brought it, Jack paid for it, picked it up and turned his back to the bar so he could watch the game. He saw that the pot was sizable, and that irritated him. They were supposed to play small stakes with Mey. He watched while Mey won another game and raked the pot over in front of herself.

"No one wins that steadily," Tompkins said.

"What do you mean?" Mey asked.

"I beg your pardon," said Conrad.

"Sir," said Jones, "if you're making an accusation, be clear about it. If you're uncomfortable with the game, you may bow out. Otherwise—"

"Let's play again," Tompkins said.

Jack heard every word. He watched carefully as Mey dealt the next hand. Tompkins waved at the bartender and called for another round of drinks. As the bartender walked toward the table with his tray, Jack did a double take on the glasses. He hadn't really been thinking about it, but his mind knew that there should be three whiskeys and one lemonade. What went past him was a tray with three whiskeys and a wineglass. He followed the bartender to the table, and as the wineglass was put down in front of Mey, Jack picked it up. He smelled it. It was wine. Suddenly enraged, Jack flung the wineglass across the room. Then with a swipe of his arm, he cleared the table of cards, money and whiskey glasses. The players all jumped up from their seats. Jack turned on Mey with a ferocity that frightened her.

"Go to your room," he said.

Mey turned and ran.

"What's the meaning of this?" said Tompkins. "There was a deal of money in that pot."

"Take back what you put into it and be damned," Jack said.

Tompkins took a step toward Jack, but Jones stepped in front of him and put a hand on his shoulder. He pushed Tompkins back a few steps and whispered into the side of his head.

"You don't want to do that, my friend," he said. "That man is Jack Spaniard, he who single-handedly killed Peek Eder and most of the rest of the Eder gang."

Tompkins's eyes opened wide, and the color drained out of his face. Conrad picked up the money and the cards and put them back onto the table. He began counting out the money into four stacks. Jones walked over to watch.

"I believe I have it right," said Conrad.

The three men each pocketed what had been theirs. Conrad picked up the fourth stack of bills and carried it over to Jack.

"This much was Mey's," he said.

Jack took the money and shuffled it.

"So much?" he said, giving Conrad a hard look.

Conrad shrugged.

"Well, yes," he said. "She kept winning, and she kept raising the stakes. What were we to do?"

"You were supposed to set a limit," said Jack. "Or don't you recall? And who ordered her a glass of wine?"

"There was no harm done," said Jones, interjecting himself into the conversation. "Just a little wine. She asked for a drink. I thought the wine would be the best choice."

"Lemonade would have been better," said Jack.

Tompkins walked to the far end of the bar and ordered himself a whiskey. Jack walked past Conrad and Jones and down to where Tompkins was standing alone. He gave Tompkins a hard look. Tompkins was visibly nervous.

"Was she cheating?" Jack said.

"What?"

"I asked you was she cheating."

"Oh, uh, no. No sir. I can't say that she was. She was just, well, remarkably lucky, I think, or she's very skillful. No. She wasn't cheating. If I said something to imply such a thing, I didn't mean it. I apologize for it."

Jack turned away from Tompkins and walked past Conrad and Jones and back out onto the deck. He walked over to the rail and leaned on it with both hands, staring at the tree-lined shore as it seemed to glide past him. Jones came out to stand beside him.

"Jack," he said, "my good friend, no one meant any harm."

"She's a child," Jack said. "I'm responsible for her. I should never have let her learn to play cards in the first place."

"Jack, there's no harm in cards."

"I'm taking her to live with a farm family. A family of— Christians."

"I see," Jones said. "I—apologize for my part in this unfortunate incident."

"No," Jack said. "I should have gone with her when you went to play. It's my fault. I should be apologizing to the rest of you. I should be, but I won't. Let's forget it."

"I'm willing," said Jones, "and I dare say, Conrad will be, but I doubt that the young lady will forget it for some time. She was acting quite the woman, Jack, and you humiliated her in front of adults."

"Yes. I suppose I did."

Jack walked straight to the door of Mey's stateroom and knocked. There was no answer. He knocked again.

"Mey," he called out. "It's Jack."

"Go away," she yelled from inside.

He tried the door and found it locked.

"Mey. Open the door. I want to talk to you."

"No," she screamed. "Leave me alone. I hate you."

A somewhat dejected Jack Spaniard walked back into the bar

and ordered himself another whiskey. He was soon joined by both Jones and Conrad.

"Jack," Conrad said.

"She said she hates me," Jack responded.

"Well," said Conrad, "that might solve one of your problems."

"What do you mean?"

"I talked to her, Jack, and Jones was absolutely correct. The girl was terribly smitten with you. Perhaps the little scene of a few moments ago has broken the spell."

"I may have a time now getting her to the Upbates," Jack said.

"And getting her to stay," said Jones. "She's had a taste of a very different kind of life, you know."

"She told me," said Conrad, "that she had no taste for the farm anymore. She's longing for the city life. The hotel room you put her in, the dresses you bought her, then the riverboat and the card games. Jack, I'm afraid you've spoiled her."

"It seems every move I've made with her has been wrong," Jack said.

"You made at least one correct move," Jones said. "You saved her life."

"But I've done nothing correctly since then."

"Don't blame yourself too much," said Conrad. "You've had no experience with young—"

"White girls?" Jack said, finishing the sentence for Conrad.

"Well, yes. And at her age, why, she'll get over it."

They did not see Mey again that day, and she did not appear the next morning for breakfast. Jack was sullen. Jones and Conrad did their best to raise his spirits, but to no avail. At last, about midmorning, Jack went back to her room and knocked again. As before, there was no answer. He tried again, and he called out to her. No sound came from inside the room. He tried the door, and was surprised when it opened. Stepping inside, Jack looked around. The room was empty. Mey's bag was gone. There was nothing of hers in the room. He rushed back to where Conrad and Jones sat in deck chairs.

"Mey's not in her room," he said. "And all of her things are gone too."

The two men jumped up from their seats.

"Let's search the boat," said Conrad.

The three men went in three different directions. In a few minutes, they were back together again. No one had seen her. Mey seemed to have vanished. They reported to the captain, and he ordered a thorough search of the boat. Jack, Conrad and Jones stood by the captain waiting impatiently as boatmen ran here and there searching for the missing girl. At last, one of the boatmen came running back to report to the captain.

"Sir," he said.

"Well?" the captain said. "Have you found her?"

"No sir, but—"

"But what, man?"

"There's a yawl missing, sir."

"What? Are you sure?"

"No question, sir. There's a yawl missing."

"But, good God, man," said Jones, "there's no way a fourteen-year-old girl could have lowered a yawl into the river and made her escape."

"I don't know anything about that, sir," said the boatman, "but the girl's not on board, and the yawl is missing."

"Wait a minute," said Jack. "What was that fellow's name?"

"Who?" asked the captain.

"The one you were playing cards with yesterday," said Jack, ignoring the captain and speaking to Jones and Conrad. "The one that accused Mey of cheating."

"Oh. Tompkins," said Conrad. "Tommy Tompkins."

"Has anyone seen him today?" Jack asked.

"Come to think of it," said Conrad, "I haven't seen him."

"Nor I," said Jones.

"Oh hell," said the captain. Then turning to the boatman, he added, "Start all over and have the men search for this Tompkins."

It was soon discovered that Mey, Tompkins and the yawl, or small boat, were all indeed missing.

"Well," the captain said, "it seems pretty clear. The girl and this Tompkins have run off together, and they have stolen my yawl in the doing of it."

"He might have taken her against her will, you know," Conrad said.

"Yes, indeed. I thought him a scoundrel from the moment I laid eyes on him," said Jones.

"Put me ashore," said Jack.

"What?" said the captain.

"Put me ashore."

17

After much persuasion from the captain, Conrad and Jones, Jack agreed to wait for the boat to reach the next landing before getting off. The captain assured him that it would be only a matter of a quarter of an hour, and Jack decided to make use of the time to change into his buckskins and prepare his weapons. He bundled up his remaining possessions and left them with Conrad.

"Carry them on to Fort Smith for me, will you?" he asked. "I'll pick them up there later."

"Of course," Conrad said. Jones stepped forward just then.

"Would you like for us to visit the Upbates," he said, "and explain what's happened?"

Jack thought for a moment. It was really his duty to see Leta and young Ish and explain what had happened to Lorn and Abry. On the other hand a considerable amount of time had passed, and they deserved to know.

"I feel like a coward," Jack said, "but yes. If you don't mind, please do that, and give this to Leta."

He pulled out all the money he had in his pocket and handed all but a few bills to Jones.

"I'll see to it," Jones promised.

The stopover was not much more than just that. It was a place for the boat crew to load on wood. Passengers could board or disembark there, but not many did. There were three buildings. At one of them, a traveler could buy food and drink. One appeared to be a stable. Jack could not guess what the other might be. He said farewell to Conrad and Jones and made his way straight to the stable. There he was able to buy a good horse and saddle, although he paid more for both than he should have. He knew it though, and he didn't care.

He was thinking about what he would do to Tompkins when he got his hands on the man, and he caught himself imagining violent scenes. He fought those images out of his brain. He tried to remind himself that he had entered a new time of his life, a time when he was going to live for something other than killing. He told himself that one of two things had happened. Either Tompkins had kidnapped Mey, in which case he should be turned over to the law for punishment, or Mey had gone with him voluntarily. The more thought he gave the matter, the more he was convinced that she had chosen to run away with the man. She was angry with Jack, and she had developed a strong taste for the lifestyle that Tompkins would seem to be able to afford her. It was even possible, Jack told himself, that Mey had been the instigator, that she had, in effect, stolen Tompkins away.

But none of that really mattered to Jack. Mey was a child, and she was his responsibility. As he had told her earlier, in a few years she could make her own decisions. For the time being, he would make them for her, until he could find someone else willing to do so. He hoped that someone would be Leta Upbate.

But he had wasted enough time. He did not think that Tompkins was an experienced sailor. He had somehow managed to steal the yawl and get it overboard and into the water, and he had gotten himself and Mey into the yawl. But Jack felt certain that just about all that Tompkins could manage after that was to drift with the current. They would be somewhere south of him, and he had allowed the captain and his two friends to talk him into going even farther north before disembarking. He mounted up and started riding.

Jack tried to stay as close to the river as he could. The riding was sometimes rough, and at times he even had to dismount and lead the horse. When he was forced to ride some distance away from the river, he tried to stay on high ground overlooking the waters. He rode the rest of that day without having seen any sign of Tompkins, Mey or the yawl, and then it started to rain. Getting himself into some thick woods as fast as he could, Jack took out his war ax and hacked some branches off the trees. He fastened them together into a makeshift lean-to for a temporary camp for the night. He built a small fire and fixed himself as comfortable a spot to sleep as he could manage. Settling down for the night, he hoped that Mey was safe and dry. He hoped that she was out of the yawl and off the river.

Jack was up and riding with the first morning light, but the first morning light was not much. It was still raining hard. It was not a good time for travel, but he kept telling himself that it was better for him on horseback than it would be for two inexperienced people in a small boat in the raging river during a hard rainstorm. He kept going. Again, he tried to stay close to the rushing waters, and tried to keep his eye out for any sign of Tompkins, Mey or the yawl. He hoped that he would find the yawl abandoned somewhere along the riverbank. That would mean that they had gotten off the river and were at least safe from that danger.

He was also thankful for the weather in that, trying to deal with the boat, Tompkins had almost certainly had no time for any other activity. With any luck at all, Jack would reach them in time to prevent any dalliance. He came to a place where the riverbank rose sharply, and he was forced to ride up on top. The good thing was that from up on the rise, he had a clear view of the river below. Then he saw them. Tompkins and Mey. They were standing in the middle of the river with rushing water up to their waists. There was no sign of the yawl. He figured that they must have hit a sandbar and lost the boat. The rushing waters had carried the boat on downstream. The sandbar was close enough to the surface of the water that they had been able to stand on it, but now, due to the hard rain, the waters were rising. He could tell that they were struggling to keep themselves from being carried off by the swift current. If he couldn't get to them soon, they would be. He had to find a way down to the water's edge.

There was no use in turning back. He had been driven to the top of the cliff back there. He rode forward as fast as he dared on the slippery ground in the driving rain. It was maybe a mile before he was able to get back down to the water. There he found a narrow trail between the face of the cliff and the rushing water. At the base of the cliff, thick brush grew, sometimes almost blocking the path. He turned the horse back north and rode the trail. For a while, the horse was walking in the rushing water, and it fought with Jack, wanting to escape the danger it sensed all around. He kept it going ahead.

At last he drew within sight of the two stranded people again, and this time they saw him. They waved and shouted frantically, but he could not understand their words. He kept riding until he was parallel with them. Taking a coil of rope off the saddle, Jack secured one end to a clump of brush. Then, remounting and taking the other end of the rope with him, he turned the horse toward the frantic pair in the river. The horse balked. Jack thought, it has good sense, but he fought it, and finally forced it into the raging waters. The horse wanted to move with the current, and he had to fight even more to make it head for the submerged island. About halfway over, Jack slipped from the saddle. He took hold of the reins and swam, pulling the horse along. Then the horse felt ground beneath its feet, and a moment later, so did Jack.

"Oh Jack," Mey cried out. She tried to rush toward him, but when she moved, the waters almost carried her away. Tompkins grabbed her.

"Stand still," Jack shouted.

He moved forward, took hold of Mey and helped her into the saddle. He took her hands and put them on the saddle horn.

"Hold tight," he said. He thought for a moment about leaving Tompkins to his fate, but he couldn't quite bring himself to do it. "Grab onto his tail," he said. Tompkins labored forward through the deep and swift water and grabbed the horse's tail. Jack took the reins in one hand and the rope's end in the other and plunged forward. They drifted some distance downstream, but at last they made it to shore.

"Thank God you came along when you did," said Tompkins.

Jack thought about telling Tompkins that he had come after them to kill him and then take Mey to Arkansas, but he kept quiet about that. Instead he said, "Come along with me. We have to try to find a place where we can dry out."

He led the horse south again on the narrow trail, Mey still in the saddle, and Tompkins taking up the rear. The water was rising fast, and the trail was growing more narrow and more slippery. Once, Tompkins lost his footing and fell into the water, but he pulled himself out quickly, and, taking hold of the horse's tail again, kept going. The rain had not let up. At the end of the narrow trail, Jack led them up on top of the cliff and headed for the woods. Once in under the trees, he built another lean-to, and he got himself, Tompkins, Mey and the horse underneath the shelter. It took him a while, but he at last got a small fire going. Mey stood close to it, shivering.

"I suppose you think me a fool," Tompkins said.

"Whatever opinion I hold of you," said Jack, "I'll keep to myself—for now."

"We were doing all right," Tompkins said, "until we hit that— island or sandbar or whatever it is. It was just beneath the surface of the water. We were trapped there. We got out of the boat, and the water was below our knees. I tried to drag the boat off the thing and back into deeper water, but the current was too strong for me, and I lost it. It was just after that when the rain started, and soon after, the water began to rise."

"That's about what I figured," said Jack. He was terse, not at all friendly. "Take off what clothes you can and try to dry them at the fire," he said. "Both of you."

"They're all I've got," Mey said. "We lost everything in the river. All my new dresses. Everything."

"We'll get more," said Tompkins. "Don't worry."

They spent the night in the lean-to, and the rain did not let up until morning. Jack spent some time cleaning, drying and reloading his long rifle and his pistols. Then he told the other two to wait for him there at their camp. He promised to return shortly. In a while he came back with a rabbit and two squirrels. He also had some greens he had gathered along the way. He prepared a meal for them, and they ate ravenously.

"It's not Parker's Hotel fare," Jack said, "but you won't starve."

"It's delicious," Mey said.

"Yes," said Tompkins. "Thank you."

When they had finished their meal, Jack put out the fire. Then he picked up the saddle and threw it on the horse's back.

"It's time we got started," he said.

"Where to?" Tompkins asked.

"Where did you think you were going when you got yourselves stranded?" Jack responded.

"Well, we were headed for the next settlement downriver," said Tompkins. "It's only about six miles from here. I know this river pretty well."

"That's where we'll go," said Jack. He helped Mey into the saddle and took the reins into his own hands. Looking over at Tompkins, he added, "We'll walk."

The settlement Tompkins had referred to was a small town, and it had the look to Jack of a growing, thriving community. There were a couple of inns, a small trading post, a saloon, a landing at the river's edge for steamboats, and a few other buildings, businesses or offices of some kind. There appeared to be a few residences, and there were buildings under construction. The streets were busy. As they made their way into the bustling community, Jack stopped the first man he came close to.

"Is there a magistrate here?" he asked. "Or some kind of law?"

The man pointed ahead to a small log house. "Sam'l Benson," he said. "Right over there."

Jack thanked the man and headed for Benson's office.

"What are you doing, Jack?" Mey said.

"You'll see," said Jack. He kept walking and leading the horse. Mey stayed in the saddle, and Tompkins walked along beside. Reaching the house, Jack lapped the reins around a hitching post. He reached up to help Mey dismount. Then he started toward the front door. "Come on," he said.

Inside a paunchy, middle-aged man with greying hair sat behind a desk. He looked up to greet the strangers who had come into his establishment.

"Hello," he said. "You're strangers in town. What can I do for you?"

"I want this man arrested," Jack said.

"What?" Mey said.

"Now, wait a minute," said Tompkins.

"All of you hold on," said Benson. "Let's start at the start. Just what is it you want this man arrested for?"

"I want him arrested for kidnapping," Jack said. "My name is Jack Spaniard. This young woman is Mey Tuckow. Her parents were murdered along the Natchez Trace, and I was taking her to live with a family in Arkansas. We were on the river, and this man slipped away in the middle of the night with her."

"He didn't kidnap me," Mey said.

"She's a child," said Jack. "Fourteen years old."

"I'm fifteen," said Mey. "I had a birthday."

"All right," said Benson. "All right. All of you calm down. Young lady, you're fifteen years old?"

"Yes."

"And did you go with this man willingly?"

"Yes."

"Sir," said Benson, facing Tompkins. "What is your name?"

"Thomas Tompkins."

"Mr. Tompkins, when you took Miss Tuckow off the boat with you, what were your intentions?"

"Why, we mean to be married," Tompkins said.

Benson looked back at Mey. "Is that your understanding as well?" he asked her.

"Yes," she said.

"But she's a child," said Jack. "She's only fourteen."

"Fifteen," Mey corrected.

"Mr. Spaniard," said Benson, "I know who you are. When you mentioned the Natchez Trace, I connected your name to it right away. I heard about the sad fate of the Tuckows, and I heard about how you sought out the culprits responsible and took care of them. I admire you for that, and I thank you for it on behalf of all the honest travelers along that road.

"But Mr. Spaniard, if Miss Tuckow is fifteen years old, has no parents, and went along willingly with Mr. Tompkins here, and they mean to be married, there is nothing I can do about it. Fifteen is legal marrying age here. Now, knowing all the circumstances, I can understand your concern. But the law is the law."

Jack stood silent. He had not considered that Mey might be old enough in the eyes of the law to make such a decision for herself. Mey stepped over to stand in front of Jack. She put her hands on his chest and looked up into his eyes.

"Jack," she said, "I don't mean to hurt you. I know what all you've done for me, and I'll be grateful to you for the rest of my life. But I know what I'm doing."

Jack patted Mey's hand and turned toward Tompkins.

"When we discovered that you were missing from the boat," he said, "my first intention was to kill you. Then after I'd had time to think more about it, I decided to let the law have you. Well, the law has spoken. And so has Mey."

"I'll take good care of her, Mr. Spaniard," said Tompkins. "I promise you."

"If I ever hear otherwise," Jack said, "I'll come looking for you." He turned to face Benson. "Is performing marriages within your legal capacities?"

"It is."

"Then can we get this done right here and now?"

"If the couple is willing," said Benson, "we can."

"They are," said Jack.

Benson performed the ceremony with little pomp, and Jack paid him. He had little cash left, but he turned to Mey and held it out to her.

"Thank you," she said, "but I really don't need it. I lost all my clothes in the river, but I didn't lose my money." Holding a hand up to her bosom, she added, "I've got it all right here."

"Where will you be going?" Jack asked.

"We're headed for New Orleans," said Tompkins. "We ought to find something to do there to make us a living."

Jack took Mey by the arm and led her to the farthest corner away from Tompkins and Benson.

"Tell me something," he said. "The other day, when Tompkins accused you of cheating, were you?"

Mey looked up at Jack and smiled.

"You know who taught me to play," she said.

Jack wasted no more time around the town. He felt defeated in his quest to give Mey a decent home where she would have a proper upbringing. Perhaps she would be happy with Tompkins, he told himself. Still, he felt the sting of defeat. He thought about making his way back to another landing and catching another riverboat back to Fort Smith. It would be faster and easier, but he'd had enough of riverboats and gamblers for a while. He was comfortable in his buckskins, and he had a good horse under him. He decided to ride back to Arkansas.

He would have to cut across the northeast corner of Louisiana and then ride diagonally across Arkansas, a good long ride, but that was all right. Jones and Conrad had taken some pressure off his shoulders by volunteering to carry the unpleasant news and the money to Lena Upbate, and there was nothing else pressing him. He had much to think about. Where was he going? What was he going to do?

18

After several days of riding Jack came into a small town in southeast Arkansas. It was like a dozen other frontier towns he had seen, but he had been alone on the trail long enough that he felt like a short stay in any town would be good for him. He found an inn and bought himself a meal. After that, he went into a saloon and had a glass of whiskey. He had little cash left, but he thought that he could survive well enough without it. He could afford to indulge himself in some pleasures before going once again into the wilds. A poker game was in progress at a table in the saloon, and when one player had been cleaned out and got up from his seat in disgust, Jack asked if he might join in the game. After a few hands, he found himself flush again. He got himself a room for the night.

The next morning, he decided to have himself a breakfast of eggs and ham and potatoes cooked by someone else before hitting the trail. The inn he selected was smoke-filled and greasy, but he decided that it would do. The place was crowded though, and he found himself seated at a table with four other men. They were white men, of course, all young, robust, rugged frontier types. Friendly enough, they dragged Jack into their conversation.

"Which way you traveling, Jack?" asked one who had introduced himself as Joey Blount.

"West," said Jack.

"Well, hell, me and the boys are headed west too. We're

headed for Fort Smith. Way out in western Arkansas. You ever been there?"

Jack nodded.

"You going thataway? Maybe going to Fort Smith?"

"I might be," Jack said.

"Why don't you ride along with us? There's strength in numbers, you know. There's outlaws and Injuns all along the way."

"I don't know," Jack said. "I usually travel alone."

"Company's good when you're traveling."

"I do all right," said Jack.

"We ain't highwaymen or nothing like that," Blount said. "Besides, we got our own horses and guns. Everything we need. Ain't nothing you got that we'd want to steal. Come on and join us. Hell, it's a long ride all the way out to Fort Smith. We'd be proud to have your company. Hell, I like you, Jack."

So in spite of his better judgment, Jack found himself riding on west toward Fort Smith in the company of Joey Blount and his three companions. The four white men talked almost constantly, usually about nothing, and always in loud voices, and while Jack found that to be an annoying habit on the one hand, on the other, it did seem to help pass the time. More than once, though, he found himself wanting to tell them to keep quiet for at least a while.

"You never did say why it was you was going to Fort Smith," Blount asked Jack. They had been riding already for two days by this time. "You got business out thataway have you? Out there at Fort Smith?"

Jack shrugged. "I'm just headed back home," he said.

"Fort Smith's your home?"

"It's close."

"Well, where you been?"

"East," said Jack. "Along the Natchez Trace."

"What was you doing out there?"

"Business," said Jack. He wanted to tell Blount that he was asking too many questions, but he held that back.

"What kind of business you in?"

"Horses."

"Say," said one who had called himself Foss, "Jack Spaniard. They call you Spanish Jack?"

"Some do."

"I heard about you. Say, Joey, I heard about him. It come back in my mind whenever he said Natchez Trace. He killed ole Peek Eder and all his gang. Just him. He didn't even have no help."

"Is that right?" Blount asked.

"Not quite," said Jack. "I had a little help."

"Well, I be damned," said Blount. "Spanish Jack. And just think. I thought back yonder that you might be afraid to ride along with us cause we might try to rob you or something. Hell, if I'd known who you really was, I might've been afraid to ride along with you, and there being four of us too."

The white men all laughed.

"Hell," said Blount, "we're riding along here with a famous man, a celebrity."

They camped alongside the road that night, and the white men all sat up late talking and laughing. Jack was relieved when they finally quieted down and went to sleep. He was tired of hearing them brag about what a killer he was. He thought about slipping away during the night and getting well ahead of them on the trail, but something kept him from it. Instead, he slept the night in their camp. In the morning, they prepared a meal, ate, cleaned up the campsite, packed and saddled their horses and started out again.

Around noon they came across a family beside the road with a broken wagon wheel. They stopped and helped repair the damage, all four white men pitching in. Then they shared a noon meal with the family, providing most of the supplies. Jack decided that they were not such a bad bunch after all. They were white frontier boys. That was all. He was uncomfortable with their constant loud talk and laughing. But they were good enough boys.

Their meal done, they rode on west, while the family in the wagon moved slowly off to the east. Later in the day, they came across a buck deer and shot it and butchered it. That evening at their camp, they had a good meal of fresh venison. The grateful family in the wagon had given them some coffee, and they boiled up a pot and sat around the fire drinking hot, fresh coffee after their meal.

"What you going to do after you get back home, Jack?" Blount asked him.

"Figure that out when I get there," Jack said.

"You said Fort Smith is near home. Just where is your home? Somewheres in Arkansas?"

Exasperated with Blount's questions, Jack took a deep breath and exhaled audibly. Again he wanted to tell Blount that he was asking too damned many questions that were none of his business. Instead he surprised himself and gave a straight and honest answer.

"The Cherokee Nation," he said. But then he thought, it really wasn't quite straight and honest, for the truth was that he had no home. He had not lived in the present location of the Cherokee Nation for long, and he was a wanted fugitive there. But that was all right. Blount's eyes opened wide in astonishment, as did those of his three companions.

"Well, I—," Blount stammered. "Well, you do have a kinda dark complexion, but I never—Well, I just never woulda figgered you for no Injun. I don't mean no offense by that. Are you an Injun? You a Cherokee?"

"I am."

"Well, damn. Now really. You being a Cherokee and all, how come you to be out there on that Natchez Trace? That's a long way from home."

"Looks like it could be kinda dangerous too," said Foss. "A lone Injun like that, and it not being too long since your people was run out of the East."

"You're a bold man to travel east outa the Cherokee Nation," Blount said. "Ole Foss there is right. It could be dangerous."

"It was dangerous," said Jack. "For some others."

The third white man, whose name was Grant, laughed out loud.

"I reckon it was," he said when he finally stopped laughing. "Sure enough. Got their heads stuck up on poles from what I heard."

"But you still ain't said what it was you was doing way out there and by your lonesome in the first place," Blount said.

"No," said Jack, "I haven't."

"Well?"

"Hey, Joey," said Grant. "Shut up. He don't want to talk about it, so don't keep on a pressing him."

At that Jack relented, and he wondered why.

"I was chasing some outlaws who'd killed some friends of mine," he said. "One thing led to another. That's all."

The fourth man, Gorman, said, "Hey. Maybe we should tell Jack how come we're all headed for Fort Smith."

There was a long space of silence before Joey Blount answered. "Nah," he said. "I don't think so. He wouldn't be interested."

Soon after that, they all went to bed for the night.

The next day the four white men were quieter than they had been since Jack had met them. They rode for long distances without talking at all. Then they would carry on a brief conversation about nothing much, and fall again into silence. Jack found the change in their behavior a bit disconcerting. He watched them carefully, and he made sure that he rode along always behind them.

At noon they stopped for a meal. They were still mostly silent as they built a fire and put the meat on to cook and the water to boil the coffee in. After they had eaten and were sitting with cups of coffee, Blount, a serious expression on his face, looked over at Gorman and spoke up.

"I been thinking about what you said last night," he said, "and I decided you were right about it after all. You know what it is I'm talking about?"

"Yeah," Gorman said. "I reckon I do."

"Anyone got any objections?" Blount asked.

No objections were voiced. Blount leaned forward toward Jack.

"Jack," Blount said, "we're fixing to take you into our confidence."

"There's no need," said Jack.

"We're on our way to Fort Smith to kill a man."

"It's none of my business," Jack said.

"Well, no," said Blount, "I guess it ain't, but we want to tell you, you being who you are and all, and we got to taking a liking to you. See, it was like this. While back, in a little ole place in Tennessee, we was cleaned out by a slick gambling fellow. All four of us. So we got to talking about it, and we decided that we was going to catch up with the no-good son of a bitch and kill him."

"We might stick his head on a pole," said Grant.

"You're talking about murder," said Jack.

"Well, technically, I reckon you're right about that too," Blount said, "but really what it is is just retribution, like what you done. I mean, it wasn't no fair game at all. He's a slick professional, and we ain't. It's the same as what you done."

"I don't think so," said Jack, "but we won't argue the point. If you'll take my advice, you'll forget it and go on back home. Killing leaves a bad taste in a man's mouth—if he's a real man."

"You done enough of it."

"What I did had to be done. I didn't enjoy it."

"Well, we kinda feel like this here has to be done."

Jack shrugged. "I won't argue with you," he said, "but I think you'll regret it."

Blount shook his head. "No, I don't think so. He cleaned us out. Slickered us good. I think we'll enjoy it all right."

"He was slick," said Foss.

"We talked it over," said Gorman. "We all agreed that it was the right thing to do—to go and kill him."

"Did the man cheat you?" Jack asked.

"I ain't sure," said Blount. "I couldn't tell."

"He was too slick for us to catch him at it," said Gorman.

"He was good, all right," Foss agreed. "I ain't never seen a better."

"Lucky too," said Blount. "Part of poker is luck, and we just didn't have none. He had it all, the son of a bitch."

"If he beat you fair," Jack said, "then you have no complaint. You shouldn't get into a gambling game if you can't afford to lose your money. Besides, what makes you think you'll find this man in Fort Smith?"

"If he ain't there, he will be," Blount said. "He rides them riverboats up and down the river looking for suckers like us."

"We heard him say so," Gorman added.

"If he ain't there when we get there," Grant said, "we'll just set and wait and watch everyone who gets off one of them big boats. He'll come around sooner or later. No question about it. We'll get him there."

"Real snitty-acting bastard," said Foss. "J. Worthington Jones. Well, he won't be so high-and-mighty when we get done with him."

Jack did not let his surprise at this sudden information register on his face. Instead, he finished his coffee and stood up. As he began cleaning up the camp, he said, "I still think you're making a mistake. I hate to see you get in trouble. I wish you'd change your minds and go on back home.'

"Ain't no way we're backing out of this," Blount said.

They rode the rest of that day away without too much more talk, and when the evening sun had dropped low in the western sky, they stopped again to camp. Jack waited until they had finished their meal, and had an extra cup of coffee. Then he got up casually and spread his blanket out on the ground. His back was to the four white men. He took hold of two of his pistols, pulled them out and cocked them, then turned to face the four.

"Don't try anything," he said. "I'll kill two of you before you can get a gun out."

The four men looked up astonished, not understanding why their traveling companion and new friend had suddenly turned on them.

"What's this all about, Jack?" Blount asked. "It's some kinda joke, ain't it?"

"Take out your guns real easy and toss them onto this blanket," Jack ordered.

They did as he told them to do. He made sure that all their guns were on the blanket.

"Foss," he said, "go saddle my horse."

"What are you going to do?" said Blount. "Kill us? What for? We ain't got nothing you want, and we ain't done nothing to you."

"Keep quiet and do as I say," said Jack, "and I won't kill anyone."

He watched until Foss had his horse saddled. Then he stepped over to check the cinch to make sure that it was tight enough. Foss had done a good job. Next, Jack made Foss tie his blanket roll behind the saddle. All he had to do was pick up his long rifle, and he was ready to ride, almost ready. There were a couple more things to be done.

"Bring me those other horses," he said.

"You ain't going to take our horses?" said Blount. "Is that what this is all about? Stealing horses?"

"Keep still," said Jack.

Foss brought the horses.

"Now get out of your clothes. All of you. Toss them in the blanket there with your guns."

"Don't do this, Jack," Blount whined.

"Clear nekkid?" asked Grant.

"Every last stitch," said Jack.

In just a few more minutes Jack was in his saddle with his long rifle and the guns and clothes of the four white men wrapped in the blanket. He had the reins of the other four horses. He looked down at the four naked and confused would-be young murderers.

"You're lucky I'm leaving you alive," he said. "J. Worthington Jones is a friend of mine. And I know that he never cheated at cards. If I had let you kill him, I'd have had to kill you, and I don't want to do that."

"Jack," said Blount, "if you leave us here like this, I swear, we'll get you. We'll kill you for this."

"Joey," said Jack, "I've killed more men than I can count. You know about some of them. Come ahead and try it if you dare."

"At least leave us our pants," said Foss.

"I don't want you to ever forget this lesson," Jack said. "I don't want to see you in Fort Smith, and if I ever hear that anything has happened to Jones, I'll come looking for you. Take my advice, and good luck to you."

He rode out of the camp leading the four horses behind him and leaving the four naked men screaming, threatening and begging. He rode on toward Fort Smith. A few miles down the road, he threw down the blanket containing their guns and clothes. He rode on. In a few more miles, he turned one horse loose. He let the other three horses go one at a time a few miles apart. The four white men could eventually get themselves armed and dressed and round up their horses, but Jack would be far ahead of them by then.

He felt good, for now he knew why he had not slipped away from them in the dark that one night. Now he knew why he had thrown in with their company and why he had put up with it for so long. There is always a reason, he told himself. We don't always understand it at the time, but there's a reason. He smiled as he rode on into the night.

19

Spanish Jack made it back to Fort Smith with no further adventures, and he stabled his horse and got himself a room at the inn. He was glad that he did not see Jones or Conrad, for he would have felt compelled to pass some time with them if he had. Instead he went to bed almost immediately and slept soundly for nearly twenty hours. When he woke up, he went looking for something to eat. It was an odd hour for a meal, but he found his two friends together having a drink. He joined them, and ordered himself coffee and food. While waiting for his meal, he told the other two the tale of Mey and Tompkins, the chase, the rescue and the conclusion. Then he told Jones about the four would-be assassins and the condition he had left them in somewhere in Arkansas.

"I don't think we'll hear any more of them," he said, "but if you should see them again, be forewarned."

"I certainly will," Jones said. "And thank you."

"You might like to know that the Upbates are doing reasonably well," said Conrad, "thanks to the money you sent them."

"How did they take the news?" Jack asked.

"Not well, of course," Conrad said. "But they'll survive. They're holding on. Leta Upbate is a strong woman, and young Ish will make a fine man one of these days."

Taking his cue from the look on Jack's face, Jones said, "They don't blame you for anything, Jack. Far from it. Believe me. They're both very grateful for everything you've done for them."

The waiter brought Jack's plate just then, so the conversation ceased for the moment. When the waiter was gone again, Jones and Conrad continued chatting as Jack ate. When he finished his meal, Jack had two more cups of coffee. Then he ordered himself a whiskey. He thought the first sip of the burning liquor tasted awfully good. The second and third would be even better. He leaned back in his chair.

"I expect there's a deal of work to be done out at the Upbates' place," he said. "I think I'll take a ride out there tomorrow morning and see if I can be of any help."

"I'll join you, if you don't mind," Conrad said. "Now, don't look so surprised. I wasn't always a fur buyer. I was raised on a farm in Virginia. Back then I couldn't wait to get off the farm and into a job in the city. Wear clean clothes and sit behind a desk. Not get my hands dirty. Now, I look back and think what a wonderful life it was on the farm. Sometimes I wish I could go back."

"All right," said Jack. "Ride out with me then. If there's work to be done, we'll get your hands dirty."

"I believe that I shall stay here," said Jones. "My hands were made for shuffling and dealing cards, not for digging postholes or shoveling manure."

Jack felt a little relief in that his dilemma, though not solved, was pushed at least a little farther into the future. He could spend some time helping the Upbates get their place in shape, and for that time, he would not have to make up his mind what to do with himself or where to go. It was some comfort.

Early the next morning, following a hearty breakfast, he rode out of Fort Smith toward the Upbate farm in the company of Morgan Conrad. Conrad was dressed for working, and his entire appearance was changed by his change of clothing. Jack thought about his own occasional transformation from buckskins to store-bought suit.

"I have a confession to make," Conrad said as they rode along. "I've already been working on the place for several days now. The latest project is digging a well, and it's a rough job. The soil is incredibly rocky."

"We'll get it done," said Jack. "So you've been working already, have you?"

"Well, yes," Conrad said. "I could tell right away that there was much to be done, and Ish is just a boy. I hadn't anything else worthwhile to do with my time, so—

"And Leta Upbate is a fine-looking young widow woman," said Jack, "with a farm, and you'd like to get back to the farm."

"Jack, please," Conrad said. "I've not made a move in that direction. Not a hint. It's much too soon. Please don't say—"

"I won't," said Jack, but he smiled as they rode on. Funny, he thought. He had not once before thought of Leta in that way. He had seen her only as a farmwife, an overworked white woman, the wife of Lorn Upbate and mother of two sons. But when he heard Conrad talking about his volunteer work at the Upbate place, it had struck him that Leta was really a fine-looking woman, and not so old either. If Leta would accept a proposal from Morgan Conrad, Jack thought, that would be good.

Leta and Ish were genuinely happy to see Jack, and he was some relieved by that. In spite of what Conrad and Jones had told him, he was feeling guilty about the fate of her husband and oldest son, and he had been apprehensive about facing the two surviving family members. After a brief conversation, Jack and Conrad went right to work on the well. It was tough digging, but with the two of them at work, they made pretty fast progress. In two more days, the well was finished, and the water was good. They began clearing another field, removing tree stumps and rocks. The work was hard, but it was good, clean, honest work. It was not like killing, and Jack felt refreshed and renewed. He noticed, too, that as the days passed by, the spirits of Leta and Ish improved. He was glad for that.

One morning as Jack and Conrad were riding out to the farm, knowing that there was really no more pressing work to be done at the place, Jack said, "I think I'll take the boy out hunting today."

"Oh? Well, yes," said Conrad. "I think that's a fine idea. Ish needs to learn to hunt, and he couldn't have a better teacher, I'm sure. Yes. I think that will be a splendid thing for you to do. Just splendid."

Jack smiled and said nothing more. When they reached the Upbate home, Jack made his proposal to Leta and Ish. Ish looked anxiously at his mother.

"Can I, Mom?" he asked. "Can I go?"

Leta glanced at Conrad, and Conrad gave her a smile and a nod.

"All right," she said, "but you be careful."

"I'll see to that," said Jack. "I won't let him out of my sight for a minute."

Conrad and Leta stood on the porch watching Jack and Ish walk into the woods. Both were smiling.

"It's good to see you smile again," Conrad said.

"I'm happy to see Ish coming around," she said. "He's been working hard, I think to keep his mind offa what happened to his paw and brother. Anyhow, this hunting will do him a world of good, I think."

"Yes," said Conrad. "I believe that it will. Leta?"

"Yes?"

"Could we—sit—and talk—for a spell?"

"I have work to do in the house," she said.

"Please. Just for a short while. I'll help with your work."

"Well, all right then," she said.

They sat in the two chairs that were already there on the porch, and for a long moment, they sat in embarrassed silence. Conrad wondered if Leta suspected his intentions. He hoped that she did. He hoped that she had been silently harboring thoughts similar to his own. But he had to find the words to open the discussion. He felt awkward, inexperienced and terribly inadequate.

"Leta, I—did I tell you that I was raised on a farm?"

"Yes," she said. "You did."

"And did I also tell you that I've been thinking lately how much I would like to get back to that life?"

"I think I recall something like that you said once."

"Leta, you're alone out here with a young son. Taking care of a farm is too much work for a woman and a boy. And raising a boy alone is too much work for a woman. You need a man around the place."

"I've had two men hanging around here lately," she said. "I couldn't ask for more help than that."

"Well, yes, but I mean, you need someone here—permanently." He stopped and gulped, his Adam's apple bobbing up and down conspicuously. "You need a husband. You're still young, Leta, and you're a very attractive woman."

"Do you have someone in mind for me?" she said. She knew very well what it was he was trying to get around to, but she felt the need to tease. It had been a long time since anyone had courted her. She was enjoying it, and she had no intention of making things any easier for him.

"I, uh, I had thought that maybe you and I—

"What, Morgan?"

"Well, we could get married. You and I. Couldn't we? I mean, would you, Leta? Would you have me?"

"I might," she said, "if you'd ask me."

Conrad suddenly turned out of his chair and dropped to one knee in front of Leta. At the same time, he whipped the hat off his head. He looked up into her eyes with the sad expression of a downtrodden beggar on his long face. He was pitiful. He was wretched. He was desperate.

"Leta," he said, "will you be my wife?"

"Yes," she said. "I will."

Walking along the road, Ish said to Jack, "I know a place where the deer come to water."

"Lead the way," said Jack.

They walked on a little farther before Ish turned off the road and into the woods. Jack followed him. Soon they came to a clear stream. Ish stopped and pointed.

"Right here," he said. "I've seen them come right here for a drink."

"Then let's get out of their way," said Jack. "We don't want them to see us and be scared off."

He took Ish a ways from the watering spot and into the trees. He checked his rifle and found it ready. He laid it in the crotch of a tree, aimed in the direction of the watering hole.

"You know how to shoot this thing?" he said.

"Yes," Ish said, his eyes wide in anticipation.

"All right then," Jack said. "We'll just settle down and wait. No more talking. No moving around. You got that?"

Ish nodded. They waited. They waited until Ish thought that they had been waiting forever. He wanted to move around. He wanted to talk. He wanted a deer to show up so that he wouldn't look like a foolish boy in front of Spanish Jack. He wanted to say, "I really have seen them here. Lots of times." But he kept still, and he kept quiet. He began to feel as if they had waited all day, clear past suppertime, but he glanced into the sky, and he could see that the sun was still low in the east. He guessed then that it really hadn't been all that long. He would have to show Spanish Jack that he had patience. A man had to have patience. He knew that, but every muscle in his body ached with inactivity. Itches came up that called for scratching. Then at last, a big buck appeared from out of the woods. It stepped out slowly and stood erect, alert. Ish reached for the rifle, but Jack touched him lightly on the shoulder and held up a hand meant to tell him to wait.

The buck stepped out into the open. Still it paused. Finally, it moved to the water's edge. Jack lifted his right arm and with his left hand tapped himself in the side just below where his arm came out from his shoulder. Then he pointed at the deer. He nodded at Ish, and Ish gripped the rifle and took aim. Jack whispered some Cherokee words. *"Yu,"* he said, and he pointed fast, and Ish pulled the trigger. There was a flash and a fizz, followed by a loud boom. The explosion of the powder in the heavy long rifle rocked Ish back. When he recovered, he looked through the cloud of smoke.

"Good shot," said Jack.

"I got him," Ish shouted.

Jack stood up and started toward the fallen deer with Ish running behind him. At the side of the dead animal, Jack knelt and said some more Cherokee words. Then he pulled out his hunting knife.

Walking back to the house, the gutted deer slung over his shoulders, Ish walking alongside him carrying the long rifle, Jack was in good spirits. Ish was so full of pride at his accomplishment, he could hardly keep himself from running ahead.

"Jack?" he said.

"What is it?"

"Just before I shot, what was it you said?"

"Oh. Well, I said a little thing in Cherokee that's meant to speed your bullet straight to its target. It worked, too, didn't it?"

"Yeah," Ish said. "I guess. And then when we got over to where the deer was at, you said something else."

"I apologized to the deer's spirit," Jack said. "I told him that we were sorry to kill it, but we needed meat."

They walked along a little farther without words. Ish seemed deep in thought.

"Jack?"

"Yeah?"

"Would you teach me them words?"

Jack smiled. "Sure I will," he said.

They sat at the table in Leta Upbate's house, having finished a sumptuous noon meal of venison, potatoes and greens, accompanied by Leta's fine biscuits. Leta had poured coffee all around, even a cup for Ish.

"That was a fine meal you provided us with, Ish," Conrad said.

Ish beamed with pride. "Thanks," he said. "Jack told me everything to do."

"Well, then," said Leta, "it looks like you had a pretty good teacher."

"I sure did. He showed me where to shoot the deer and everything. He taught me how to sit still for a long time and wait. And then, he even taught me to say some Cherokee words: words to make your bullet go straight and words to tell the deer you're sorry you had to kill it. Jack says you don't go killing anything without a good reason, and even then, you don't do it lightly. You got to have respect for all of life."

Jack thought about all the men he had killed, and he wondered about his own words. He also wondered how Leta, with her Christian beliefs, would take the words that Ish had just spoken. Then Conrad broke into his revery.

"Leta and I have some news," he said. "We want to tell it now, because we want the two of you to be the very first to hear it. We're going to be married."

Ish's jaw dropped.

"Congratulations," said Jack. "I think that's wonderful."

"Does that mean you'll be my paw?" Ish said.

"Something like that," said Conrad. "I'll never really be your paw, Ish. Your paw was a fine man, and we'll all always miss him. I know I can never take his place. But I'll be here for you, and I'll do my very best to take care of you and your mother the way he would have done. Is that all right with you?"

Ish looked across the table at Jack, and Jack gave him a smile and a nod.

"Yeah," said Ish. "Yeah. It's fine."

Leta was pouring another round of coffee when they heard the horse come up in front of the house. Conrad stood up and moved to the door. When he opened it, a young lieutenant was standing there.

"Excuse me, sir," he said. "Is this the home of Mrs. Upbate?"

"It is," said Conrad.

"Is Mr. Jack Spaniard here?"

"Yes, he is."

Conrad turned to look at Jack, who, having heard the lieutenant's words, was already up from his chair and walking toward the door.

"I'm Spaniard," he said.

"Mr. Spaniard, Major Bradford sent me. He respectfully requests that you come to his office for a visit at your earliest convenience."

"What's it all about, soldier?" Jack asked.

"Sir, I'm not at liberty to say. I'm only authorized to pass along to you the major's request that you visit him in his office. As soon as possible, sir."

"All right. You can say I'm on my way," said Jack.

"Thank you, sir," the young officer said, and he turned and went back to his horse.

"Well," Jack said, turning back into the room, "I think I'll ride on in and see what this is all about. Will you be staying, Conrad?"

"I'll stay for a while," Conrad said, "but not the night. That wouldn't be quite proper—yet. But tomorrow morning, we'll all be driving into Fort Smith to find a preacher. You will attend the wedding, won't you?"

"I wouldn't miss it," Jack said.

———

Riding back toward Fort Smith alone, Jack wondered what Bradford might want of him. He could think of nothing. At the same
time he felt a new freedom, a tremendous sense of relief. For a
long time, he had felt obligations, first to the Upbates, and then
to Mey. Now, all of a sudden, all of those obligations were lifted
from his shoulders. He was free. But free to do what? To go where?
He still had no idea.

20

J ack went straight to the major's office on arriving at Fort Smith, and he found the major in. Bradford welcomed him like an old friend.

"Come in. Come in," he said, and he took Jack's hand and pumped it vigorously.

He offered Jack a chair and had an orderly bring coffee. Then he asked Jack where he had been and what he had been doing, and Jack gave the major an abbreviated version of all his recent adventures.

"I knew part of it already," Bradford said. "Word reached us all the way out here regarding your killing of the outlaw Peek Eder. You've become quite a hero along the Natchez Trace, as I understand it."

"I don't feel heroic," Jack said. "There were just some things I had to do, and now, having done them, well, I'm not especially proud of all the killing."

"It's a rough frontier, Jack. Sometimes it just has to be done. But that's not why I asked you to come to see me."

The orderly came in with the coffee just then, and the major stopped talking until it was served and the orderly was again out of the office.

"Jack," Bradford said, "I've had a letter from Lieutenant Colonel Gustavus Loomis in command of Fort Towson down in the Choctaw Nation."

"Yes, I know the place," said Jack.

"Good. Lately they've had a great deal of trouble from Co-manche raiding parties stealing horses from the Choctaws. Loomis has green troops, Jack. They haven't been able to catch these Co-manches or stop the raids. They haven't recovered a single horse. There's been no killing yet that we know of, but the situation is serious. I'd like for you to go down there as chief of scouts and see if you can't find a way to stop these raids. You'll be paid by the U.S. Army of course. What do you say?"

"How do they know the thieves are Comanches?" Jack asked.

"Ah, well now," said Bradford, "it's my feeling that they're just guessing. I don't believe that Loomis or anyone in his command would know a Comanche from an Osage. That's the way the letter was written, and that's the way I repeated it to you."

"Will I be taking orders from this Loomis, or will I be free to follow my best instincts?"

"The letter I send along with you will order Loomis to take your advice on this matter," Bradford said. "I'll not put you in a position of taking orders from an inexperienced—Well, that's the way my letter will read."

"Has the Choctaw Light Horse tried to chase down these horse thieves?"

"If they have tried, they've not been successful. Perhaps they're busy in other parts of the nation, or perhaps there are simply not enough of them. My letter from Loomis makes no mention of them. The Choctaws are looking to the U.S. Army for protection, and we are obligated to furnish it. It's the same with your—well, with the Cherokee Nation. The Light Horse is for maintaining domestic quiet. It's not really set up to protect citizens from out-side invasions. Any other questions?"

"I guess not."

"Will you take the job?"

Jack considered the irony of the fact that at one time he had made his primary living by stealing horses from the Comanches. Now he was to stop Comanches from stealing horses from the Choctaws. He also considered the situation he was in, not know-ing where he would go or what he would do, not having any ties or responsibilities. He was weary of killing, but according to Bradford, there had been no killing, just horse stealing. It was a situation that might be resolved peacefully. He accepted Bradford's offer.

Jack spent the rest of that day gathering the supplies he would need for the trip south to Fort Towson. He knew that it would take him back very close to the country where he had gone with the two Upbates on their ill-fated hunting and trapping venture. Fort Towson was within six miles of the Red River in the southern Choctaw Nation. He loaded up on ammunition, extra clothing, food, coffee and cooking utensils all from the post store and all at army expense. He drew a small advance on his pay, and the army furnished him with an extra horse and saddle. Bradford prepared the letter for Jack to carry along with him to deliver to Lieutenant Colonel Loomis.

With all his preparations for travel made, Jack went back to the inn. It was too late in the day to start traveling, so he decided to have a good meal and perhaps a glass of whiskey or two with his friends. He would get an early start in the morning. He found Conrad and Jones sitting at one of the tables outside, and he joined them there.

"Did you give Mr. Jones your big news?" he said.

"Yes, I did," Conrad answered.

"I think it's just marvelous," Jones said. "Our Conrad here is changing his whole life in one stroke. From single man, he'll go to husband and father, and from city-dwelling businessman, he'll be transformed back to a farmer. And all at once, by speaking two words. It's an absolute marvel."

"Well, both of you will always have a home to come to when you're in the area," Conrad said. "I've enough cash saved up from my life as a businessman that the farm will be secure enough. Oh, we'll continue working it, but if there should come another crop failure, I'll have extra money in the bank."

"It sounds ideal," Jack said.

"We should be well fixed, all right," Conrad said.

"So, my friend," said Jones, turning to Jack, "Conrad tells me that you were summoned to the presence of the major. Are you at liberty to tell us what that was all about?"

"Of course," said Jack. "It's no secret."

"Well, tell us then, man," Jones said. "Don't keep us in suspense. I don't suppose they're going to put you in front of a firing squad or hang you or anything like that, because you're walking around free."

"I've just signed on with the army as a scout," Jack said. "They're having some trouble with Comanche horse thieves down south in the Choctaw Nation, and the boys at Fort Towson can't seem to put a stop to it."

"And you will?" Jones said.

"That's what I've hired on to do," said Jack.

"What caused the major to select you for the job?" Conrad asked.

Jack smiled. "Perhaps it takes an old horse thief to catch a horse thief," he said.

He ordered his meal and a round of drinks, and after his meal was finished, he ordered another round.

"How will you go about it, Jack?" Jones asked.

"What?"

"This new thief-catching job of yours. What will you do when you get there?"

Jack gave a shrug. "I don't know," he said. "First I'll have a talk with the commander there, Loomis is his name, and I'll find out where the latest thievery was done. I'll see if I can track the Comanches, and then I'll see if I can't have a talk with them."

"Will they talk?" Conrad said. "How will you approach them to prevent their simply killing you? They are wild Indians, aren't they?"

"They haven't killed anyone down there yet on these horse raids," Jack said. "I'll just have to see what develops."

"Well, I'm glad it's your job and not mine," Conrad said, "and I do hope you'll be careful. Good friends are few and far between."

"When you've accomplished your mission," said Jones, "and I'm sure you will, I hope you'll be coming back this way."

"You'll both see me back here again," said Jack.

He finished his whiskey and ordered another round.

"I think we three should get drunk tonight," he said. He thought about all he had been through, and he considered that this would be his last chance for a fling before starting his new job. But he didn't say any of that. Instead, he said, "Conrad is getting married, and I'm going south in the morning."

"By God, sir," said Jones. "A splendid idea."

"I think so too," Conrad agreed. "It may be my last chance."

"The new Mrs. Conrad will undoubtedly put a short leash on him," Jones said.

"I'm sure of it," said Jack.

"Now, see here," Conrad started, but Jack stopped him.

"You'll wear it well," he said.

By the time they were ready for yet another round, they told the waiter to stop fooling around and just bring a bottle. He did, and Jones poured the next round of drinks at the table. Then he lifted his own glass high.

"To friendships and to new adventures," he said.

Jack and Conrad raised their glasses.

"Here, here," they both said. They all drank.

"Well," Conrad said, and his speech was beginning to slur, "we've talked about me and we've talked about Jack. What about you, our river-roving friend? Are you just going to ride the river and play cards until you die? What plans do you have?"

"Interesting you should ask at just this time," said Jones. "A month ago I'd have said that I have no plans, that I'll just continue to do the same as I've been doing, riding the boats and playing cards, until I die, as you say. But here lately I've been thinking of settling down. I have a little nest egg, and I'm thinking of opening an establishment of some kind right here at Fort Smith. I shall become a respectable businessman, just as you have been."

"What kind of establishment?" Conrad asked.

"Drinking and gambling, of course," Jones said. "I know nothing else."

At that they all laughed, and Jack picked up the bottle and poured some more into each of the three glasses.

"Let's drink to that," he said.

And they did.

"Conrad, my friend," said Jones. "do you really think that you can leave the city life behind you and settle down happily on the farm?"

"Do you think you can settle down from your life on the river?"

"It's not the same thing. I shall still have my cards and whiskey and women. You, on the other hand, will be—

"Living in wedded bliss," said Jack. In his drunkenness, he

thought of his own short marriage, and he felt tears well up in his eyes. He fought them back as best he could, but his eyes remained watery.

"Yes," said Jones. 'But still on a farm. With pigs and chickens and digging in the dirt. Let me see your hands. I'll bet they're as soft as my own."

Jones reached for Conrad's hand, and Conrad jerked it away.

"Never mind my hands," he snapped. "Of course, I can do it. I was raised on a farm. I know what I'm doing."

"I know you were raised on a farm," Jones said, "but you escaped it. You've said so yourself many times. You escaped. To the city. And now you've grown used to the city and the so-called finer things in life, as well as, shall we say, some of the seamier pleasures. Won't you miss them?"

"Not a bit. I spend most of my time as it is out at places like this," Conrad said. "My trips back into St. Louis are few, and they're short. I do some paperwork in the office, visit my bankers, and then I'm back out onto the frontier. I'm not so citified as you might think me to be."

"Besides," said Jack, "our friend just told us he has money in the bank. He'll likely hire someone to do all the hard work. He's going to be a gentleman farmer."

They all laughed at that, and Jones poured another round.

"Here's to the life of a gentleman farmer," he said.

Jack woke up the next morning lying on the ground in front of the inn. The ground was wet with dew. The sun was still low in the eastern sky. He rolled over onto his back and tried to recall the events of the night before. The last thing he could remember was the toast to the life of a gentleman farmer. Nothing after that came back into his mind. He was still lying there breathing deeply when J. Worthington Jones walked up looking as fresh and dapper as ever. Jones stood over Jack and smiled down at him.

"I see you're still alive," Jones said. "May I offer you a hand up?"

"Slowly and carefully," said Jack. He raised his right arm, and Jones took him by the hand and pulled him to his feet. Jack moaned, and his right hand went to his forehead. For a moment, he seemed unsteady on his feet.

"You seem a bit worse for the wear," Jones said. "You were the one who first suggested that we all get drunk, if you recall. Now just look at you."

"Coffee and breakfast will fix that," said Jack. "Where's Conrad?"

"He hasn't yet come out of his room," said Jones. "He may be worse off than you are. Come on over here and sit down. We'll soon get some coffee."

Just as they sat down, Conrad came out. He walked slowly and looked as if his head was aching. They all ordered coffee, but when Jack started to order some breakfast, Conrad stopped him.

"Let's all go out to the farm for breakfast," he said. "Leta will be happy to have you. We'll have ham and eggs. Jack, you can't leave without saying good-bye to Leta and Ish."

"Well, I—

"Oh, please, Jack," Conrad said. He turned to Jones. "Help me convince him, will you? He can't just go riding out of people's lives."

"Conrad is right, Jack," Jones said. "I accept his kind invitation, and I insist that you do the same."

"I guess my start won't be quite as early as I had thought," Jack said. "All right. We'll go."

They had one cup of coffee each, and Jack excused himself to go to his room, get cleaned up and change clothes. While he was doing that, the other two had more coffee.

"I'll go down to the stable and order the horses ready," said Jones.

When Jack reemerged from his room, the other two men were waiting for him with three saddled horses. They mounted up and rode out to the Upbate farm. Conrad had been right. Leta was more than pleased to have the company. So was Ish. They had a hearty breakfast and more coffee. When Leta found out about Jack's new plans, she was especially glad he had come out for breakfast.

"You wouldn't have left without telling us good-bye, would you?" she said. Then before Jack could answer, she turned to Conrad. "Morgan," she said, "why don't we go in and get married to-day—before Jack leaves? Otherwise, we'd have to wait for him to come back, or else he'd miss the wedding."

"That's a splendid idea, my dear," Conrad said. "We'll do it today. Jack, will you wait long enough for the wedding?"

Jack smiled and gave a shrug.

"What's a few more stolen Choctaw horses," he said. "Of course I'll wait. I told you I wouldn't miss it, didn't I?"

Back at Fort Smith, Jack went to see Major Bradford and inform him that his trip was being slightly delayed. He also invited Bradford to the wedding. Other officers and their wives were invited. The services of the post chaplain were acquired. Leta and Ish went shopping for new clothes, which Conrad paid for. Jones arranged with the innkeeper for the use of the patio, and by early afternoon everything and everyone was ready. Jones produced a fiddle and, amazing everyone with a talent hidden until that very moment, played the wedding march, after which the chaplain read the words. When the service was over, Jones's fiddling grew more lively, and the bride and groom danced together. At the second tune, officers and their wives joined in the dancing. Before they were done, Leta danced with Jack and with Major Bradford.

While all that was going on, Ish made some new acquaintances among the boys who lived at Fort Smith. They ran around together throwing rocks into the river and at squirrels. Then as the festive crowd at last grew weary, Jack drew Conrad aside.

"You're not going back to the farm until morning, are you?" he said.

"Why, I, I hadn't thought of it," Conrad said.

"You have a room here," said Jack. "Stay the night."

"But there's Ish," Conrad said.

"I'll give him my room," said Jack. "I've already paid for one more night."

When Conrad and Leta at last went to the room, Jack found Ish. He took the boy with him to his room, pretending that he needed his help. Jack and Ish packed Jack's supplies on one horse and saddled the other. Then Jack handed the room key to Ish.

"Your mother and your new father will be sleeping here in a room tonight," he said. "You can have my room for the night. This is the key. When everyone comes out in the morning, tell them that I said good-bye. When my job is over with, I'll come back by and see you again."

"Promise?"

"Yes. I promise."

Without saying anything to anyone else, Jack mounted up and rode out of Fort Smith, headed south. The Texas Road going through the Cherokee Nation and on down into the Choctaw Nation would have been a better route, but Jack wanted to avoid any contact with Cherokee Nation Light Horse Police. He thought about crossing over in time to stop by Tom Starr's place, but then he decided that he would not reach Starr's place until well after dark, so he dismissed that plan. He would simply ride until nearly dark and make himself a camp for the night. He could stop and visit Starr on his way back.

21

Fort Towson, not being walled in, had the appearance of a small frontier settlement. The buildings were of hewn log and whitewashed, the main cluster standing in a square with a row of separate buildings in a line a short distance away from the square. Everything was neat and orderly, and the large gardens were well tended. A creek ran nearby. A number of Choctaw Indians were hanging around the place, as well as a few white civilians. Jack rode over to the blacksmith's shop, where the smith was busy shoeing a horse. A bearded man stood by watching. Jack figured it was his horse being shod. He dismounted and stepped toward the man.

"Howdy," the man said, smiling wide. "You just ride in, did you?"

"That's right," Jack answered. "Name's Jack Spaniard."

"Birchfield," said the other, extending his hand. Jack took it.

"Are you resident here?"

"Naw. I got my place up on the Muddy Boggy. Just come down here now and then to get some business took care of. Too many folks around for my taste."

"I know just what you mean," Jack said. "Can you direct me to the commander's office?"

"Why, sure. Hell, this ole boy's going to be busy here for a little while. I'll just walk you on over there."

"Thanks," said Jack. "I sure appreciate it."

Birchfield started walking and Jack followed along, leading his horses. They walked down the road to the square and then inside the square. Birchfield led the way across the square to a building with a soldier standing guard at the front door on a roofed-over veranda.

"Hi, Joe," said Birchfield. "Mr. Spaniard here just rode in, and he wants to see the colonel. He in, is he?"

"Yes, sir. Go right in."

Birchfield was obviously well-known around Fort Towson. He opened the door and stepped aside. Jack walked in. Birchfield followed and closed the door after himself. He spoke to another soldier, who was sitting at a desk in the front room. The soldier stood up and opened a door to another room and announced Birchfield and Jack. Then he stepped aside, leaving the door open, and told them to go on in. When they went through the door, the soldier waited there. Lieutenant Colonel Gustavus Loomis stood up and walked around his desk to shake hands with his visitors.

"Mr. Birchfield," he said, "it's a great pleasure. What can I do for you?"

"Nothing at all," Birchfield said. "Not for me. Mr. Spaniard here was looking for you, and I just brought him along."

"I see," said Loomis. "And so, what can I do for you, Mr. Spaniard?"

Jack pulled out the letter from Major Bradford and handed it to Loomis. Loomis read it over quickly and handed it back to Jack.

"So you're just down from Fort Smith?" he said.

"That's right," Jack said.

"Well, have a seat, gentlemen. Birchfield, this will interest you too. Corporal, bring us all some coffee."

"Yes sir," said the soldier at the door. By the time Loomis was seated back behind his desk, and Jack and Birchfield were seated across from him, the corporal returned with a tray of cups, coffeepot, milk and sugar. When everyone was served, he put the tray on a table to the side, left the room and shut the door. Loomis looked at Birchfield with a serious expression on his face.

"Fort Smith has sent Mr. Spaniard here down to help us out with the problem of the Comanche horse thieves," he said. Then he looked at Jack. "Mr. Birchfield is a very prominent Choctaw citizen. He's been concerned about this problem for some time now. I thought it would be all right to let him in on this conversation."

Jack shrugged. "It's all right with me," he said.

"They got some of my horses on their last raid," Birchfield said. "Most of them, in fact. In fact, all of them except the one you seen over at the blacksmith's."

"When was that?" Jack asked.

"It was just four nights ago," Birchfield said.

"And you say that was their latest raid?" Jack asked.

"Most recent I know of," Birchfield said.

"We haven't had any more recent reports," the colonel added.

"Mr. Birchfield, I'd like to ride back to your place with you when you go and have myself a look around," Jack said.

"Well, I'll be headed that way just as soon as my horse is ready, but don't you want to get settled in here first?"

"There's plenty of time for that," Jack said. "I wouldn't mind putting up my horses, if I could borrow a fresh one."

"I'll see to that," Loomis said. "And we'll have quarters ready for you."

"In that case," Birchfield said, "we just as well head on out. My horse will likely be ready by the time we get back over there."

Jack thanked Loomis and left the office with Birchfield and the corporal, who accompanied them to the stables. The soldier at the stable was introduced to Jack and given the orders from Loomis. He showed the horses to Jack and allowed Jack to pick out the one he wanted. Then, while Jack unpacked the packhorse, the stableman switched Jack's saddle to the fresh horse.

"I'll stow your gear right over here for you, sir," the stableman said. "You can get it whenever you want."

Jack and Birchfield made the ride out to Birchfield's place on the Muddy Boggy River, and Birchfield showed Jack the corral off to one side of his house where his horses had been kept up until four nights ago. Jack noticed that Birchfield was not the best of housekeepers. He wondered if there was a Mrs. Birchfield, but he doubted it. He kept the question to himself.

"The only reason I have this here ole nag left," Birchfield said, referring to the horse he was riding, "is 'cause I was away from home and riding on her when they hit the place. Anyhow, I come home, and the gate was down, and the horses was all gone."

"How many?"

"Even dozen."

"Shod?"

"Yep. Ever' one."

Jack rode slowly over to the corral, watching the ground closely in case of any telltale tracks. There were none the way he rode. At the corral, he dismounted and lapped the reins of his mount around the top rail of the corral fence. Then he walked toward the gate. The pole that served as gate was on the ground. The tracks of Birchfield's shod horses were clear enough as they left the corral and were driven southwest. They obscured most of the approaching tracks of the horse thieves, but there were some Indian pony tracks showing where some of the thieves had turned their horses and taken up the rear in order to drive Birchfield's horses off. Among those unshod tracks were the tracks of one horse with shoes. Birchfield came up behind Jack.

"Finding anything?" he asked.

"Yeah," said Jack, "but I'm not sure what it means. Most of these tracks were made by Indian ponies all right, but there's one shod horse among them. Now, the way this bunch has been stealing horses, it could be a Comanche riding a shod horse that he stole, but I kind of don't think so."

"You don't?"

"No. I think there's a white man with them."

"A white man with Comanches?"

"I could be wrong," said Jack. "That horse with shoes, and a gut instinct. That's all I have. If I'm right, it could be a bigger problem than we thought."

"Well, I'll be damned. How come you say it could be a bigger problem?"

"I've been hoping to find the Comanches and talk them into returning those horses and cutting out the raids. They might listen. A white horse thief won't."

Birchfield scratched the side of his head and wrinkled his face. "I guess maybe that's right," he said.

Jack remounted his horse. "Thanks for the help, Mr. Birchfield," he said. "I'm going to see how far I can follow these tracks. They might lead me to something."

"Good luck with it," Birchfield said. As Jack rode off, Birchfield's voice got louder with each sentence. "I hope they lead you to my horses. Be careful now. Don't try to fight no overwhelming odds. If it looks like a fight, ride back to Towson for help. Them soldier boys ain't too bright, but they'll help you out in a fight."

Jack rode along at a fair clip as long as the tracks were clear. They led him west beyond Fort Towson and then angled southwest toward the Red River. As he moved farther from the dark mountains to the east, the ground flattened out into a rolling prairie, rich with tall green grass. There were no more tracks to be followed, so Jack just continued riding in the same direction the tracks had been going. It was midafternoon when he reached the river. Thinking that the horse thieves might have crossed over to the Texas side with their ill-gotten gains, he began to ride the riverbank looking for signs that would support his guess. He found none.

Locating a place where he could easily ride across, he forded the river and moved along the Texas side for a while. He found no sign there either. He turned and rode for a distance in the opposite direction. Still nothing. He was about to recross the river when he saw a half dozen white men riding in his direction. He sat still in the saddle and waited for them. They rode hard until they were nearly on him, and then they reined in fast, scattering rocks and dirt. It was a move calculated to intimidate. Jack sat still giving no sign of nervousness.

"Howdy, stranger," said a big man with a red beard.

Jack nodded a greeting. He didn't like the looks of these men, nor did he like their manners, and it came into his mind that as soon as he had seen them, he should have crossed back over into the Choctaw Nation. He called himself twelve kinds of a fool, but it was too late now.

"What's your business in Texas?" red beard asked.

"I'm looking for stolen horses," Jack said. "I'm a scout out of Fort Towson up in the Choctaw Nation."

"What's your name?"

"Jack Spaniard."

"Spaniard," the red beard said, squinting, "are you an Injun? You kinda got that look about you."

"I'm a Cherokee," Jack said.

"We run all you Cherokees out of Texas not long ago," the red beard said. "Leastways, we thought we did."

"I'm not resident here," said Jack. "Like I said, I'm working for the U.S. Army, and I'm looking for stolen horses. I thought maybe they'd crossed the river, but I didn't find any sign that they'd come out on this side. In fact, I was just getting ready to cross back over when I saw you coming."

"That there's a U.S. Army horse he's setting on, Red," said a Texan with a stubby black beard.

"Yeah," Red agreed. "I can see that. Could be, he stole it. Could be, he ain't hunting horse thieves at all. Could be he's the horse thief."

"I have a letter on me from the commander at Fort Smith introducing me to the commander at Fort Towson," Jack said. "That should be proof enough of what I'm saying."

Red rode forward until he was right beside Jack. He held a hand out.

"Let me see it," he said. "By the way, we're Texas Rangers. We're interested in them same horse thieves you was talking about. Them and any other wild Injuns that comes into Texas. Including Cherokees. Was you with old Bowles?"

"No," said Jack. "I wasn't."

Jack knew that when the new Republic of Texas refused to honor Sam Houston's treaty with the Texas Cherokees, an offshoot of the Western Cherokee Nation in Arkansas, and ordered Chief Bowles and all his people out, the Texas Rangers had demanded that the Cherokees surrender their gunlocks. Bowles had refused to surrender the gunlocks, but he was leading his people out of Texas. Texas Rangers attacked them along the way and killed many, including the eighty-year-old chief. Jack wondered if these bastards had been with that bunch of Rangers. He felt hatred well up inside him.

"Well, let me see the goddamn letter," Red said.

Jack pulled out the letter and handed it to Red, who squinted at it for some minutes, making Jack wonder if the man could even read. Then Red folded it and stuffed it into his own shirt.

"I'd like to have my letter back," Jack said.

"Yeah, I reckon you would. How the hell do I know that you're really this Jack Spaniard? That don't sound like no Injun name to me. Maybe you killed the real Spaniard and stole his horse and his letter. Maybe you—"

Before Red knew what was happening, Jack's left arm was around his throat, and Jack's right hand was holding a knife up to the side of his head. Red was being pulled almost out of the saddle, stretched between his own horse and Jack's. He gurgled and coughed trying to catch his breath. He held on to his horse as tightly as he could with his legs.

"Tell those others not to make a move for their guns," Jack said, "or I'll slice the side of your face off. Tell them."

"Don't make a move, boys," Red said.

"Now tell them to turn their horses around and ride like hell."

"You heard him, boys," said Red. "Go on. Do it."

"But Red—"

"Just get out a here. He's going to cut my face off."

The other five Rangers turned their horses and rode away hard and fast. Jack waited until they were well off in the distance.

"Now, you son of a bitch," he said, "take your pistol out of your belt and drop it."

Red did as he was told.

"Now your knife."

Again Red obeyed.

"Now unloose that rifle from your saddle and drop it."

Red did that, and he was totally disarmed.

"I done what you said. Don't hurt me now."

"I want my letter," said Jack.

Red pulled out the letter and held it up to Jack's left hand. Jack took the letter, then slowly released Red, who sat up straight in his saddle again and rubbed his throat. He was gasping for breath and coughing.

"Were you with the cowardly bastards who killed Chief Bowles?" Jack asked.

"No. I swear it. I wasn't nowhere near that place when that happened."

"I ought to kill you anyway," said Jack, "but I won't. Now ride after your friends."

"What about my guns?"

"I'll take care of them for you. Get moving."

Red raced after the other five Rangers, who were already out of sight. Jack dismounted and picked up Red's weapons. Then he turned his horse and rode back into the river. About halfway across, he dropped Red's guns and knife into the water. He rode back out of the water on the Choctaw Nation side of the river. He rode the north side of the Red a little farther, but he saw no more sign of the stolen horses or of the horse thieves. He turned around and headed back toward Fort Towson.

It was late when he arrived back at Towson, and Loomis was just leaving his office as Jack rode up. The officer looked up at the scout.

"Any luck?" he asked.

Jack dismounted.

"Not much," he admitted. "I followed tracks from Mr. Birch-field's place on down close to the Red before I lost them. Rode the river a while hoping to pick them up again, but I never did. I crossed over to look on the south bank thinking that if they had gone into Texas I might see some sign where they came out of the river. Not only did I not find any sign, I was set on by a ruffian gang who called themselves Texas Rangers. That made me think that if the men I'm after are really Comanches, they wouldn't likely ride down into Texas unless they were ready for a fight. Last I heard, the Comanches didn't have any guns, and there seem to be armed gangs of Texans just waiting for Indians to come down."

"Well, I suppose that all makes some sense," Loomis said. "So what do you do next?"

"I'll just ride around the countryside watching for them," Jack said. "I'll find out where there are any horses yet to be stolen and watch those places as close as I can. I'll scout out farther west to see if I can pick up any sign of a wandering band of Comanches— or some other western tribe."

"I guess you know best," said Loomis. "That's what Major Bradford said in his letter. Is there anything I can do to help?"

"Not just yet," Jack said. "I'll let you know."

"I'll get a man to show you to your quarters," Loomis said.

22

Jack scouted the area for several miles around Fort Towson pretty thoroughly for the next three days without sighting anything that would be of any help to him in his search for the horse thieves. Everyone in the area, including Birchfield, who helped him some in his scouting, seemed convinced that the thieves were Comanche, but Jack wasn't sure of even that. No one had actually seen them, no one that Jack could find. It seemed to be an assumption based on the fact that some years earlier, the Choctaws had indeed had trouble with Comanches stealing their horses. The problem had been solved with the help of the U.S. Army. The Comanches had explained that they needed the horses for fighting the Texans, and they had agreed to back off. In the present situation, the stolen horses disappeared at night or in the daytime when the owners were away from home.

On the fourth day of Jack's scouting, a Choctaw man whose home was a few miles west of Fort Towson came into the fort to report his horses stolen. The tracks, he said, led off to the west, toward Comanche country. Jack rode out to follow them while they were still fresh. It was the closest he had been to the thieves. The horses had been taken sometime during the night before. The owner believed that it had been early morning. He had heard some noises in his sleep, but he had not gotten up. He had waited for daylight before venturing out to check. When Jack had asked him why, he had explained that if it had been the Comanches, and he had gone out to see what was going on, they would likely have killed him.

From the man's directions, Jack easily enough found the house and the nearby corral from which the horses had been stolen. As the owner had said, the tracks did go west, and Jack followed them. Eventually they turned south, and this time Jack found evidence that the horses had been driven across the Red River into Texas. Sitting in his saddle on the north bank of the Red River, he hesitated, recalling the belligerent Texas Rangers he had encountered the last time he had dared to cross the river. But he wanted to know where the horses had been taken, and he wanted to find out who the thieves actually were. He had signed on to do a job, and he meant to do it well. He rode on across, and soon he picked up the tracks there where they came out on the Texas side. They were easy to follow, almost too easy. Whoever these thieves were, they were cocky. They obviously felt safe and secure in Texas.

Even so, Spanish Jack rode carefully in Texas, watching all around for any sign of riders. It wouldn't pay to be surprised by either the horse thieves or a band of those rangers. The tracks led him farther west for a few miles, then turned north onto a road that cut through the trees there by the river. Moving onto the shaded road, Jack suddenly felt vulnerable. He was on a narrow, closed-in trail following a band of horse thieves, and he could easily ride up on a difficult situation. He stopped his horse, dismounted and led it into the trees. He left it there tied to piece of brush and began walking through the woods, picking his way carefully. He was wearing his four pistols and carrying his long rifle, so he had five shots. His knife and his war ax were at his belt.

He stayed close enough to the road, so that he could look out and see what might be at its end, and before long he found himself looking at a small frame house with a couple of small outbuildings behind it. He could hear the river running not far beyond the house. A corral was off to one side, and the corral was full of horses. At least some of them had to be the ones he had just tracked. He figured that the entire herd was made up of the stolen Choctaw horses. He stopped there at the edge of the woods to study the situation. Smoke was rising from the chimney on top of the house, and just in front of the house, five saddled horses stood patiently waiting at a hitching rail. Someone was home. At least five of them, and they were almost certainly the horse thieves he was after.

Jack thought about the shod tracks he had seen at Birchfield's corral and his own surmise that at least one white man had been among the thieves. That became an even stronger conviction looking at the stolen horses in the corral at a white man's house in Texas. The next question was who were the others? Could a white man be working with Comanches? Or any other Indians? It was possible but not likely. The setup looked to Jack like one from which these stolen horses would be sold. Comanches would want the horses for themselves, not to sell for cash. He was now convinced that everyone around Fort Towson who had decided that Comanches were the culprits was wrong. Standing there in the woods beside the road, Jack was convinced that he was dealing with a gang of white outlaws.

While he was contemplating all these things, the front door of the house opened and five white men came walking out. They were talking as they walked. Jack was not able to get a good look at them, but one turned as he mounted his horse, and then Jack recognized the Texas Ranger called Red. Their voices got louder as they mounted up, because a sixth man was complaining in a loud but whiny voice from the doorway.

"How come I got to stay here by my lonesome?" the man said. "I always get left behind."

"Quit your bellyaching," said Red. "We'll be back here after a while with that buyer from down south. Meantime, you got plenty of food and whiskey in there. Hell, boy, you got it soft. We're the ones doing all the hard work, and you'll still get your share of the money."

"Yeah? Well, what if I was to have to defend this here place all alone, just me by my own self? What if a posse or something was to come riding in here after them stole horses? What could I do all by myself against a whole posse?"

"What kind a posse's going to come riding in here looking for them horses?" Red said. "Hell, we're outside a the U.S. Ain't no Choctaws going to come into Texas looking for their horses, and besides that, they think that Comanches got them, thanks to some phony sign I left around here and there. And Texas law ain't got nothing against us. We got them horses outside a Texas. Hell, just go on back inside and get your ass drunk. By the time you do that, we'll be back here with that buyer. We'll be back come nightfall, and we'll all have cash money in our pockets."

Jack watched while Red and the others rode off. He waited for a couple more minutes. Then he moved away from the house a distance before crossing the road into the woods on the other side. From there, he would be able to work his way to a spot back behind the house. It took him a few minutes. He had to move slowly through the thicket to keep from making too much noise. He did not think the whiny-voiced man in the house would cause him much of a problem, but there was no reason to get careless. Finally, he was behind the house, and he moved out cautiously into the open space between the house and the woods. The corral was over to his left. He hurried across the clearing to stand at the back wall of the house. There was a back door. Easing his way over to it, he leaned his rifle against the wall, pulled out and cocked a pistol, then tried the door.

It was not latched, so he shoved it hard and jumped into the room, his pistol held out ready. The man was seated at a table with a bottle and a glass in front of him and both his hands on the table.

"Don't move," Jack said.

The man's eyes opened wide. Jack walked over for a closer look. The man was not wearing any weapons, but a pistol was on the tabletop within his reach. Jack stepped over and picked it up. He tossed it out through the open back door.

"You can go ahead and finish that drink now," he said.

The man picked up the glass and drained it in a gulp.

"Have another one," Jack said. "Pour it full."

The frightened and puzzled man poured himself another drink and turned that one down as quickly as the first. When Jack told him to pour again, the man protested in his whiny voice, but Jack insisted. Soon the bottle was empty, and the man's head was lolling loosely on top of his shoulders, and he was weaving from side to side from his waist up. Jack put his own pistol back in his belt and found a piece of rope hanging on the wall. He pulled the drunken man's arms behind him and tied him securely to the back of the chair.

"Tell your friends when they come back that Jack Spaniard

was here," he said. "Tell them they can find me and the horses up in the Choctaw Nation. Tell them I'll be waiting for them. Jack Spaniard. Don't forget."

Then he went outside through the back door, picked up his rifle, and walked down the road to where he had left his horse. He mounted up and rode back to the corral, threw down the gate pole and started the horses out and onto the road. It was a sizable herd, but Jack had been handling horses for about as long as he could remember. He'd get them home all right.

Mass confusion and excitement reigned at Fort Towson when the large horse herd came thundering down the road trailing a dust cloud past the line of buildings there, headed straight for the square. Soldiers came running from every direction. Officers shouted orders at sergeants who shouted at corporals who in turn shouted at privates. Some soldiers managed to get on their own horses. Everyone was either shouting orders or trying to get the horse herd under control, or trying to get out of its way to avoid being trampled.

"Round them up," someone yelled. "Round them up."

"Stop them."

"Get them in the corral."

"Watch out."

"What the hell's going on?"

Then Spanish Jack came riding out of the dust cloud from behind the herd. He looked around for the highest-ranking officer he could find and rode over to him.

"I got the horses back," he said. "You can take it from here."

He rode on over to Colonel Loomis's office and dismounted. Loomis had just stepped out the front door, having heard all the commotion.

"I don't know if I got them all," Jack said, "but I would guess that I did. They were being held for some big buyer down in Texas. And the horse thieves are not Comanches. They're white men. Texans. They're the same bunch I had trouble with the other day. Called themselves Texas Rangers."

"Well, I'll be," Loomis said. "Maybe they lied to you about being Rangers."

"Maybe," said Jack.

He looked back over his shoulder at the pandemonium still in progress.

"You think your boys can get that herd under control?" he asked.

"They will," Loomis said, "but it will take them the rest of the day. Come on inside and relax."

They went into Loomis's office, where Loomis ordered them some coffee. Sitting in the office, sipping coffee, Loomis said, "You've done a fine job, Mr. Spaniard. I'll see that Major Bradford is informed. He said you were the right man for the job, and I can see now why he said that. Congratulations."

"Thank you," said Jack, "but the job's only half-done. I brought back the horses but not the thieves."

"But you've identified them for us," Loomis said.

"I got a good look at one of them, and recognized him," Jack said. "I didn't get a good enough look at any of the others, but I'd guess they were the same ones who were with him when I ran into them before. The only thing I know for certain is that the one is called Red, and they claim to be Texas Rangers."

"I see. Well then, what do you propose we do from here? I can't ride down into Texas with U.S. Army troops. It's out of my jurisdiction."

"I know that, and I may have already set a plan into motion," Jack said. "There was one man left alone at their place. I left him there alive. I told him my name and said to tell his friends they could find me and the horses back up here in the Choctaw Nation. I have a pretty good idea that they'll be coming back. They'll want to get their hands on me, and they'll want to start stealing the horses back. I think I know which way they'll come riding in, so if you'll give me a squad of good men, I think we can lay an ambush for them."

"That sounds reasonable to me," Loomis said. "How soon do you want them?"

"Tomorrow morning," said Jack. "Those outlaws won't find out what happened until after dark tonight. They won't likely head up this way till morning, if that soon. If we can get out there and get ready for them sometime in the morning, though, I think we'll stand a good chance of catching them as they ride in. But we'll have to move early in the morning. They're really not very far away from us."

"Be back here in front of my office right after morning mess," Loomis said. "I'll have your men waiting for you and ready to go. I'll also send word out tomorrow to all the victims of the horse thieves to come in here and identify their stock."

The squad of soldiers was armed and waiting in front of Loomis's office with their horses saddled when Jack arrived. They packed food, for they had no idea how long they would be out on this mission. Loomis met Jack and introduced him to Sergeant Daniel Kilpatrick, who was in charge of the squad. He also made it clear to Kilpatrick that Jack was in charge of the operation. Jack looked over the soldiers. They seemed awfully young. He hoped that they would be up to the job.

"Let's mount up and ride then," Jack said.

He already had a good idea where he wanted to lay his ambush. It was only a few miles away from the fort. There was a spot where the trail wound through some rocky and hilly country, the hillsides covered with trees and brush. He would be able to conceal the men in the brush on the hillsides, and he would also be able to post a man high enough on one side of the road to be able to see the approach of the outlaws. When they reached the spot, Jack stopped them. He had them get their horses out of sight, he put men on both sides of the road, and he posted his lookout. They waited all day, ready for action, and nothing happened.

Jack set up rotating sentries for the night. He didn't think that the gang would come in during the night, but he didn't want to take any chances. At least some of the horses had been stolen under cover of darkness. His guess turned out to be right though. No one came down the road that night.

It was almost noon on the second day when the posted sentry came running to Jack.

"Riders coming," he said. "Six of them."

Taking field glasses from Sergeant Kilpatrick, Jack hurried to the lookout post. He spotted the riders right away, and looking through the glasses, he saw Red riding at the head of the group. He hurried back down to where the others waited. They were anxious and tense, perhaps a little frightened. They were all young soldiers who had seen no real action, all except Kilpatrick.

"It's them all right," Jack said. "Take up your positions and be ready, but wait for my word. If we play this right, we ought to be able to take them all alive."

The soldiers took their places at the sides of the road and hid themselves, and Jack mounted his horse and waited in plain sight, right in the middle of the road. He held his long rifle loosely across his saddle. Soon Red and the others came into view. When they saw Jack, they pulled up. Red wrinkled his face in puzzlement.

"When Beefy told me your name," he yelled, "I thought it was you he was talking about. What the hell are you trying to pull anyhow?"

"I told you I'm working for the army," Jack said. "I told you I was looking for stolen horses. Well, I found them. Now I want you all to throw down your guns and ride peacefully into Fort Towson with me. You'll get a fair trial there."

"You must be some tetched," Red said. "The only reason I don't just shoot you dead right now is 'cause I want to make you suffer a little for what you done, stealing them horses from me. You put me to some trouble. It took a while to round up all them horses. Now we got to do it all over again."

"You mean steal them, don't you?" Jack said.

"It ain't stealing to take Indian horses," Red said. "Now you throw down your guns or all six of us will shoot you to pieces."

"Boys," said Jack, raising his voice, "show yourselves."

Soldiers stood up or stepped out from behind their cover on both sides of the road, their guns cocked and trained on the outlaws. Red jerked a pistol out of his belt, and Sergeant Kilpatrick fired a rifle ball into his chest. As Red twitched and jerked in his saddle, dark blood gushing from the fresh wound and running down his belly, the other outlaws quickly raised their hands.

"Don't shoot," they cried. "Don't shoot."

"We'll go peaceful."

But one man at the back of the group yelled, jerked his horse around and started racing back in the direction from which they had come. Jack shouted, "Take charge, Sergeant," and rode through the group of outlaws in pursuit of the fleeing man. Red fell from the saddle just as Jack rode past him, and Jack heard

Kilpatrick order the outlaws to throw their guns to the ground. The escaping outlaw had a good start on Jack, but Jack kept after him. He could see, though, that his army-issued horse was not going to catch up with the other one. He waited until the road was straight for a distance, pulled back on the reins, dismounted quickly, and dropped to one knee. Raising his long rifle to his shoulder, he took careful aim. It was a long shot, and his target was moving, but he fired.

Ahead, the man flinched, slowed, then turned his horse. He held a hand to the side of his face for a moment. Then, knowing that Jack's rifle was empty, he started riding back toward Jack. Jack climbed back into his saddle and rode toward the outlaw, pulling out a pistol as he rode. The outlaw stopped riding and took aim from his saddle with his long rifle. The distance was far too great for a pistol shot. Jack jerked the reins of his horse to turn it off the road, but he was not quick enough. The outlaw's rifle ball tore through his left thigh and into the side of the horse. The horse squealed and fell over, pinning Jack's right leg underneath it.

The outlaw came riding toward Jack, pulling out a pistol. Jack readied his own pistol. Suddenly the outlaw stopped, but he was close enough by then for Jack to get a good look at him. It was Walker, the ex-soldier, the last survivor of the Peek Eder gang. He was still too far away for a pistol shot. Jack waited, wondering why Walker had stopped riding toward him. Then Walker turned his horse again and rode away fast. Jack looked the other direction to see two mounted soldiers coming. The soldiers stopped there where Jack was down.

"Do you want us to go after him, sir?" one said.

"No," Jack said. "He's got too great a start on you. Just get me out of here."

Jack was lying in bed in the hospital at Fort Towson when Lieutenant Colonel Loomis walked in. Loomis made it straight to Jack's bedside.

"They taking good care of you?" he asked.

"They patched me up," Jack said. "I'll mend."

"You did a real fine job once again," Loomis said. "We have the horse thieves all locked up in the stockade—all except the one that shot you and escaped."

"I think I shot him too," said Jack. "I think I creased his face along the left side. And I got a good look at him. I know who he is."

"Oh? That's good. Who is he?"

"He's a former soldier from Fort Smith named Walker," Jack said. "I don't know the first name, but Major Bradford will know it. He was cashiered from the army for general bad behavior. That's only because they couldn't prove assault and robbery charges on him. Since then he's done some murders. Until he shot me, the last I'd seen of him was on the Natchez Trace where he'd been running with the Peek Eder gang."

"We'll watch for him," Loomis said, "and we'll put out the word on him too. We'll run him down sooner or later."

"The sooner the better," said Jack.

"Well, in the meantime, you just take it easy and let the U.S. Army wait on you till you're well mended. I'll write a letter back to Major Bradford informing him of what a fine job you did for us down here."

"Thank you, Colonel," said Jack.

Jack lay staring at the ceiling after Loomis left. He was thinking about Walker. It seemed that all his troubles, after he had made his peace with the Osages, all of his troubles had involved Walker. Part of him wanted to get out and run the man down and kill him, but there was that other part, the part that had seen himself as turning bloodthirsty, as cold-blooded as the Natchez Trace outlaws. That was the part that wanted to stop killing and settle down to some kind of peaceful life somewhere. But then there was that damned Walker.

23

Spanish Jack was up and around in a matter of a few days. The lead ball had missed the bone in his thigh and gone all the way through, leaving a clean wound. He was sore and stiff. He was limping, of course, and using a walking stick, but he was getting around. He became restless in just another couple of days. His job with the army was over and done, and his wound was healing nicely. He had been paid for his work, and there was no more reason for his hanging around the fort and being an expense to the U.S. Army. He wanted to be moving on. He had Walker on his mind.

He thought about tracking Walker, but he really had no idea where to start. The man could be anywhere. In just the time Jack had known him, he had gone from Fort Smith down to the Red River and from there to the Natchez Trace and back again to the Red River country. Too many days had passed since Jack had last seen him running away for it to do any good to try to follow an actual trail. Any attempt at tracking him down that way would be nothing more than guesswork.

He decided to shove Walker to some remote place in the back of his mind. Stay alert. Watch for any sign of him that might appear and listen for any word that might come his way, but abandon any idea of active pursuit. Sooner or later, he figured, he would get his chance. Or the army would get him. They were also alerted and had put the word out on the man. It didn't matter anymore. Either way would do. Jack packed up his belongings, saddled his horse and said his good-byes to the friends he had made at Towson. He rode out of the fort without any particular destination in mind.

Since he was a fugitive in the Cherokee Nation, he soon found himself on the road to Fort Smith, riding on the Arkansas side of the line. But after riding north for some time, he suddenly took it into his head to pay a visit to Tom Starr. That would mean watching out along the way for the Cherokee Nation Light Horse Police, but he had dealt with them before. He felt confident that he could successfully elude or escape them, and he would not have to ride very far through the Cherokee Nation before arriving at the security of the Starr stronghold. Having made the decision, he crossed over the border.

Even so, Jack was instantly alert back in the jurisdiction of the Cherokee Light Horse, but he ran into no problems. No Light Horse patrols were around. At least, he did not see any. In fact, he made it all the way to the outlaw stronghold of Tom Starr without having seen anyone along the way. As he wound his way down the dark and narrow trail leading to Starr's house, he heard a voice hail him by name.

"Spanish Jack," it called out. "Ride on in."

Jack waved an arm and rode on up to the house, and before he had swung down out of his saddle, Tom Starr himself stepped out the front door, his face wearing a broad smile and his arms outstretched. As Jack stepped down on solid ground, Starr wrapped his arms around him and hugged him like a big bear.

"Welcome," Starr said. "Steal any good horses lately?"

"I've given that up," said Jack. "How are you, Tom?"

"I'm doing real fine," Starr said. "Business has never been better. I don't know why you'd want to give up a good business like horses, but then, it's your life."

Tom Starr called out over his shoulder for someone to take care of Jack's horse, and a man came running to do that little chore. Then Starr took Jack by the arm and led him into the house. He indicated a chair at a table, and Jack pulled it out and sat down.

"Coffee or whiskey?" Starr asked.

"This time of day," said Jack, "coffee."

Starr poured two cups and put them on the table. He took a chair across the table from Jack. Jack took a tentative sip of coffee while Starr gave him a hard stare. Starr leaned forward resting his elbows on the table.

"What do you mean you've given up stealing horses?" he said.

"Well, I didn't swear an oath or anything like that," Jack said. "I've just been busy doing other things. That's all."

"Tell me about it," said Starr. "What have you been up to lately?"

Jack went on to tell Starr the history of his adventures since they had last spoken together, bringing the tale right up to date with the horse thieves around Fort Towson and the bullet wound to his leg. Starr frowned as he listened.

"You sound almost like a lawman, Jack," he said. "Running down outlaws and horse thieves. You didn't come in here to try to clean out my place, did you?"

"Oh, hell, Tom, I'm no lawman," said Jack. "I got into all this because friends of mine had been hurt and killed. Then I took this last job because I had nothing else to do at the time. And it was a scouting job. That's all. I didn't go out looking for any of this to happen. It all just kind of came my way."

"Jack," Starr said, "you know how it is I make my living."

Jack shrugged. "The same way I used to make mine," he said. "You pick up—stray horses and then sell them."

"What if you had tracked those stolen horses from down there in the Choctaw country up here to me?" Starr asked.

"Oh, come on, Tom," said Jack. "I knew it wasn't you. Besides, like I told you, I tracked them to Texas."

"But what if you had?" Starr insisted.

Jack sighed. He didn't like this line of questioning, and he was beginning to think that he had made a mistake stopping by for this visit. It seemed to be turning into more than just a friendly visit.

"Well," he said, "I guess I would have told the army that I just couldn't find any evidence. I'd have quit my job."

"Are you sure about that?" Starr asked.

"Sure, Tom."

"Well, that's only part of the way I earn my keep around here," Starr said. "The horse business. The other thing I do is I run a safe haven here for fugitives. Anyone is safe here as long as he pays his way. Anyone. Indian, Black, White. I don't give a damn. I don't care what it is he's done either. From cheating at cards to murder. Jack, I like you, and I'd sure enough hate to wake up and find you standing on the other side of the fence from me, and us shooting at one another."

"That's not going to happen, Tom," said Jack. "All that other stuff that I told you about, that all happened outside the Cherokee Nation. Hell, you know as well as I do that I'm a wanted man here. I'm an outlaw. I'm just another one of your fugitives while I'm in this country."

Starr heaved a long sigh and leaned back in his chair.

"Yeah," he said. "That's right. Forget all that talk. Hey. Let's have a real drink. What do you say?"

"All right," Jack said. "That sounds good."

He turned up his coffee cup and emptied it as Starr went for the glasses and a whiskey bottle. Starr put the glasses on the table and poured them full. He put the bottle between Jack and himself and sat down again.

"Jack," he said, "let's get drunk tonight, you and me. You can stay the night here—no charge. After you sober up tomorrow, if you decide to stay longer, we'll talk about money then. What do you say?"

"I say this is good whiskey, Tom Starr."

As they sat and drank, every now and then, Jack heard a rider go past the house, but Starr told him to pay no attention.

"I have a bunkhouse out back where my paying guests stay," he said. "No one gets in here that I don't know about. You've come down that path yourself. You know that. It's the only way in here. So anyone riding past the house here is just one of my paying guests going back to the bunkhouse. I told you business has never been better."

Jack nodded his head in understanding, muttered something, and took another drink. The whiskey felt good burning its way down his throat and then warming his belly. Before long though, he was feeling a bit woozy. He was also feeling something else. He stood up on unsteady legs.

"I have to go pee," he said.

"You lose the contest," Starr said.

"What contest?"

"Who can hold out the longest," Starr said. "Go on outside. I'm the winner."

"I guess you are," Jack said, heading for the front door at an angle. He made it outside and around to the side of the house all right. Then he staggered a few more feet to get himself over to the edge of the thick woods that surrounded the house. He took care of his business and was about to turn to walk back to the front door when he heard someone come walking toward him. Jack turned his head slowly to see Tom Starr approaching.

"I won the contest," Starr said, "but not by much."

Jack laughed but not raucously. He was too drunk for that. His head was hanging so that his chin almost rested on his chest. He stood on weak legs and wobbled from side to side. Now and then a knee would buckle, and he would jerk to keep himself standing upright. Waiting there for Starr, he heard a rider coming. Another of Starr's "guests," he thought. He raised his head casually, and he saw the rider clearly. It was Walker. Jack reached, fumbling, for a pistol, pulled it out and thumbed back the hammer, but before he could point it, Starr's big hand enclosed his, gripping it tight, preventing the hammer of the pistol from falling, holding Jack's hand so that the barrel of the gun pointed up into the air.

"Jack," Starr said, "what the hell do you think you're doing?"

"I need to kill that son of a bitch," Jack said.

"I told you already that I get paid to provide a safe haven here," Starr said. "I can't let you do that. You're acting like a lawman again."

"Tom," said Jack, "this has nothing to do with the law. That no good son of a bitch has killed and robbed friends of mine. He's tried to kill me more than once. He's the bastard I told you about that put that hole in my leg."

"I still can't let you do it," said Starr, his voice quiet but stern. "Not here. If the word ever got out, it would ruin my business. Come on. Put the pistol away. God damn it, I've got my reputation to protect. Put it away."

Starr was a big man, and he was strong. As he talked, he still held tight his powerful grip on Jack's fist. Jack could not move his arm to take aim, could not pull the trigger. Walker was gone anyway, having ridden on back to the bunkhouse. Jack stopped straining against Starr's grasp and relaxed.

"Ease the hammer down now," said Starr. "Real easy."

Jack did, and Starr was forcing Jack's gunhand down. He turned loose of Jack's hand, but stayed close and kept himself ready, just in case.

"Now put the pistol away," he said.

Jack did that. He was trembling with rage, even in his drunkenness. Starr took hold of him and turned him.

"Come on," he said. "Let's go back in the house."

Back at the table with another drink, Jack still fumed.

"Relax," said Starr. "I don't give a damn about that man, but you can't kill him here on my place. When he leaves here, kill him, with my blessing. You're my friend, Jack, but business is business. You understand?"

"I'm all right," Jack said. "I need to go to sleep."

Jack was up early, outside saddling his horse. Tom Starr came out of the house and found him there.

"You don't seem any worse for the wear," Starr said.

"I'm just fine," said Jack.

"You leaving?" Starr said.

"I can't stay in the same place as that son of a bitch," Jack said. "And you told me I can't kill him in here, so I got to go outside and wait for him to come out. He can't stay in here forever."

"All right, Jack, but be careful. He's a mean one."

"I know all about that," said Jack, swinging up into the saddle. "Thanks for the hospitality."

As Jack turned his horse to head for the trail that would take him out of Starr's property, Starr called after him, "Jack, he might be in here for several days. You could get awful hungry waiting for him to ride out."

The trail led back to the road, and across the road and down not far was a large boulder. Behind the boulder and all along the side of the road was thick brush and woods. Jack rode to the boulder and turned to look back where the trail to Starr's house came out. He had a good view. He dismounted and led his horse through the thicket. He found a small clearing, and there he unsaddled the horse and left it to graze. He walked back to the boulder. He would wait there for Walker to come out. He would wait as long as it took. In spite of all his claims to the contrary, the old rage was returning. He remembered Lorn and Abry. He thought about the Tuckows, and the least of it all was the scar on his leg.

Tom Starr had said that Walker might stay in there for several days. Well, so be it. Spanish Jack knew that he could easily wait for four days without food. He had fasted for that long on several different occasions in his life. There was nothing to it. And if he could fast for four days easily, he was sure he could last even longer than that if he had reason to, and he had damn good reason. He was a little worried about water for his horse though. He decided to wait it out for a while and deal with that problem later. He settled down against the boulder to wait and watch.

It was midmorning the second day, and as yet there had been no sign of Walker. Two strangers had come riding out of the narrow trail and gone their ways. They looked like white men, white outlaws, Jack thought, two more of Tom Starr's "guests." Jack decided to take care of his horse, even though he hated the thought of leaving the trail unwatched for even a short while. He went back for the horse and led it out to the road. He studied the tracks going in and out of the trail closely. Then he jumped on the horse's bare back and rode east on the road. He knew there was a clear stream not far in that direction. When he reached the stream, he left the horse again and trotted on foot back to the trail to Starr's house. He studied the tracks again. They had not changed. He went back to his post at the boulder to wait.

It was high noon on the fourth day, and the bright sun was blazing down from overhead. The ground was wet, and the air was muggy, heavy and humid. Jack was soaked with sweat. He felt a little weak from hunger and the oppresive heat, but he was confident that he could handle his weapons well enough. He was strong enough to kill. He was looking at the entrance to the trail, and he saw a horse's head emerge. Then half the horse came into view, and then the rider, and it was Walker. Jack felt a thrill run through his body. He waited a moment to see which direction Walker would turn. He turned west onto the road, riding toward Jack. Jack stood up with his long rifle in his hands. He thumbed back the hammer and stepped out into the open. He could see the scar where his rifle ball had creased Walker's cheek.

"Walker," he shouted.

Walker stiffened and halted his horse. He was sitting straight in the saddle holding his own long rifle casually across his thighs. He cocked his head to one side and squinted in the bright daylight.

"Spanish Jack, is it?" he said.

"That's right," Jack said. "I mean to end this right here."

"Just what is it you mean to end?" said Walker. "What is it you're talking about?"

"You know well enough," Jack said.

"You might have me all confused with someone else," said Walker. "Why don't you just tell me what it is that's gnawing at you?"

"You've killed friends of mine," Jack said.

"You sure of that, are you?"

"I'm sure."

"Aw, hell, I was just making a living is all. You can't hold that against a man, can you?"

"You've tried to kill me."

"Just defending myself is all. Put your gun down now. All that's in the past. Put it down, and I'll ride on down that road. Ain't no need for one of us to die here. Put it down. We don't have to see each other again."

"No," said Jack. "That's not the way it's going to be."

As Jack raised his rifle to his shoulder, Walker swung his long barrel up and over his horse's head in order to get the rifle in firing position, but before either man could take a bead on the other, there was a loud boom from behind Walker, and Jack saw the puff of smoke from over at the entrance to the trail. An instant later, he saw the stream of blood and brains blast out of the side of Walker's head. Walker's bloody head bounced loosely on his shoulders, and his lifeless body leaned slowly sideways and slid out of the saddle to drop and then land hard with a dull thud in the middle of the road. A puff of dust rose up around it when it dropped. Jack looked over toward the trail just as Tom Starr stepped out, a smoking musket in his hands.

"Tom?"

"I figured you'd try to fight him fair," Starr said. "You got that about you. I also figured that if you did, there was at least a good chance that he might win. I couldn't let that happen."

Jack eased the hammer down on his long rifle and walked over to stand by the body of Walker. He looked down at it thinking that it had been a long road since that day Walker and his buddies had beaten him and robbed him. Starr walked over to stand beside him, and Jack held his rifle out toward Starr.

"Hold this for me, will you?" he said.

Starr took the rifle, and Jack pulled his hunting knife out of its sheath and knelt beside the body. He took a handful of hair and made a quick cut just below the hairline on the forehead and ripped back, pulling loose the scalp.

"God damn," said Starr. "When did you take up that practice?"

"I got to show the proof of it," Jack said. "That's all. And I don't mean to carry that carcass along with me to Fort Smith."

"Well, I don't blame you none for that," said Starr. "It'd get smelly before you were back into Arkansas. Well, get on your way. I'll get rid of this body."

"Tom," said Jack. "Thanks."

He took his rifle back from Tom Starr, and carrying the bloody scalp, started walking down the road toward the stream where he had left his horse.

"Where you going?" Starr said.

"I left my horse down there at water," said Jack.

Starr nodded at the horse Walker had been riding.

"Take this one," he said.

"All right. I'll bring it back here. I left my saddle over there behind that boulder."

"Don't fool around out here any longer than you have to," Starr said. "I don't want you getting caught by no Light Horse."

Jack stepped into Major Bradford's office and tossed the scalp onto the desk. Bradford looked up astonished. Then he looked back down at the grisly trophy and shivered in disgust.

"That came off the top of Walker's head," said Jack. "I thought you'd want to see some proof."

"Well, I'm glad to know that you finally got him," Bradford said. "I'd have taken your word for it though."

"I didn't kill him," said Jack. "I saw him killed, and I brought that back here to show you."

"Either way, it's a relief," Bradford said. "Did you receive your pay?"

"Loomis paid me. I'm done now. The job's over."

"I've received a letter from Loomis," Bradford said. "He wrote that you did a fine job at Towson. All the stolen horses were recovered. All but one of the thieves arrested or killed. Now that one is taken care of as well. Have a drink?"

"Thank you," Jack said. "I don't mind."

Jack pulled a straight chair up close to the major's desk, and Bradford opened a desk drawer and brought out a bottle of brandy. He held it up for Jack to see.

"This all right?" he asked.

"It'll do just fine," Jack said.

The major then took two glasses out of the drawer, shut the drawer and poured the glasses full. He reached across the desk to hand one to Jack. Then he held his up for a toast.

"To a job well done," he said.

Jack lifted his glass in response and then took a drink.

"You have good liquor, Major," he said.

"Where do you go from here, Jack?" Bradford asked.

"I don't exactly know," said Jack. "I haven't thought much about it. I guess I'll get something figured out before I run out of money though."

"The army needs a good scout over at Fort Gibson," Bradford said. "They've asked me for a recommendation. I can't think of a better man for the job."

"That's in the Cherokee Nation," said Jack, shaking his head. "I can't go back there. You know that. I'm a wanted man in my own country."

"I have news for you, Jack. Good news. While you were down at Fort Towson, I took a trip over to Tahlequah. I had a very pleasant visit with your chief. There were some Osages there visiting with us. One man of them said that you would know him by the name of Broken Legs, and he called you Broken Arms. I don't know what he meant by that. He didn't explain it."

"I know the man," said Jack.

"Well, this Broken Legs said that you had made your peace with the Osages. He was very definite about it. I told Chief Ross of the great service you've done for the travelers along the Natchez Trace, and how at the very time we were speaking, you were involved in helping the United States Army down at Fort Towson. We had a long talk about you. The upshot of all of it—you've been pardoned, Jack. You're free to go home—to the Cherokee Nation. You're no longer a wanted man, no longer a fugitive."

Jack didn't know what to say. He wasn't even sure whether or not he could believe what Bradford had just said to him. But why would Bradford tell him such a lie? Perhaps he had been to visit Chief John Ross. Perhaps it was a conspiracy between Ross and Bradford to get Jack back inside the boundaries of the Cherokee Nation so that he could be arrested. But how would they have known about Broken Legs? This was unexpected, and Jack did not know how to react. He finished his drink, put down the glass and stood up.

"I'll give it some thought," he said, and he walked out of the major's office. Almost without thinking about it, he walked back to the inn where he had spent so much of his time in recent months. Jones was there. Jack didn't really want to talk to him, not just then.

"I'm going to have a bath and change my clothes," he said. "I'll be out later to have a drink with you if you're still here."

"You do look as if you need a good hot bath," Jones said. "I'll be here."

It was an hour later when Jack reemerged looking like a new man. He was still confused, though, about his new station in life, that was, if he could believe it. He found Jones still sitting at an outside table with a bottle of whiskey and two glasses.

"I'm ready for you, you see," Jones said. He poured whiskey into the two glasses.

"Yes," said Jack. "I need a drink."

"Is there something bothering you, my friend?"

"Yes," Jack said. "When I first arrived, I stopped by the major's office to report on the progress of my job."

"Did all go well?"

"With the job? Oh, yeah. It's all done. I had a drink with Bradford, and he told me that I have a pardon from Chief Ross. I'm free to go back into the Cherokee Nation."

"That's wonderful. Of course, we've already heard the news. But what's bothering you then?"

"I don't know whether to believe it or not," Jack said.

"Oh, you can believe it all right," Jones said. "Look at this. I've been saving it for you."

Jones pulled a folded newspaper out from under his coat and tossed it on the table in front of Jack. Jack picked it up and opened it out. It was the latest copy of the *Arkansas Banner*, and it was opened to a story with the headline, "Notorious Spanish Jack Pardoned." Jack started to read the article. "In Tahlequah, Principal Chief John Ross of the Cherokee Nation issued a pardon for the notorious Jack Spaniard, also known as Spanish Jack, giving Jack for the first time in years the freedom to go wherever he pleases." Jack put down the paper. He didn't bother reading further. So it was true. He could go home. He was no longer an outlaw and a fugitive. Not anywhere.

He considered the idea of home, though, and he reminded himself that this new Cherokee Nation had never been his home. His Cherokee Nation, the Cherokee Nation he had grown to manhood in, was the Western Cherokee Nation, and it had been in Arkansas. It no longer existed. It had been uprooted and absorbed into the larger Cherokee Nation, and when that had happened, Jack had been outlawed. Of course, his old friends, other Western Cheokees, were living over there in the new Cherokee Nation. He would be able to look them up, maybe find a place to live among them. Maybe. But what would he do then? Farm? The idea had no appeal to him.

"Well, Jack," Jones said, jerking Jack back out of his revery. "How do you feel? You look stunned."

"Yes," said Jack. "I feel—stunned. I never thought to see this day."

"What will you do now that you're a free man?"

Major Bradford's last offer came back into Jack's mind just then.

"I think I'll go back to work as a scout for the U.S. Army," he said. "At Fort Gibson. That's in the Cherokee Nation."